The Kiss of Death

An Anthology of Vampire Stories

THE DESIGNIMAGE GROUP, INC.

This book contains works of fiction.
Persons' names, characters, places, organizations or incidents are used fictitiously, and are only the products of the authors' imaginations. Any resemblance to actual events, locations, businesses or persons living or dead is purely coincidental.

Inquiries may be directed to:
The Design Image Group, Inc.
P.O. Box 2325, Darien, Illinois 60561.

ISBN: 1-891946-05-6

First Edition

Visit us on the web at
www.designimagegroup.com

Printed in the U.S.A.

10 9 8 7 6 5 4 3 2 1

The Kiss of Death

I shall give you, my dark one,
Kisses frozen as the moon

Charles Baudelaire,
The Ghost

Contents

Oh sweet delicious lips
From which I fancy all the
world's blood drips!

John Barlas,
Terrible Love

Acknowledgements

Night And Day, © 1990, Barb Hendee - Previously published in *After Hours #5*

Morbidly Obese, © 1998, Rick R. Reed

Prey For The Dead, © 1998, Don D'Ammassa

To Die For, © 1998, Dominick Cancilla

The Pale Hill's Side, © 1998, Margaret L. Carter

Friends, © 1998, Christine DeLong Miller

Blood Feud, © 1998, C.W. Johnson

Winding The Clock, © 1998, Deborah Markus

Who Was Jane Dalotz?, © 1998, Sukie de la Croix

Bongo Bobbie's Bel Air, © 1998, Kyle Marffin

Sixteen Candles, © 1998, Kiel Stuart - Previously published in *The Fifth Di Anthology*

Pet Consultation, © 1998, Mia Fields

Something I Can Never Have, © 1998, Lynda Licina

A Month Of Bleeding, © 1998, Tippi N. Blevins

Poster Man, © 1997, Sandra Black - Previously published in *Nocturnal Ecstasy: Vampire Coven,* Volume 8

La Petite Morte, © 1998, D.G.K. Goldberg

Introduction

Did you miss me?
Come and kiss me.
Never mind the bruises,
Hug me, kiss me, suck my juices
Squeezed from Goblin fruits for you.

Christina Rossetti,
Goblin Market

"The kiss of death"...that is what's at the core of the perplexing allure of vampires, isn't it?

Other horrors can thrill us, chill us, delight us in countless gruesome ways. But there's always something oddly enticing about vampires that perversely blends a shudder of fear and trembling arousal at the same time. It's a kiss – but a cold and vicious kiss that pierces the skin and dives down to the veins till the rich red warmth bubbles out. It's a kiss, an enticing, lethal kiss that begs for acquiescence, demands surrender, and exacts the ultimate payment...death. Inviting this cold embrace is a disturbing acknowledgment of dark desires that may best have been kept hidden. A macabre wish to live in the darkness, to experience whatever delicious madness may lurk on the other side of life, the scents and sounds and sights and touch of undead pleasures and pains. It's desire and doom, it's love at its most brutal. It is a kiss of death.

In this anthology, sixteen writers invite you to welcome their own dark embrace with vampire tales that are sometimes frightening, sometimes funny...stories that delight in arousal or plumb darker horrors than vampires themselves to provoke us, to leave us brooding over our own dark sides.

The literary vampire is no longer just another "monster"...clearly they've become an archetype, much more so perhaps than any other "monster" in the horror canon. Here, familiar horror favorites and fresh emerging talents twist and tweak and manipulate the vampire in their own special ways, celebrating the traditional blood drinking creatures of the night, spoofing the icon and all its trappings, and even toying with your very notions of vampires and victims, good and evil. In these stories, vampires lurk among the murkiest shadows in grimy city streets, they reveal their horror amidst our own man-made terrors, they rise from the darkness in fog shrouded forests, and may even hide in the house right next door. But wherever these stories find them, the undead will mirror our most secret dreams and our most terrifying nightmares. They may weave their dark magic of sin and lust and delicious violence around us, ever hovering in the shadows beside us, always waiting to embrace us with that kiss of madness and desire and death.

Turn the page, step into the darkness, yield to cold and outstretched pale hands, lean into the icy lips and the sharp and painful pleasure of the undead's bite. Each tale is its own cool embrace, its own delightfully dangerous kiss of death.

Kiss me; – oh! thy lips are cold:
Round my neck thine arms enfold –
They are soft, but chill and dead;
And thy tears upon my head
Burn like points of frozen lead.

Percy Byshe Shelley,
Invocation To Misery

His lips were soft and warm, like new puppies. They moved across my face with a purpose, and his muscles began tightening to granite. Something told me I should stop him, but I didn't. He caressed my cheek, then moved down my neck. His touch made me shiver, and I tried to kiss him back. He stopped moving at my throat.

Night and Day

Barb Hendee

The first of many nights began the night I finally met him, when the leaves turned blood-red in the October cold, and everyone in my world put their clock back an hour, and it would be dark when I got home from school to do my chores for the next four months.

Four months.

I stood outside the back door staring into the night, coat on, boots fastened, flashlight in hand.

Oh God I'm going to have to do it.

I could picture him waiting, his black decayed clothes hanging in tatters from a white body. He stayed among the trees, watching from shadows, never coming close, but never straying far. I wondered what he had been doing since last February. Had he missed me? Maybe he had found someone else to torment during those months.

I'd known about him for three years now, but nobody in my entire town had died or disappeared (except for the oldest

Mervyn boy who'd gotten drunk and driven his car off a cliff). That's why I never told anyone, because even if they did believe me, they probably wouldn't care.

I took a deep breath, gathered up my skirt, and slipped through the gate. I always walked to the barn. I knew that if I ran, he would feel my panic and catch me from behind.

Dark cedar trees cast flickering shadows across my path, which gave the ground a life of its own. I glanced around, wondering why he had waited so long. Why didn't he just do it and get it over with?

Through the night, I could only see a few feet away, but I was afraid to turn on the flashlight. He hated the light, and I was saving it for an emergency – like shining it into his eyes.

Lost in thought, I felt surprise when the worn trail suddenly ended, and the old, moss-covered barn stood looming up before me. I hadn't seen one sign of him the whole way down.

Where is he?

I could hear Rosy inside pushing softly at her stanchion as she waited for me to come in and feed her. I didn't have a choice. If I had, I never would have come down here. Hand shaking, I opened the door and stepped into the equipment room. It smelled musty and was full of spiders. Dad never put anything back where he got it, so there were tools lying all over the place. The main body of the barn lay in the next room, but I stayed where I was for a moment, listening.

Where is he?

I made my way to the inner door and pushed it open. Rosy's large, black eyes were the first things I saw. She was real. She was the reason I'd come down here. I just wanted to get it over with and get back home where I was safe.

"Sorry I'm late," I whispered. "I'll be just a minute."

The other cattle heard my voice and began pushing at each other to jostle up to the front. I quickly found my knife stuck in its usual beam and cut the twine; the bale fell apart into loose leaves, easy to pick up and throw into the manger. Rosy sniffed the hay, then lifted her head suddenly to stare at the wall behind me.

A stale, sweet smell drifted into my nostrils.

Oh God, he's in the barn. The flashlight! Where's the flashlight?

My pocket...I shoved it in my coat pocket to pick up the hay leaves. Silently pulling it out, I locked my eyes on the ground and started for the door.

Click.

No light came. It had been sitting in the closet since last February. The batteries must have gone dead.

My breath came fast and shallow as I turned to follow Rosy's stare. Stark white hands gripped the loft ladder. A dark figure hung there motionless.

I screamed. Fear poured out my mouth in the form of sound, and I slid on the hay in a panic to reach the door.

"No!" His wild cry sounded behind me. My fingernails dug into the latch, driving small slivers of wood under my skin. Ignoring the pain, I jerked the door open.

Two arms shot over my head and slammed it shut. The wall shook from the force, and I heard tools clatter to the ground in the next room.

"No!" he cried again, his mouth so close to my ear that the cry deafened me. He dropped his hands and pinned me against the door, pressing his face into the top of my hair. I was sobbing so hard all I could hear was myself and the little incoherent noises he was making in his throat.

I'm going to die.

His hand moved up to my wrist and gripped it tightly until I dropped the knife. Then he forced me to turn around. His chest was against my face, but I could smell the exhalation of stale breath when he whispered.

"Look at me."

I wouldn't look. He would hypnotize me. His hand

moved to my chin and forced it up.

"Look at *me*."

I screamed again and pushed at him wildly. He held fast and felt like stone. When I tried to wrench my head away, I saw his face. It was so close. I fell silent.

He wasn't much older than me. His eyes were dark and wild, glowing out of white, tightly stretched skin.

"Don't run away." His voice sounded hard. "Don't run away, or I'll hurt you."

He let go and stepped back. A tangled mess of red-brown hair hung to his shoulders, resting on a soiled and torn Levi jean jacket. His expression turned to confusion as tears ran down my face.

"My name is Troy," he whispered.

I didn't hear him. Too lost in fear to understand what he was saying, I started begging. "Let me out...I want to...I want my father!"

His eyes flashed in anger, possibly frustration, and then he leaped the few feet between us. I swung at him, but he sidestepped my fist, picked me up, and walked across the barn carrying me with one arm. He grabbed the first rung of the loft ladder and started climbing. I grew numb from shock and the sharp coldness of his body and the darkness. We came up into the loft through an opening in its floor. He jumped off the ladder and moved quickly enough for me to realize that he could see where he was going. Finally stopping, he put me down on a rough wool blanket.

"You'll be able to see in a minute," he whispered.

Frozen, I slowly began to make out the lines of his pale face. "What do you want?" I whispered.

He leaned back against the hay. "What you want. What everybody wants." I could feel his eyes.

He was a tall, pale version of the boys I went to high school with. His frame was gaunt, but heavy enough to keep him from looking fragile. I didn't know what to say. He crossed the floor quickly and crouched down beside me.

"What's your name?"

I sniffed. "Rachel."

"I'm Troy," he said again. "I...I didn't mean what I said about hurting you. I just didn't want you to go away, like you always do."

He glanced covertly at me. His voice strained as if he were trying to find the right words. "I can't leave. I mean I can't go where there's people." He paused for a moment. "I'm alone all the time. Not dead, not alive. I'm nowhere."

The pain in his voice made me listen. He had been living in my shadows for such a long time, as a vision, a nightmare. Now he was real and touchable, something to be feared, but pitied. I wiped the tears from my face.

"I don't know what to say."

"Say anything. I don't care. Just talk to me."

My mind was racing for words when a long call sounded from outside. "Rachel!"

I jumped. "That's my father. I have to go."

"No, not yet! You can't tell anyone about me." He grabbed my arm. "You can't tell *anyone.*" His face twisted with fear. "Come back tomorrow. Promise me."

My dad would open the barn door any minute. "I promise," I whispered, hoping he'd let go of me, but actually wanting to protect him at the same time.

His face relaxed a little. He ran a hand through his dull hair. "Tell him you came up to get hay, the flashlight went dead, and it took you a while to find your way out. He'll believe you."

He stepped forward to guide me as I walked to the ladder. I turned towards him. "Do you...do you need anything?" My head didn't even reach his shoulder.

He stared at me for a moment, lost in thought. "Books," he said, becoming excited. "Novels, comics." Then he sobered and finished lamely, "anything".

I nodded and then hurried onto the ladder. Halfway down I heard him whisper, "and some candles."

◆

A little past midnight, I slipped out of the house. Every move I made sounded like a blaring announcement. I carried a clean blanket under one arm and a stuffed pillowcase under the other. I was barefoot and hadn't risked putting my coat on. Afraid, I hardly felt the rough dry grass beneath my feet as I hurried back to the barn. A few feet away, I slowed down, so that if he were watching, he could see me. "Troy," I called softly.

No answer. I opened the door and stepped in slowly. The tool room was empty.

"I brought some things for you."

A soft thud sounded in the feed room. He must have jumped down from the loft. Before I reached the inner door, he jerked it open and stared out at me in shock, his expression uncertain. I clung to the belief that he was trustworthy, but my stomach lurched just the same.

"You came back already," he whispered.

"I didn't want you to have to wait until tomorrow. Do you usually stay up in the loft?"

He nodded. "I can see if anyone's coming. Nobody ever goes up except at harvest time or to get hay for the cattle."

"Well, let's go up, and I'll show you what I brought."

He motioned me up the ladder. The loft was darker than before, so I waited for him at the top.

"This way," he murmured. I grabbed his jacket and let him lead me to an open space in the hay bales. He crouched down on the wool blanket.

"Is this where you sleep?"

He glanced at me cautiously. "No, I sleep when the sun's up, and I have to hide then. Almost nothing wakes me up. If someone found me, I couldn't fight."

He looked at my pillowcase. I started pulling candles out.

"Can't you see in the dark?"

"Not well enough to read small print," he said.

I lit one with a match. Shadows flickered on the cobwebbed walls. I looked up and gasped. Troy's face was pale. Worse than pale, light blue. His hair hung limply with the dullness of ill health, and his skin stretched smoothly over his bones as if he were starving. Not horrible, he was pitiful.

"What's wrong?" He tilted his head in puzzlement.

"Nothing." I turned back to the pillowcase. "Here, I thought you'd like this." Excited at the thought of pleasing him, I held out a faded, dusty copy of *Great Expectations.*

His eyes scanned the title, and he snatched it out of my hand. His breathing quickened.

Can he cry? I wondered silently.

He ran his slim fingers over the worn cover, feeling the binding.

I wasn't sure what to say. "Here Troy, try this on." I pulled out a long, brown coat. "My dad's a lot shorter than you are, but he's heavier."

His attention shifted back to me reluctantly, and then he smiled. "You took your dad's coat?"

"Yeah, but he never wears this one anymore. It's getting too tight on him."

Troy leaned forward and pulled his torn Levi jacket off. Underneath he was wearing a sleeveless tee-shirt that must have once been white. The flesh on his arms glowed in the darkness. They were thin, but not bony. Tight muscles flowed from his shoulders to his forearms, and I knew that he was stronger than he looked. He fingered the brown wool and then slipped into it.

"How's it look?"

I smiled. "How's it feel?"

"The sleeves are a little short." He stopped apologetically.

"It's good, it's perfect. The only things I've had for years are what I scrounged from other people's garbage."

I twisted the prickly blanket with my hands. "Well, if you really needed something badly enough, couldn't you steal it?"

"I'm not a thief." He gestured toward the book. "These things are miracles." He dropped his eyes and whispered, "I can't explain it. You wouldn't understand."

I reached out to touch his face. From the corner of his eye he saw my hand coming and jumped back.

"Don't!" he snapped, and I pulled away in confusion.

He looked angry, but not at me. "I'm sorry. It's just that you don't want to touch my skin." He whispered, "I feel cold. I feel dead."

"You look pretty alive to me."

He stared at me for a long time.

◆

Two weeks later, it started to snow. The world became covered in a mass of white powder. The barn would be cold that night.

As soon as the bus dropped me off, I ran down to see him. We spent a few minutes talking and went outside for a snowball fight. Even without wearing gloves, he won. I ran home, cooked dinner, and rushed through my homework. In the kitchen, my dad was sweating over his monthly tractor payment. So I went to my bedroom, closed the door, and set the clock for midnight. I would stay with Troy until four and then come home and reset it for six.

I had gradually adjusted to falling asleep around eight, but my mind was so full that night I stared at the ceiling until I heard my father's bedroom door close. Sighing, I got up. Might as well go see Troy early.

I picked up my cassette deck and the newest John Cougar Mellencamp tape. It'd been a long time since Troy heard any music, and I thought he'd like it.

It was freezing. The cold seeped quickly into my worn boots, so I ran faster than usual. Without bothering to call for him, I hurried up the loft ladder to find a blanket.

A full moon shone brightly through the single upstairs window. I crawled off the ladder and called. "Troy, where are...?" The last word never came out.

He crouched a few feet from me pressing something against his mouth. He jumped at my voice and dropped what he'd been holding. Blood covered his face, and his eyes were so glazed that I hardly recognized him.

I looked down. It was a cat. I stumbled backward. He had torn its throat open. A white daisy-chain of neck vertebrae poked through red, gristly tendons. The fur covering its legs was ripped and loose, yet matted, lumped without form like a wrinkled, empty balloon. Its fangs were spread wide, its claws distended, as if it had tried to fight him.

Troy cried out once.

I didn't want to listen. All I could see was the mutilated cat on the loft floor. He grabbed it suddenly, ran to the window and threw it out.

"Rachel, I..." His face was hysterical now, and he was begging. "Don't look at me like that."

I couldn't help it. Bile forced its way up in a rush. I turned away to be sick. He moved back to me and reached out for my arm.

"Troy, don't."

The room felt even colder, and he stepped away. His blood-smeared face turned hard, flat, and angry. I moved toward the ladder. Being afraid of Troy was an odd feeling. I hated it.

"What in the hell did you expect?" His voice was soft and yet violent. "Roast chicken and potatoes? You know what I am."

"How am I supposed to know what to expect?" I shouted

at him more from shock than anger. "You won't talk about any of it. You won't tell me where you sleep! You won't even tell me what happened to you."

"You don't want to hear it." His words jerked out like hooks from netted fish. "You'd crawl away and never come back."

I didn't care what he was. I just wanted that look off his face. "I'll be right back, Troy," I whispered. "Sit down, and I'll be right back."

I tore off a piece of blanket, crawled weakly down the ladder and went to the hose outside. Though cold, the lines hadn't frozen yet. When I cam back, he was sitting on the floor.

He let me clean off his face. As I wiped away the blood, his tension washed away with it. His eyes grew soft again. Then he reached out and pulled me up against his chest. I had grown accustomed to him doing that when he was lonely or sad. It bothered me at first since my father is not affectionate, but it didn't anymore.

"I grew up about twenty miles south of here," he whispered. "My dad raises horses. It happened three summers ago. She was so beautiful."

He stopped talking for a minute and started sobbing without tears.

"When I woke up, I was in a wooden box in the ground. They buried me! I thought I was going to die of suffocation and thirst, and nobody would ever know. I clawed at the lid and it moved. I didn't stop to think. I just tore it to pieces and dug like a scared animal. After I got out, I sat in the darkness, in the middle of a cemetery with tombstones all around."

I wrapped my hand around two of his fingers.

He went on. "The graveyard was two miles from my house. When I fell through the front screen door to find help, my mother tipped her chair over backwards trying to get away from me and started screaming. 'You're already dead! We buried you!'"

"Troy stop," I whispered, leaning my forehead against him. "You don't have to say anymore."

He went on as if I hadn't spoken. "I ran as far away as I could. For days I stumbled around the woods, wanting to die. The hunger was faint at first, but then it started to hurt. It began to blind me. I caught a rabbit and tried to eat it raw. The meat made me vomit, but the blood left in my mouth was warm. So warm. I sucked the whole carcass dry."

He trailed off, lost in memory. I stayed frozen against his chest. He wrapped both arms around me and shivered.

"I wandered around the woods catching small animals and sleeping wherever I found cover. Then one night I found this place and saw you. There's a hidden hole behind the barn that goes underground. That's where I sleep. I used to come out and sneak up near the house just to watch you."

He took my head in both hands and turned it up to look at him. "But I've never killed anyone." His face was intense. "I promised myself that no mater what happened, I'd never feed on people."

I dropped my gaze, "I'm sorry about the way I acted when I saw the cat."

"Just don't leave." He gripped my face a little tighter. "Do you still feel the same about me?"

I nestled back into his chest. "Nothing could make me feel differently."

He stroked my hair. "You're tired. Sleep for a few hours, and I'll wake you in time to go home."

I closed my eyes. He liked it when I slept up against him. Sometimes he'd read to himself by candlelight and hold me for hours. I fell asleep right away.

Nothing can wear you out like loving someone.

The spring rains came hard that year. I could no longer see Troy after school because it stayed light too long. I did some yard work for a neighbor in between rain storms and bought him a new pair of Levi's. When my father asked what I had done with the money, I panicked and told him I'd lost it. He slapped me. Money was really tight.

Troy didn't mind the cold, but he didn't like to get wet. We stayed in the barn and read to each other or played board games. Once we even wrote a radio play and taped it on my cassette deck. It was fun. I kept the tape.

Sometimes when I got to the barn, his clothes were wet. I figured he had been out hunting. He was doing the best he could with what he had, like everyone else.

"You won't have to stay down here forever, you know," I murmured one night in late spring.

He rolled over and looked at me curiously. "What do you mean?"

"I'll be out of school in a year and a half. We'll go to the city and get an apartment. You can sleep inside for once. With the right make-up, you might even be able to go out at night."

He looked stunned, sitting up as his mind absorbed what I was saying. Then he shook his head. "No, you're going to college. I'm not going to have you waste your life on some white trash job because of me."

It was my turn to be stunned. "Troy, my father can't afford to send me to college. He can barely afford to buy us food."

"I know that! You have to apply for a loan –"

We heard a muffled motor running and stopped talking. He jumped up and reached the window before I could move.

"What is it?" I whispered, frightened.

"Come here."

I ran over softly and looked out. A large truck came through the upper pasture. Nobody in my house would hear it. It stopped next to my father's tractor, and a man got out.

Troy hissed through his teeth. "Has your father made his payments on that tractor?"

I went cold. "I don't know. Is that a repo man?"

"Yeah," he whispered. "Your dad won't know until it's too late. They just want their money."

I grabbed Troy's shirt. "We've got to stop him."

He stared at me. "Rachel, I can't let him see me."

Letting go of him, I ran for the ladder.

"No." His voice cracked like a whip behind me. "I'll do it."

Crouching down on the window's edge, he tensed, then jumped silently. His movements were fluid and natural, like a drop of dark wine sliding down crystal. I rushed back over and searched the ground wildly but couldn't see him.

As the repo man was heading toward the tractor, Troy jumped him from behind. From the awful crack the man made when he hit the ground, I was certain he wasn't going to get up again. His head lay at an unnatural angle, eyes staring vacantly at the sky. His partner was just getting out of the truck; Troy didn't see him.

"Watch out!" I yelled. Bolting down the ladder and out through the tool room, I grabbed a pitchfork. I seemed to be moving in slow motion.

When I reached the pair, the man had Troy pinned down with a long knife poised right above his eyes. Their faces were locked in identical expressions of fear and desperation. Then Troy grabbed the intruder's wrist, jerked him forward, and somehow whirled up behind him. Blood sprayed briefly from the man's head as Troy drove both fangs into the base of his skull. They both fell, with Troy on top.

I walked up to them slowly. Troy was ravenously draining the man's blood. His eyes were euphoric, enraptured, his gaze locked straight ahead. His lips were pressed tightly against the open wound; he was gulping in mouthfuls.

I dropped the pitchfork. "Stop it. You're killing him!"

He threw my hand off and snarled. The sky behind him misted between black and neon purple. He held the body effortlessly in one hand and didn't seem to even know who I was. I ran back into the barn and crouched down in the feed room.

After a while the sucking noise stopped, and then he reeled through the door yelling my name. My fear melted into shock.

His face had filled out and it had color. His glossy hair hung glorious and ebony with red highlights. "Rachel, you gotta get outta here." He was slurring like my dad after too many rum and Cokes. "I gotta get rid of them and that truck."

A murderer, but was awe inspiring now – and beautiful.

"Stay away," I whispered.

"No. You gotta go home." He stepped forward and grabbed my arm.

Somehow I thought that he would try and explain the horrible act he had just committed, that he would make sure I still loved him and understood. But he didn't. He just pulled me out the door, stopping only long enough to grab a sharp edged shovel.

"You go home and don't turn around."

I stumbled up the field. The sound of two wet, heavy thuds followed behind me, and then the truck started. I didn't turn around.

Two nights passed before I forced myself to go back. I hadn't been able to sleep. The police had found the abandoned truck about fifteen miles away and were organizing an investigation to locate the men. I had a feeling no one would ever find them.

"Troy?"

The feed room was empty.

"Where are you?" I climbed to the loft.

"Over here."

He sat on his blanket. I felt around quickly for my lighter and lit a candle before he could stop me.

"God, Troy, what's wrong with you?"

His skin was stretched so tightly across his bones that I hardly recognized him. His hair was stringy and dead. He looked so weak I wasn't sure he could stand up. Fear made me incoherent.

"Listen to me. It was an accident. You had to do it! I never should have let you go." When he didn't respond, I grabbed his shirt. "It's my fault, not yours. I asked you to stop them. Nothing's changed."

"You don't even know what happened," he whispered indifferently. "You can't help me. You're tired. Go home and go to sleep."

"I'm not leaving." I tried to lay my head against his chest, but his hand stopped me like a stone.

"No, Rachel, not now. I have to think. I want you to go home."

Panic rose in my throat. "Have you eaten? I'll get a rabbit out of our hutch. Then I'll go."

"It wouldn't do any good." He closed his eyes. "Just go home. I'll talk to you tomorrow."

Miserable, I stood up. "Tomorrow, I'll go buy some new comics."

He nodded without opening his eyes.

◆

I woke up the next morning to the sound of someone ringing our doorbell. My dad was already opening the front door as I walked down the cold hallway. Our neighbor Thomas Walker stepped in; his face was drawn. I felt sick before he said a word.

"Mornin' Ben," he murmured to my father. "My boy didn't come home last night. The town is settin' up a search party. I was hoping you could come and help me." He choked. "It ain't like him. He ain't the kind to worry his mama."

My dad had grabbed his boots and coat before Thomas even finished. "I'll be home when I can," he called over his shoulder on the way out.

I sat down shivering and hoped to God that Stephen had gotten drunk and was passed out somewhere.

It was raining, and I sat on the living room couch staring out at the gray, clean world until about six that night, trying not to think, just waiting for my dad to come back home. Then I got up and made a pot of stew to keep warm on the stove for him.

At ten-thirty, he staggered in wet, tired, and dirty. I looked at his face and knew they hadn't found Stephen.

"Is he dead?"

Dad shrugged. "I don't know. We didn't find anything. He was working on his Honda late last night and took it for a test run. He just never came back."

"Did you find the bike?"

"Nothing." He looked sad. "Poor Thomas. It's for the police now."

Ten minutes later I was on my way to the barn. As I stepped up to the tool room, I heard a clinking noise and looked in the window. Troy had hung a flashlight from a barn rafter and laid out all my dad's tools. He was lying on the floor, working on a red motorcycle. His face glowed, and his hair was spread out across the wood planks like dark crimson satin. I walked back home.

A shadow passed over me. My eyelids clicked open. The

bedroom was dark, but moonlight shone through my open window.

In front of my maple vanity, Troy stood brushing his long hair. When I sat up, he glanced icily at me through phosphorescent eyes. He had never come within fifty feet of the house before – due to fear of being seen.

"What are you doing?"

"Shhh." He put down the brush and walked toward me. He was wearing a clean tee-shirt and a black leather jacket. The supple sleeves hugged his arms like a second skin, contrasting with the flat white of his chest. He pulled something from the pocket. "Give this to your dad and tell him you found it. It should cover the tractor payment till the end of this summer."

I looked at his hand. "Where did you get that?"

He dropped it on my nightstand. "Never mind, just do it." He crouched down. "I came to say goodbye."

I went numb. "You can't leave. What if somebody sees you?"

"What if somebody sees me? Am I frightening now? Am I horrible?"

I looked away. He was a glorious stranger with pale, creamy skin and shining, silken hair, a flaming lost angel who would draw countless people to his warmth and light.

I couldn't answer his questions. "You killed Stephen Walker, didn't you?"

He blinked. "Of course."

I started to cry softly. "He could turn into what you are. Have you thought about that?"

"He won't."

My voice rose. "How do you know?"

His expression darkened. "Because I made sure. I cut off his head with a shovel and buried it fifty feet away from his body." He bit off each word as if they hurt.

I was shaking. "What's happening to you? What are you

becoming?"

He leaned close to me and cupped my chin in his hands, as if he were a collector considering a purchase. "What I am," he replied, his teeth glinting almost blue. The skin around his cheekbones tightened. His smile was as quick as the flicker of a bird's wing. He released my chin, and I fell backwards, fascinated yet terrified.

"Words can't describe what is happening to me," he went on. "I thought that having you would make me happy. We'd live somewhere in between what I couldn't go back to and wouldn't become. Until now I had no idea what a disgusting existence that was."

He raised his arms. "I'm alive again!" Then he stopped and stared at me sadly. "I am what I am. Nothing can deny what it is forever."

Tears ran down my face. "Don't do this. Light a candle and we'll read for a while." Then an impulse struck me. "Why can't I come with you?"

Indecision clouded his face. A momentary battle raged, but I had no idea who was fighting. Then he leaned forward. "You can," he whispered, kissing me on the lips. "Just lie still, and I'll make sure it doesn't hurt."

His lips were soft and warm, like new puppies. They moved across my face with a purpose, and his muscles began tightening to granite. Something told me I should stop him, but I didn't. He caressed my cheek, then moved down my neck. His touch made me shiver, and I tried to kiss him back. He stopped moving at my throat. His mouth opened, and I felt the wet pressure of his tongue probing.

My heart pounded in my ears, and I went cold.

"No!" I tried to twist out from underneath him.

He pinned me against the bed with his chest. "Sssh," he murmured through my hair. "It's like a hard kiss, that's all. A moment, and you'll go to sleep. When you wake, you'll be like me."

I stopped fighting. "I don't want to be like you."

He stiffened and jumped away, angry. "But you want to come with me. How could you keep up like..." He gestured at my body, small and human, with his hand, "like that."

I pulled the blanket up around my neck. "Have you forgotten who I am?"

Frustration replaced condescension. "No!" he cried. "But you can't come with me in that form. I'll have to keep moving, maybe into the city." He seemed to be waiting expectantly, tense and tight, as though it were an effort to keep away from me.

I shook my head slowly, and the smooth skin over his cheekbones pulled up. For a moment I thought he was going to do it anyway, but he stepped back and walked to the window instead. "I can't stay here." Yellow moonlight washed across his shoulders. "I won't forget you. I won't forget any of it."

Part of me died. "Will I see you again?"

He nodded slowly. "Whenever you close your eyes."

Then he leaped up onto the sill and disappeared into the night.

"Greetings, friend," a woman glided up beside him so silently that Milton jumped. She looked more like a suburban housewife who was a little too fond of coffee cake and bon bons than one of the damned.

Morbidly Obese

Rick R. Reed

Milton Bradley was not your typical vampire. First, there was his name. Milton Bradley? The moniker didn't exactly conjure up images of sparkling fangs, rivers of gore, batwings, unspeakable deeds done in shadows. No, the name conjured up a whole panopoly of board games. Milton's only consolation was that he pre-dated the game company by about 100 years...so he could always claim he was the original. Next on the list came Milton's looks. No, he was no Anne Rice hero, full of angst and forbidden sexuality...the embodiment of carnal desire, someone to be played in the movies by a Tom Cruise or Brad Pitt. No, if a movie were to be made of Milton's life, the lead role would probably go to someone like Peter Ustinov or Dom Deluise. Milton was 6'4" tall and weighed close to 400 lbs. "I can't control my eating," Milton would often complain, as the bodies around him fell like so many McDonald's wrappers. "I can't control my eating and I hate myself," Milton would say, imagining himself the "before" subject of a television commercial, his teary, ashen face in close-up. Then he would imagine the "after" shot of the commercial...one of the svelte undead. Gaunt, even, to the point of elegance.

Milton belched and picked a bit of flesh out of his teeth. Another binge, he thought. You'll pay when you step on the scales tomorrow evening. His ample belly was full, but his heart was empty. The corpses, seven in all, lay strewn around him: disgusting, drained reminders of his inability to "control his food." Why couldn't he push himself away from the table so to speak, as others of his kind did, after drinking the blood of one, maybe two (if they were small) humans? He wondered if it was a glandular problem. If only it were so simple, he thought, but to have a glandular problem, one must have glands that function. No, the truth, painful as it was, lay there before him in the seven members of the Daughters of the American Revolution. Milton had expected a larger gathering. He wondered if he had cavorted with some of his victims' ancestors. But such mysteries were lost in a wave of remorse...Milton was a pig, a glutton...perhaps it had something to do with his upbringing? No, he had no one to point a finger at but himself...two hundred years roaming the earth, searching for the ideal meal, would teach anyone enough about themselves that they could make intelligent choices. "I can't control my food," Milton moaned, kicking one of the matronly husks away.

It wasn't until about a week later that Milton saw the flyer. It was posted on a kiosk outside one of those "goth" clubs that had become so popular lately with the youngsters. Pallid youths who liked to dress up in black, wear heavy eye make-up and pretend they were one of the undead. He wished he could be one of them, who really had no idea what being a vampire was all about, if only to be as rail-thin as all of them seemed to be.

The kiosk was covered with flyers advertising new clubs,

bands, apartments to sublet and solicitations for various get rich quick schemes.

But one stood out. Printed on blood red paper, emblazoned with a border of black bat wings, the headline read: *Are You Morbidly Obese?* At first, Milton almost discounted it and moved on. He was getting hungry and knew there was a meeting of Alcoholics Anonymous coming up in the neighborhood in about an hour. AA was a rare treat for Milton, who enjoyed killing two birds with one stone: dinner and cocktails, all rolled into one repentant corpse. It was only the bat wings that gave him pause, made him think this was more than just a come-on for Jenny Craig.

He continued reading: *As one of the undead, do you have trouble controlling your intake? Are you finding it hard to stop at a pint? a quart? a gallon? Have you ballooned? Have other weight loss schemes failed...only to end in binges of epic proportions (think of Jonestown, the My Lai massacre, downed airplanes and other misconceived "disasters" which were really nothing more than some out of control Dracula making a pig of himself)? If you answered yes to any of these questions...help is possible. Just remember: dieting doesn't work...often initial losses of weight are not due to a true change in physique, but mere plasma loss. In order to acquire that gaunt, emaciated look associated with our kind in countless novels, stories, plays and films...you need to CHANGE YOUR BEHAVIOR! Morbidly Obese is a 12-step program designed to change your whole way of thinking and thus, result in lasting weight management. Attend one of our next meetings at one of the following locations on ________ 13, 19____.*

Milton looked around once and then snatched the flyer from the kiosk. There was still time to get to the AA meeting and find out in advance what this 12 step mumbo jumbo was all about. To him, it sounded like something one would do in a country western bar, something a lot more complicated than the two step. And even that was complicated for one of

Milton's girth.

And, Milton smiled grimly, after learning a little about the principles behind the 12 step program, there would still be time for a light snack or maybe, God forbid, a meal.

It was two nights later that Milton attended his first meeting of Morbidly Obese. The meeting was held just after dusk in the large mausoleum on the west side of Chicago's famous Rosehill Cemetery; enter through the side.

Milton was surprised to see many others of his kind: pasty faced ghouls with multiple chins, broad hips, bulging bellies and dimpled knees. That alone made Milton have the vampire equivalent of a warm flush: a cold shiver. The shiver let Milton know he was alive, in a way, and capable of change.

"Greetings, friend," a woman glided up beside him so silently that Milton jumped. She looked more like a suburban housewife who was a little too fond of coffee cake and bon bons than one of the damned. Her blond hair was sprayed stiffly into an upsweep that seemed to have vague First Lady aspirations. Her broad face broke into a smile that Milton couldn't decide was kindly or predatory. From the looks of her thighs, encased in mint green polyester, neither could many of her victims. "You're new here, aren't you?" She leaned back, looking him over. Milton was glad he had worn black.

"Why, yes, yes I am. But I'm here just to observe tonight."

"That's fine. Take your time." She handed him a blood red flyer, then glided away to descend upon a group of laughing fat men, too jolly for vampires...but then everyone in this room was too *something* for a vampire.

Milton took a seat on one of the folding chairs near the back. His stomach rumbled. Usually, by now, he had had at least an appetizer...perhaps a pretty girl with anorexia or a hyperactive child, whose blood was full of Ritalin, which always gave Milton a boost. Losing weight, he could tell already, was not going to be easy.

He glanced down at the flyer. Across the top, in bold

Gothic letters were the words: The 12 Steps. He began reading:

1. We admitted we were powerless over our compulsive death and dining behavior – our lives had become unmanageable.

Well, that much was true, but it didn't change the fact that Milton was very hungry. He could barely make out the words on the page, his vision was so clouded by red, images of flowing blood, rivers of it. He licked his lips and tried to concentrate on the second step: "We came to believe that a Power greater than ourselves could restore us to slenderness." Milton didn't know about restoring himself to slenderness... but he wouldn't mind restoring the blood that was sorely lacking in his system.

And then he noticed it, before they even came into the room: the smell of humans. Two middle-aged women entered through the back and Milton turned to look at them. Like the rest of the crowd, they too were overweight, but the ruddy glow in their cheeks and the sound Milton could just barely pick up, which was of their beating hearts, told him that maybe they had stumbled into the wrong self-help group.

"Marie...why couldn't we just go to TOPS?" The woman with a black bubble cut and blue eye shadow wondered. She had the broad, flat accent of a Chicago southsider.

"Look at yourself, Sheila...is TOPS doing you any good? Did Weight Watchers? God forbid we should hook up with that Richard Simmons fella again! And what did Jenny Craig do for us other than empty our pockets and add twenty pounds to our frames?"

Sheila, a woman with a pear shape, and a salt and pepper hair-do similar to her friend's except hers was more of a woven upsweep, accented with two spit curls, stared at the floor, then picked some lint off her yellow cardigan sweater. Her preoccupation with her sweater told a tale of low self-esteem. Milton thought this one would never lose weight.

And as the hunger rose to fever pitch, he thought that neither of them would ever lose weight, but that had nothing to do with their self-esteem.

He licked his lips.

The smell of them, the heat radiating off their bodies... these things almost transported Milton out of the room. He didn't hear the greeting, he didn't hear the invocation and he heard only a few words from the man who bore an unhealthy resemblance to Sebastian Cabot of *Family Affair* fame, when he stood to testify in a trembling voice.

"Hello, I'm Martin and I'm a hemoholic."

Milton started as the entire group became one in saying: "Hi Martin!"

Milton shook his head and tried to look away from the women, who truth be told, weren't paying much attention to what was going on either. Sheila was looking at herself in a compact mirror as she applied fresh lipstick and Marie dug for something in a voluminous brown vinyl bag.

"I fell off the wagon last week. But I know that one slip does not a failure make." Martin cast his eyes down. "I couldn't help it...I was so hungry and I thought if I got away, into the woods, you know, I might remove myself from temptation. How was I to know the Webelows were having their campout at the very spot I went looking for solitude?" Martin burst into tears and couldn't go on for several minutes.

Milton couldn't care less, he was becoming more and more preoccupied with the women, knowing their blood would be rich, clotted with saturated fats and oils. That Martin character should get a life.

It seemed that Marie and Sheila had suddenly tuned in to the meeting and were more than a little stunned by what was going on. They exchanged glances. They sucked in some air. Together, they cried out, stood and hurried from the room.

Milton made himself count to five, then slid out silently behind them.

Milton sat near his coffin, a custom job crafted from oak, wearing a blood moustache and feeling miserable. It was a vicious circle, he thought, I *am* an addict. The hunger gets out of control, I binge, then feel horrible, then binge again to ease the guilt and remorse.

It was the blue gray hour just before the sun rose and Milton recalled Sheila and Marie, the surprised looks on their faces when he approached them and tried to convince them that he too, had stumbled into the wrong meeting, suggesting they still their beating hearts by having a few slices of pie at the Baker's Square which was just around the corner. The women had been leery, but the promise of French Silk pie made them abandon their good sense when Milton suggested a shortcut through a dark alley from which they never emerged.

Milton climbed into his coffin and pulled the lid shut. He promised himself that he would begin his diet tomorrow. Tomorrow, he told himself, was another night.

But when the sun set the next night, Milton found himself rising with hunger pangs. It was hard squeezing out of the coffin and Milton told himself mildew must be getting into the crypt somehow because the wood was surely beginning to contract.

He tried to deny the hunger pangs, telling himself that it was too difficult for him to have just one. He could never stop at just one...no, he had to have a battalion, a troupe, a club, a group, a squad, a regiment, an assembly, a crew...drinking, drinking, drinking until he felt bloated, until the sharp copper tang of freshly-let blood filled the air...it was only then that Milton felt sated.

And just look where it's gotten me, he thought with despair, I can't even see my feet! *Thank God I don't ever have to look in a mirror.*

Milton struggled into his XXXlarge black canvas pants and black sweat shirt. Even these were beginning to feel snug and soon he would have to find a tailor, because he had gone as big as he could go with off the rack clothes.

Something had to be done. My God, how would he ever find a female companion to see him through eternity?

And in spite of all these sensible thoughts, Milton still craved blood...large quantities of blood. Why weren't there vampire diet pills? Why couldn't there be an undead equivalent of Slim Fast? He'd heard of liposuction...but how could he find a physician to perform the operation?

The first step of Morbidly Obese, the self-help group came back to him, haunting: *We admitted we were powerless over our compulsive death and dining behavior – our lives had become unmanageable.* Milton felt a tear at the corner of his eye and reached up to wipe it away: his finger came back smeared with blood, greedily he licked it from his own tantalizing digit.

The tiny taste of blood made him crazy, filled him with blood lust. In the midst of his red-misted fervor, he thought: this is the way it is for addicts...the yearning controls them instead of the other way around. He realized he was powerless. And a tiny voice inside said: "Yes, Milton you are powerless...so go with it. Why fight it? Lay down the sword and the shield and drink until you're full. Go on, you deserve it."

Milton was out of the crypt as fast as his pudgy legs could carry him. There was no gliding on air for a 400-lb. vampire. His hunger warred with his desire to be thin. I'll start tomorrow night, he told himself, heading toward a little theater he knew of, one that was in rehearsal for a production of *Twelve Angry Men.* Twelve was such a lovely number, he thought, and licked his chops. These twelve men won't be so angry when I get through with them!

But as he neared the theater, his conscience made him sick to his stomach. The rolls of blubber on his large frame shook with every step. Milton could appeal only to his vanity, though. When you're immortal, you really don't have to worry about the health concerns of being overweight.

He stopped, panting, in the shadows and wiped some sweat from his brow. The little theater was just ahead and Milton could see the warm glow of yellow lights. The rehearsal was in progress. Two actors stood outside the stage door and the smell of their blood and hot flesh combined with cigarette smoke and adrenalin to make Milton weak.

He could just barely hear their voices, born up on the night's warm air. How easy it would be to entice them.

The two actors on their smoke break had gone back inside, leaving the stage door slightly ajar. Silently, Milton moved toward it, the smell of human blood wafting out on the current of air coming from inside the warm theater. Saliva gathered in his mouth.

He opened the door, wincing when it creaked, and slipped in the darkened backstage area. One of the difficulties of transforming any group into a trip down the smorgasbord line at a sort of vampire Old Country Buffet was maintaining control over prospective dinner courses. they could often be so unruly, screaming their silly little heads off and running every which way one dinner had begun. Jesus, it was getting so a guy couldn't even enjoy a meal in peace.

The actors were all on stage. They must have been early into rehearsals because they were sitting on folding chairs and reading their lines from scripts.

Milton paused and suddenly his hunger took a nose dive. One of the men looked familiar. Milton immediately thought: Mr. French...Family Affair. And then shook his head as the memory came back from just last night. this was Martin, from the Morbidly Obese 12-step group, the one who had tearfully addressed the crowd, but Milton hadn't heard, because he was too busy thinking how he could open a vein on Sheila and Marie.

And here Martin sat, with a group of humans, rehearsing. He was obviously in control of himself enough to be able to have hobbies with humans like community theater.

Milton was ashamed. Suddenly, this group didn't look as appetizing. He hung his head, staring at the scarred wooden floorboards. He thought then of Morbidly Obese and how his addiction never even gave him the chance to see if he could help himself.

Milton hadn't noticed it had gone quiet in the treater. He turned to leave. Perhaps there was another meeting of Morbidly Obese. Maybe he wouldn't be too late to get up in front of the crowd and admit his weakness. He couldn't wait to hear them all say, "Hi, Milton!"

But as he turned, he tan into a solid wall of flesh. He gave out a little cry and looked up into the feral yellow eyes of...Martin. Martin grinned and put a finger to his lips, then winked.

He leaned close, whispering: "They're ripe for the harvest. Know what I mean?"

Milton was at a crossroads. Martin had turned out to be a disappointment. Becoming an actor so he could feed on unsuspecting community players...and the angle was pretty clever, if one didn't linger too long in one place. But what did it mean? Martin sorrowfully confessing one night and ready to binge the next? And there was another matter: Milton had always felt so lonely, so desperately lonely, shunned for his weight by most others of his kind. It wasn't fair. Yet, here seemed to be a vampire who had come to terms with is obesity, maybe even accepted himself for who he was.

And Milton saw that he might have a sort of mate in his lonely immortality. He pictured the two of them feeding together...how much easier crowd control would be with two large, burly vampires to keep the food in line!

Yes, maybe what Milton needed was not a 12-step group, but a self-acceptance and another like-minded souls with whom to share his life. It was all anybody really needed, he thought, dead or alive.

So he leaned close to Martin's broad back and whispered, "Let's eat, Martin."

And Martin said, out of the corner of his mouth, "Call me Sebastian."

There was a man lying on the floor behind the cartons, hands folded on his chest. Jessie had seen dead men before, had huddled next to a man on a grate one night for warmth, only to find him stiff and cold in the morning.

Prey For The Dead

Don D'Ammassa

The smell was so awful, Jessie almost stopped looking before she found the body. But she hadn't eaten all day, the sun was dropping fast, and the basement looked promising.

There was a broken window in the back of the deserted warehouse, almost completely concealed by crumbling packing crates. Jessie removed the remaining shards of glass carefully. It was going to be a tight fit even for her slim body and she didn't want to do any damage to her last intact pair of jeans.

It was a longer drop than expected and she landed painfully. The basement was dark, but she had the stub of a candle and some matches. It didn't do much to banish the gloom, but at least she could see well enough to avoid tripping over the debris. And there was plenty of that – broken cartons, disconnected electrical wiring, pieces of mechanical equipment she couldn't identify. Jessie examined it all with an experienced eye. Anything she took must fit through the narrow window. There were some nice aluminum shutters she could have sold at the scrapyard, but they were too wide. She slipped a crescent wrench into the canvas shoulder bag where she carried her only change of clothing, along with a package of electrical fuses, two paperback mystery novels, and a pair of sunglasses. They'd earn some small change at the thrift store, but not enough for a decent meal.

The basement was a series of linked chambers stretching off in every direction. Most of these were empty except for layers of dust. Others contained stacks of wooden crates encasing enigmatic machines. Jessie made her way among them, moving slowly to avoid extinguishing her candle, cursing silently under her breath as she realized this wasn't going to be the treasure trove she'd hoped for.

The rancid odor was strong enough to be noticeable at the first main cross corridor. Jessie sniffed, rubbed her upper lip and turned in the opposite direction, explored all the way to one side wall, adding a screwdriver to her stash. She returned to the intersection and advanced into the unexplored branch, but within a few steps the smell was so bad that she stopped.

"I don't need this." She half turned to go back, but the truth was that she did need to explore further. What she'd found so far wouldn't bring much more than a dollar. A decent burger and fries cost three times that. Sighing with exaggerated resignation, she advanced as rapidly as possible into the darkness. The candle was nearly gone so she had an additional incentive to hurry.

A minute later she found herself in a narrow dead end filled with corrugated boxes. The smell of decay and corruption was so intense she felt lightheaded. Obviously some animal had crawled into a corner and died; the air was thick with the sweet smell of rotten flesh. Jessie wanted desperately to leave, but she deliberately set her candle on top of one carton and began prying open another.

The first two contained rags, the second cotton

workgloves. That was promising though not ideal. The next box was filled with coiled electrical cables. Jessie used two arms to shift it to one side so that she could open the one below, and that's when she spotted the dead body.

Two dead hands, actually, one on top of the other.

At first she thought it was just a pair of gloves, but she moved the candle closer and the body's outline became more obvious. There was a man lying on the floor behind the cartons, hands folded on his chest. Jessie had seen dead men before, had huddled next to a man on a grate one night for warmth, only to find him stiff and cold in the morning.

The smell was overpowering.

Jessie shifted a box to one side and slipped through the gap. Her stomach was rebelling now, but there wasn't enough in it to be worth vomiting. Crouching, she let her hands explore the corpse, not allowing herself to think about what she was doing. There was a wallet, and she removed it quickly, slipping it into her own pocket without examining the contents. The dead man wore a suit and tie, the former a heavy tweed, the latter such a brilliant red that she noticed it even in the wan candlelight, and a quite substantial digital wristwatch with a luminescent display. This wasn't a street person who had crawled into a hole to die.

Jessie was suddenly nervous. She removed the watch quickly, retrieved her candle, and retreated to the broken window. It took a few seconds to find a box she could move so that she could climb back up, and while searching for one, she had the uneasy feeling that she wasn't alone. The window seemed tighter on the way out, her hips wouldn't quite fit through.

"Don't panic," she told herself. "You came in, you can go out. Just calm down and do it."

Something brushed her left leg.

She kicked out with both feet, struggling to extricate herself. Her jeans snagged on something, held for a second, then tore free. With a final surge of effort, Jessie pulled herself completely out of the window and lay breathless on the ground.

The sun was almost completely gone.

With a wary glance around to confirm that she was unobserved, Jessie walked deliberately around the side of the building to the main road. Pedestrian traffic was still heavy, but the exodus from the city had begun. The streets were filled with commuters headed for the on-ramps.

There was an empty bench in front of a bank. Jessie's clothing was still in sufficiently good condition that she could appear in public without attracting attention so long as the beat cops who knew her face weren't around. She moved the wallet from her pocket to her bag, then opened it within that shelter. Experience warned her not to count her take where it could be seen. No credit cards. No driver's license. No identification card. No family pictures. But there was money. A lot of money. Almost a thousand dollars.

Jessie closed the bag and then her eyes, and leaned back. "Yes," she said softly. "Yes. Yes. Yes." She could buy a new set of clothing, rent a hotel room for a night or two and take a real bath instead of a shower at the YWCA. Sleep the night through without worrying that some drug addict or sex maniac or violence junkie would turn her into an uncounted crime statistic. Maybe even eat in a restaurant, a real one where they came and served you and you had to leave a tip. Just once though, to celebrate. If carefully managed, she had enough money to last through the beginning of winter.

The fish and chips at Antonelli's were delicious and the waitress never gave her a second look. For the first time in months, Jessie didn't feel acutely self conscious while in a public place.

It was full dark outside when she emerged onto the street, and the traffic level had dropped appreciably. Jessie had been sleeping in an abandoned building on the east side, but tonight she was going to stay at a cheap hotel. The cash would have to be concealed somewhere, but that could wait till morning. It wouldn't do to keep it on her person; the regular street people knew she had nothing worth stealing, but there were still the crazies, and the runaways, and she had no intention of getting mugged out of what was, in her frame of reference, a considerable fortune.

Someone was watching her.

Jessie stopped in the middle of the sidewalk, convinced beyond any shadow of doubt of that fact. She'd developed a sixth sense about danger since losing her job, her boyfriend, and her apartment. Slowly she turned her head, trying not to be obvious.

There were two teenagers with their heads together in front of a hardware store, laughing at some private joke. An elderly woman stood at the curbside, apparently watching for a taxi. Two well dressed men were approaching, one three steps behind the other. A third man, wearing a dark grey suit, stood at the corner, staring into the distance.

Jessie waited until the two men passed, then pressed on.

The feeling persisted, grew in intensity. She crossed to the opposite side of the street and hesitated, pretending to examine the contents of a jewelry store window. Actually she was trying to catch sight of anything suspicious by watching the reflections. After a few fruitless seconds, she turned away, and almost bumped into the man with the newspaper.

"Sorry," he said apologetically, hesitating for a second. He wore grey tweed and a bright red tie, and his breath stank of corruption.

She shrank back, breathless, convinced that this was the man she'd robbed earlier. But that was impossible, of course. He'd been stone cold dead, several days dead judging by the smell. It was just a coincidence that this man happened to be dressed similarly.

And smelled the same.

"No problem," she whispered, refusing to look into his face, glancing to one side until she sensed that he had moved on. She waited until the man was out of sight, then deliberately turned and walked off in the opposite direction.

McGuire's Hotel didn't look like much on the outside, and as a matter of fact, it didn't look like much on the inside either. But Jessie had lived there for several months while collecting the last of her unemployment. The wallpaper was faded and the ceiling plaster was cracked, but the door locks worked and there was plenty of hot water and that's all she cared about at the moment.

She checked in, paid for the night in advance, and found herself in a front room overlooking the street. There was very little traffic now, pedestrian or vehicular. The downtown had been declining for years, the shops closing earlier or altogether, the jobs fleeing to the suburbs along with the job holders. Jessie undressed quickly and showered to get the worst of the dirt off, then drained the tub and drew a bath, in which she lay with her eyes closed until the water had dropped to room temperature. Her clothes were soaking in the sink.

Eventually she rose from the bath, toweled herself dry, and slipped into her alternate outfit. The slacks were threadbare and there were tiny holes in the blouse, but they covered her too thin body adequately enough in private. Jessie wrung out her dirty clothes and draped them over the shower rod, then walked into the bedroom to see if the television worked. It did, after a fashion, but the picture was grainy and fluttered periodically. She watched all of one sitcom and part of another, eventually realizing that the world these characters lived in was so totally alien to her now that she could no longer understand the jokes.

She turned off the television, wandered to the window and trailed her eyes from the garish neon sign on the building opposite down to the empty street.

Almost empty.

A man stood in the shadows on the opposite corner, a tall man in a grey tweed suit. He was wrapped in darkness and remained so motionless that it was several seconds before she realized he was there, but once she had spotted him, she had the distinct feeling that he was returning her gaze.

She wondered what color tie he was wearing.

Anger and fear pumped adrenaline through her body. She wrenched the curtain across the window so harshly that it jammed in the track halfway across. Her efforts to tug it free were unsuccessful.

"Great," she said softly.

The night was warm and humid and there was no air conditioning. Jessie stripped to her underwear and folded the blanket down to the foot of the bed. The feel of cool, relatively clean sheets top and bottom was a luxury she had never appreciated until it was gone. With two pillows under her head, she settled back to sleep.

The window rattled.

Jessie's eyes opened but she was otherwise motionless, waiting for the sound to repeat itself. Sometimes there was a brisk breeze at night, like a night owl wandering through a concrete forest. She started to lower her lids, but then it came again, as though something knocked on the glass with leathery knuckles.

She was on the fourth floor.

"Close the window if it bothers you," she told herself. But that would make the room even more stifling. If the curtain had been completely closed, she could have ignored it, but that two foot section of exposed glass seemed like a gigantic lens through which unfriendly eyes might be watching.

"Damn it!" Angry with herself, with the fear that had become an inescapable part of her life these past two years, Jessie threw back the sheet and stood up, took several deep breaths, and walked directly to the window.

There was nothing to see. The window was untouched, as

was the narrow ledge below. Impulsively she glanced down to where she'd seen the man in tweed standing, but the spot was empty now. Nor could she see him or anyone else in either direction. There was distant traffic noise, but no movement.

Thoughtfully, Jessie leaned out and glanced to her left. The fire escape loomed above and below, so close she could have reached out and touched it. For a fraction of a second, it seemed to her that something moved there, but it was impossible to see clearly. The neon sign from the beauty parlor across the street had been extinguished now and the nearest streetlight had burned out.

She had barely made it back to the bed when the window trembled again.

"God damn it to hell!" Without hesitation this time, she walked directly to the window, started to pull it closed. The frame moved about two inches before coming to a halt, jammed in the track. Jessie tugged on it tentatively, then determinedly, but it wouldn't budge.

With one shoulder pressed against the glass, she reached outside, trying to find the obstruction with her fingers. As she did so, something incredibly cold caught hold of her wrist, something very much like a human hand except that its substance was so hard and unyielding that it felt like metal spikes against her flesh. She jumped at the touch, lost her footing, and fell to her knees with her captured arm extended awkwardly. There was a sudden sharp pain and she tore her arm free, falling flat on her back.

There were two parallel scratches across her left wrist, from both of which beads of blood were visibly forming.

"Great!" Jessie had a terrible fear of illness or injury. Supposedly the local hospitals treated the homeless regardless of medical coverage, but she knew in practice the treatment was minimal at best and delivered with notable reluctance. She washed the small wounds thoroughly, then used toilet paper to staunch the flow of blood until scabs began to form.

The moment she turned off the bathroom light, the window rattled louder than before, continued for three or four seconds, stopped for the same length of time, then rattled again.

Jessie turned on all the lamps in the room. Two worked, two did not, and the light from those that did only seemed to emphasize the gloominess. She tried to pull the curtain wide open, but it was jammed in that direction as well. Frustrated, she dropped into a cushioned chair and tried to regain her composure.

Someone was whispering. At first she didn't recognize it, thought it might be some other sound made indistinct by the night. Then she realized it had the cadence of speech, and she thought perhaps someone in one of the other rooms had left the television on. But it seemed too close at hand, as if someone were hovering just outside. She leaned forward, straining to hear the words more distinctly, and after a few minutes, she began to understand.

"Little thief," the voice was saying. And "Let me in" and other phrases. She turned each sound over in her mind until it was understandable, and then pieced them together into the same sequence, repeated over and over. "Let me in, little thief. What was mine cannot be yours. What is yours will soon be mine." But Jessie wasn't certain how much of that she was actually hearing and how much was order she had superimposed on meaningless noise.

If only she could close the window, then perhaps she could go back to sleep.

That's when she remembered the wrench and screwdriver she'd scavenged from the basement. She wasn't the handiest person in the world, but it was just possible that she might be able to force it back onto the track and lock it closed. That would shut out the frightening whispering, and anything else that might lurk outside.

Jessie stood on the narrow table and examined the source

of her frustration. The wood had splintered at the top of the frame and her first effort to close the window had forced it to move in a direction that had never been intended. In order to get it closed, she would first have to move it back to its original position, and the closeness of the wall made it very difficult to get enough leverage. After a moment's thoughtful hesitation, she lifted her left foot onto the windowsill and shifted her weight in that direction, swinging her body up and partly out the window. As she did so, Jessie sensed rather than saw something large and dark moving just beside her, and then something caught hold of her left elbow and started to pull her out into the night.

"Little thief!" it whispered harshly, and then she was trying to pull free and her feet went out from under her. Desperately, she reached for the drapes and one hand closed on the harsh synthetic and the other caught hold of a woven material. Like tweed. And then she was falling back into the room, dragging something with her, something heavy and cold and with breath that stank of corruption.

The table overturned and she fell heavily, half sprawled across the bed. Briefly there was a weight on her chest, then it was gone and the room was silent again.

But not empty.

"Thanks for inviting me in," whispered the darkness.

Jessie hastily retrieved the screwdriver and raised it menacingly. She knew that something was there among the shadows, something that could blend in too perfectly for human eyes to detect. She edged slowly toward the door, her back to the wall, and was almost close enough to reach for the knob when he appeared out of nowhere.

It was the dead man from the warehouse, tweed suit and red tie, the same man who'd brushed against her on the street. Except that he didn't look so much like a man now. His eyes were deepset and almost as red as his tie, his jaw seemed unnaturally extended below flared nostrils, and his skin was pale and unhealthy looking.

The stench was suddenly overpowering.

"Caught you, my little thief," the man whispered and reached toward her.

Jessie danced back, retreated into the bathroom and tried to slam the door, but he was there too quickly, gliding effortlessly across the floor, and he threw the door back. Jessie's instinct was to retreat again, but she knew there was no escape behind her, only death. She swung her right arm with all the strength she could manage and drove the point of the screwdriver up through the underside of his chin out through the right cheek and into the doorjamb. He hissed and clutched at her arm, but Jessie danced away, relinquishing her hold on the screwdriver.

She squeezed past the struggling body but his fist caught her in the small of the back with bruising force and she lost her balance, slammed into the dresser so hard that she was momentarily stunned.

Then he was coming toward her and she saw his mouth open, crimson lips with pearl white teeth that were unnaturally long and sharp and she was throwing things at him, the lamp, the telephone, anything that came to hand and he kept on coming, his face growing larger and larger and Jessie thought she could read the end of her life in those dead eyes and smell her own body's corruption in that rotten breath.

And then he was backing away from her, his face suddenly swelling obscenely, the dead flesh splitting bloodlessly open and she realized that she was holding the Gideon Bible in her hand. The intruder's head turned toward the window, but this time she was quicker, interposing herself between her attacker and his freedom. She opened the Bible and held it forward, slowly advancing, forcing the man to retreat into the bathroom.

"Not this time," she said harshly. "This time I'm not

going to lose."

The man in tweed shrank back further, seeming somehow smaller, less threatening. "Let me go, little thief, and I'll spare your life."

"Why should I? It looks to me like I just wait for morning and I'll never have to worry about you again." She saw his surprised expression and laughed. "Oh, I know what you are, all right. There was a time when I wouldn't have believed any of this, but living on the street for a while changes things. You get to understand how much evil there really is in the world."

For a moment, it looked like he would speak again, but then he subsided, and seemed to grow even smaller. Jessie righted a toppled chair and moved it directly in front of the bathroom door, settled in with the Bible in her lap, watched her prisoner shrink back to the far corner. Dawn was a long way off but she was safe so long as she remained awake and she had enough money to last for months, months before she'd have to search dumpsters and abandoned buildings for things to sell at the thrift center. The other street people would realize something was up, of course, when she abandoned her usual habits, so she'd have to be on guard all the time. They'd corner her some night in a dark alley or follow her back to wherever she was currently sleeping, hoping to discover where she kept her money.

Jessie thought about her future for a long time, and her smile of satisfaction inverted itself, and sometime an hour or so before dawn, she closed the Bible and set it aside and went to meet her guest in the bathroom.

It was better to become a predator than remain the prey.

Tyler awoke in darkness, lying on his back, surrounded by wood. He could feel the walls to his sides, and found the box's lid by trying to sit up – much to the discomfort of his forehead.

To Die For

Dominick Cancilla

At first, what Tyler hated most about being a vampire was the teeth. They kept getting caught on his lower lip and, even worse, made him sound like an idiot when he tried to talk. He'd been a creature of the night for only two days when he discovered that the teeth were nothing compared to the groupies.

When he applied for the job, Tyler had hoped for a position as a Texas chainsaw maniac. Chasing screaming teenage girls through one of the theme park's many "Halloween Terror Nights" mazes with a roaring *faux* chainsaw in hand sounded like a decent way to earn some extra cash over four October weekends, and if he could imagine that some of the girls he chased were among the legions who'd dated and dumped him for something with more cash to flash, so much the better. Unfortunately, this preference wasn't of much import to the powers that be, and when he was offered the Dracula position he snapped it up. It was a hackneyed and less active part, but he could do the stupid accent and wasn't in a position to turn away anything that might pay for another round of textbooks to perpetuate the myth that he might make it through college and give him an excuse not to sit up all night wondering when his parents were going to come stumbling home.

The act was pretty easy. All he had to do was lie in a big wooden coffin, arms crossed, eyes closed, until a group reached his station in the maze. Then he'd "awaken," sit up, bare his teeth, and hope the kids ran screaming to the next scene. At first he'd found it difficult to work in a room lit only by a strobe light, but his argument that it made no sense to light an outdoor crypt with anything but moon or torch light earned him only an annoyed glance from his supervisor, so he bit the bullet and dealt with it.

For the most part, guests played along just fine. They screamed, they ran, they gave Tyler the respect due an essentially immortal thing of evil from beyond the grave. Aside from his cape getting caught on everything, the fact that the coffin was a bit too short to fit him comfortably, and the way pancake makeup made his face sweat, everything went well up until the second shift on his third night as the Count. After that, it was pretty much a freefall straight to hell.

That's when the woman with the pendant showed up.

Tyler knew he was in trouble the moment he laid eyes on her. The silver bat she wore on a chain around her neck caught his eye immediately – first because it seemed to be perched on an ample bosom pushed up by a tight black camisole; then because it started rushing toward him, bosom and all, when everyone was supposed to be running away.

Because of the strobe light, it took Tyler a second to realize that the woman was coming at him. He had only a glimpse of her face – beautiful and alight with a look both erotic and hungry – before she was within grappling distance and his world became nothing but throbbing bosom and a touch of cool silver against his forehead.

"Count," she cooed, pressing his face into her. "You have drawn me to you despite my weakening will. I'm yours, to do with as you will."

It was not the kind of behavior that Tyler had come to expect from park patrons, but he thought he wouldn't mind it becoming a trend.

The part of Tyler that wanted to keep his job overcame the part that would have paid good money to keep his face right where it was, and he managed to break her embrace by placing his hands on her well-tapered waist and pushing with all he had.

The woman glanced down at the pancake makeup smearing her chest but didn't seem to be bothered by this mark of rejection. Her hands rested on his caped shoulders as he held her away, and her steel-blue eyes bore hungrily into him. With calculated sensuousness, she tilted her head to one side, baring her neck, and tried to press herself closer.

"Bite me, Count," she said. "Drink of me. I am in your power and cannot resist." She closed her eyes and parted her lips in a way that ensured Tyler would be unable to stand up in his costume's loose silk pants any time soon without significant embarassment.

Tyler had watched Lugosi's *Dracula* several times to ready himself for his part, but this was a situation he hadn't prepared for. As much as he might have liked to comply with the woman's request under normal circumstances, that really wasn't an option, so he tried to return to more familiar territory.

"I cannot, my dear," he said in the best Lugosi voice he could manage around the teeth. "It is on these shores that I first met Van Helsing, and I must remain ever vigilant!"

The woman's grip on Tyler's shoulders loosened, and between flashes of the strobe light, her eyes, suddenly cold and almost lifeless, opened. "What do you mean, 'on these shores?'" she asked in a suspicious tone, striking compared to the breathy voice she'd used up to that point.

"This country – America," Tyler explained.

Her arms lifted from his shoulders and crossed, dramatically changing the scenery. "Don't you mean England? Dracula met Van Helsing in England."

Tyler rolled his eyes. "Give me a break, will you?" he said in his own, slightly irritated, voice. "I'm just an actor, not a vampire expert." It was a step out of character that would have gotten him fired on the spot if he'd worked for Disney.

"Well!" the girl huffed. She kicked the base on which the coffin sat and stomped out of the room, followed closely by those who'd hung around to gawk at the scene she'd made. The next group came in just in time to catch Tyler sitting up in his coffin looking more annoyed that vampiric, and with a seriously smeared countenance.

The incident was bizarre and certainly memorable, but Tyler had no idea that would be only the beginning of a much longer, eventually fatal, problem until he headed out of the maze at the end of his half-hour shift.

The night air and steady light outside the maze tent was refreshing, but Tyler's relief didn't last long. The woman with the pendant was waiting for him, standing still-crossarmed by the path which led toward the break room where Tyler intended to get a little rest and touch up his face. Any lingering fantasies he harbored about what might have happened if he had let her go about playing her vampire game turned to dust under the weight of her nearly-insane-with-rage glare.

His first impulse was to just walk on by, hoping that by paying no attention to her he would provoke no action. Obviously that did not fit her plan; she stepped into his path at the last possible moment and held out a fistful of white paper toward him as if it were an accusation.

Reflex brought Tyler's hand up to take what was offered,

and once the transfer was complete the woman with the pendant turned to continue the angry exit she'd begun back at the coffin.

Tyler had to get to the break room before he could get a good look at what the woman had handed him. It was napkins, seven of them, from one of the refreshment stands. On them, the woman had written – in great detail – just how a classical vampire should act. It was all written with a delicate hand, notable for the fact that it was near perfect despite the unusual media and that not a single "t" was crossed.

"Whatcha got?" Julie was sitting on the break-room couch in her sports bra and bicycle pants, Bride of Frankenstein from the neck up only.

"Oh," Tyler said, any glibness he once had lost in embarrassment that he'd been caught standing in a doorway reading napkins. "It's just a – it's a note from a guest. I guess she didn't much like my performance."

"Well, don't sweat it." She patted the couch beside her. "Take a load off and tell me about it?"

Tyler took her up on her offer. He plopped down on the sofa and held the wad out to Julie. "Take a look."

She did, really reading the words where Tyler had pretty much just skimmed. "Man, this girl should write Cliff's notes," Julie commented after napkin four. She didn't say anything else until she finished reading.

"Oooh, I don't like this," she said.

"What?"

"'Learn your part for tomorrow you may die.' That is some serious weirdo talk."

"Let me see that." Tyler took the napkins back. The threatening sentence was written on the back of the last page; he hadn't noticed it before. "Damn," was all he could think of to say.

"You've got to show this one to security."

"I guess. I just don't want to make a big deal out of

something stupid. It's probably nothing."

"This is Hollywood, honey. We've got every kind of nut here. You can't be too careful."

"I guess. Still–"

"I hope I'm not interrupting a tender intermonster moment here." Joey, one of the wolfmen, came into the room, made up in full fur. "And I hope you aren't leading the bride on when you're already spoken for, you smooth vampire you."

"You're a funny man," Tyler said as Joey took a seat in the make-up table's director's chair. "But don't taunt the prince of darkness when he's having a bad night."

"Bad night my ass. Julie, you should see the sweet thing that's after our Tyler here."

"Oh great," Tyler said, sinking back in the sofa. "So just how many people saw what happened?"

"I don't know that one," Joey said. "But your foxy lady asked a whole bunch of us about you – she's obviously got it bad. So what happened? Something hideously perverted, I hope."

Tyler ignored the question. "What do you mean she was asking about me? You didn't tell her my name, did you?"

Joey winked. "You'll thank me in the morning. Besides, it's not like it's a state secret, and I didn't think you'd want to let someone like that –"

"That's great; that's just fabulous," Tyler interrupted. "I am so doomed."

"The girl's some kind of weird Dracula groupie," Julie said by way of inadequate explanation. "She got all upset that Tyler's performance wasn't picture perfect, and now she wants to stake him or something."

"Oops."

"No kidding, oops," Tyler said, holding a hand across his eyes for a moment to squeeze back a forming headache. "Now what am I supposed to do?"

"Tell security and go on with your life," Julie said. "Odds

are she's had her little snit and isn't coming back. But if she does, security can pick her up easy if she's as gorgeous as Dick Puppet the Wolfman says."

"That's '*Mr.* Wolfman, Dick Puppet' to you, honey. Like 'Ace Ventura, Pet Detective.' But seriously Tyler, she's right. The girl's gone, and if she comes back, you can tell her the wolfman's waiting to make her howl. Awooo!" He finished the bay with a grin to match his mask.

Tyler was still uptight but couldn't help grinning at his friend's performance. "Thanks, that's really helpful," he said. After a moment he sighed away the last smile, got up, and headed for the phone in the corner. "Okay, let's get this over with."

◆

It went just as Julie had predicted. Security treated his story seriously – at least to his face – and nobody reported seeing the woman with the pendant for the rest of the night. Tyler had trouble getting into the part of Dracula again, but he managed to make it through the rest of his shifts without embarrassing himself further.

It was two in the morning when he finally got back to his car, exhausted and more than ready to head home. As he put the keys in the ignition, the hair on the back of his neck prickled, accompanied by a creepy feeling of being watched. He glanced into the rearview mirror. Nothing unusual showed in the silvered glass and Tyler had been ready to write it all off to stress and paranoia when a soft voice whispered, "Sleep, my Count," and something hard struck the back of his head.

◆

Tyler awoke in darkness, lying on his back, surrounded by

wood. He could feel the walls to his sides, and found the box's lid by trying to sit up – much to the discomfort of his forehead. He realized where he was almost immediately, and when he discovered that the box was somehow sealed shut, he lapsed into screaming, pounding panic with equal speed.

The coffin wasn't of first-class construction, but it proved more than equal to resist his feeble efforts. At some point while he was bruising his fists against the fiberboard panels, Tyler became aware that he was no longer in his street clothes but in the slick, pseudo-silk Dracula costume he'd so recently freed himself of. Even worse, the vampire-teeth prosthesis had been placed in his mouth (he couldn't believe it had taken him more than an instant to notice *that*). The change of clothes implied so many disturbing things that Tyler was forced into new, heretofore unexplored heights of panic, and his screams and struggles to escape redoubled appropriately.

The air in the coffin was quickly becoming hot, stale, and thick with CO_2. Tyler's breathing tightened – whether due to the failing air or stress he couldn't tell. It was obvious that a few minutes more of heavy exertion would suffocate him, but lying in silence, hoping to be discovered and rescued, would most likely prove suicidal.

Tyler had been awake in the box for a subjective hour some sixty seconds long when that miniscule part of his mind not overcome by the sharpening face of death realized that some of the pounding on the coffin lid was not coming from his fists, but from the other side of the wood. He became instantly still and silent, his dread of suffocation replaced by fear of what his captor had planned for him – and realistically, who but his captor would have found him so quickly.

"For God's sake," a voice said. The words, resonated by the box, were muffled but seemed to surround him. He immediately recognized the voice of the woman with the pendant, despite the distortion caused by his prison. "If you can't do better than that I'm just going to leave you in there until sunrise. Understand?"

Tyler didn't, but figured he didn't have much choice. He answered "Yes" in what felt like little more than a whisper, but she apparently heard.

"Good. Now count ten, open the lid, and we'll see how well you've learned. Do well and I promise we'll have a good time – a *very* good time. Fail, and I'll be – upset." The way she said that last word made Tyler shiver in a way mere cold could never match.

He began to count. Just after "two" there was a sharp impact on the coffin lid which made him jump.

"Count silently," the woman said, obviously annoyed. She followed the command with "Moron," barely loud enough for him to hear.

Tyler ran ten seconds by in his mind, taking a shallow breath after every other. He hesitated when the time came, fearing the hopefulness that would overtake him if the lid didn't give at his touch. For a heart-stopping moment he did indeed think the lid would resist him, but when he put the full of his remaining strength into it, it rose easily.

Cool evening air rushed over him as the lid opened, feeding his starving lungs and turning the sweat-pasted back of his shirt to ice. He sat up quickly, upper body flopping over the coffin's side to let his arms hang free. He sucked in great wheezing gulps of air and took in his surroundings.

He was in the Dracula set of the classic monster maze, just as he'd assumed. Thankfully, the work lights were neon instead of strobes, albeit only enough of them to give the room a twilight glow.

The woman with the pendant stood by the coffin dressed in the black silk and lace of hideously confining underclothes that no woman in her right mind wore unless she was preparing to drive a man insane.

In no time flat Tyler went from wondering if security would find him before things got even worse to hoping that the entire night staff had forgotten to show up for work. His eyes ran from the crush of her full bosom to where garter belt and g-string hugged her hips, and were falling lower still when she crossed the distance between them with a single long stride. As she closed on him, Tyler tried to do the right thing – he sat up straight and forced himself to look at her face.

There was just enough time for him to register her very unsexy, highly annoyed expression before he caught the flash of her right fist speeding toward his face.

The impact was like a sledgehammer to his forehead, driving him back into the coffin so suddenly that his head whacked the wooden bottom hard enough to bring the lid crashing down on him. Even in the renewed blackness Tyler saw lights; at least he now knew what the woman with the pendant had used to knock him out in the car.

"Wrong!" The woman's voice engulfed Tyler. "You're Count Dracula, not some damned obscene-phone-call pervert at a sorority sleepover. Jesus!" The coffin shook as she kicked its base for emphasis. "Count to ten and start over."

His head still reeling from the blow, Tyler had to restart twice before he reached ten, but when he did, he opened the coffin lid in the slow, deliberate manner he'd been taught by parks staff. He sat up slowly and straight, and by exerting what he thought was admirable control only turned his head toward her after he was sitting up completely.

She stood with hands loosely crossed over crotch looking so innocent and demure that Tyler could almost believe it.

He bared his teeth, and was pleased to see her full lips quiver ever so slightly. Then with a grin Tyler hoped was a cross between evil and seductive he said, "Well, now, what have we here?"

The woman with the pendant shot forward like a snake, and Tyler was seeing stars and falling backwards before he realized where he'd misstepped.

"'Well, now, what have we here?'" the woman asked as the

lid slammed down. "Jesus Christ, why not, 'Hey hot mama,' or 'Woo baby' while you're at it? Huh? Look, just stick with the classics – 'Good evening,' or just 'Welcome.' And where's the accent? You're not god-damned Count Malibu. Now try it again and no screw ups. I'm seriously losing the mood here."

Tyler certainly didn't want that. The woman was certifiable, but she was hotter than anyone Tyler had seen outside a magazine bought on the sly, and was obviously prepared to put out big time if he'd play along with her little fantasy. Not only that, but she could obviously kick his ass, and if Tyler wasn't going anywhere, he figured he might as well make the most of it.

He counted ten, took several deep breaths, opened the coffin, and rose.

Perhaps a few good blows to the head were what Tyler had needed to clear his mind. He concentrated on the role, visualized his reward, and tried not to think about what would happen if he screwed up again.

"Good evening," Tyler said after sitting up and turning toward her. "I am...Count Dracula."

"I am in your power, Count," the woman with the pendant said, her voice dangerously husky. "I awoke with the sound of your summons in my mind, and was drawn here with no will but your own."

Tyler wasn't sure if he was supposed to get out of the coffin, but he couldn't think of any way to do it that wouldn't be awkward at best. Instead, he reached out a hand and did his best Lugosi arthritic-looking "I'm drawing you to me" gesture. "Come to me, child, and feel the night's embrace."

He'd made that up but it seemed to do the trick. She walked toward him slowly, her hips rolling in a way that made him react in a very un-undead fashion. Absently, Tyler wondered how she could walk so perfectly over a graveyard-dirt floor on stiletto heels.

When she was close enough, Tyler reached out and placed his hands gently on her waspish waist. The cold of her, reflecting, he was certain, the cold of the night, was easy to feel through the thin fabric and stiff stays of her outfit.

She allowed herself to be drawn to him. When her belly reached the coffin edge and her breasts brushed Tyler's chest, she held his eyes with the deep blue of hers and whispered to him. "Take me. Drink of me, this first time of three, and we'll consummate the bed of my life to come." She closed her eyes and tilted her head to one side, baring her throat.

Tyler wondered what would happen when his plastic tooth extensions snapped off against her neck, but figured he'd cross that bridge when he came to it.

The woman shivered in his hands as he leaned forward, and her lips parted sensuously, just enough for him to see her needle-sharp incisors reaching down from sockets in her gums in a way no makeup master could hope to duplicate.

The woman's eyes snapped open at almost the same instant Tyler blurted "Oh, shit!" There followed a blur of motion, a sense of falling, and the slam of the coffin lid. Tyler didn't feel the pain in his face until he was again in darkness, but it was strong enough to squeeze tears from his eyes. It felt like his nose was broken.

"You idiot," she railed outside the box. "I can't believe you let me get so worked up and then pulled a bonehead move like that. Jesus! You look hot as hell but you're dumb as a post! What did I ever see in you?"

Tyler didn't dare say a word. He just lay where he was, listening to the woman stomp about and waiting to find out what would happen. After a short but interminable period, she calmed down a bit and returned to the coffin's side.

"Okay," she said. "We try one more time. If it works, it works. If it doesn't, we move on to the fantasy where I break the spell and drive a hunk of wood through your chest – got it?"

Tyler nodded agreement, for all the good it would do.

Apparently taking silence for assent, the woman told Tyler to count to ten once again.

Things were much, much weirder and more dangerous than Tyler had imagined. The woman wasn't insane – or not *just* insane. She was what Tyler only pretended to be. At least, she appeared to be. It explained the cold flesh, the speed, the strength, and the teeth, but it begged a lot of really, really heavy questions.

Tyler supposed that if the woman with the pendant really was – that – it explained her obsession: she was looking to relive a past experience, or maybe just pretend she was part of the mortal world for one night. It wasn't much different from anyone else's little sex fantasies. Aside, of course, from the fact that she'd kill her partner if he didn't play his part well enough.

Tyler couldn't believe he was entertaining such thoughts. They sounded insane even to him. There was no way the woman drank blood, feared the sun, or slept in a box. Still, Tyler was beginning to think he'd be safer staying in the coffin and risking suffocation than opening it and risking death at the hands of a woman who, in the best possible case, was just a homicidal maniac with a good right jab and mutant teeth.

"I'm waiting," the woman growled with a deep, animalistic timbre that erased any doubts Tyler had about her nature and made him drastically reevaluate his position. Inaction was surely death; he took a deep breath, reached out a hand, and pushed the lid open.

Tyler was up before he realized that everything was moving much too fast. He'd shoved the lid away instead of opening it with menacing slowness, and had popped upright like a tuxedoed jack-in-the-box. He received his wage of indiscretion when the lid rebounded from the block of wood against which it was supposed to settle and returned to deal him a nasty blow to the back of his head. A second, more serious, blow – this one from the woman – came a heartbeat later, sending him to darkness of sight, mind, and hope.

Insensate for a few seconds at most, Tyler found himself half wishing the condition had been permanent. He could feel a slow crawl of blood moving down his cheeks from a broken-twice-over nose, and the wiggle of two loose teeth. His head hurt from all directions, one eye had begun to swell, and he felt like throwing up, but those problems contained within Tyler's coffin were nothing compared to those waiting beyond its walls.

"You're dead! Christ-sure dead, actor boy!" The woman with the pendant sounded far beyond merely upset and well into psychotic. Tyler's fingers fumbled dumbly to find something he could hold the coffin's lid closed with, knowing full well there was nothing of the sort.

"You know, there were two ways this fantasy could have gone," she continued. "And since you don't seem interested in the one that's fun for two, we're going to do the one that's just fun for me. And I'll bet that even a screwup like you can die just *great!*"

From outside the coffin Tyler could hear the sound of the woman stomping about. It lasted only a moment, ending right beside Tyler with the light tap of a hand coming to rest on the wood just above his face.

"Oh my, a coffin," the woman said, giving no effort toward sounding anything but sarcastic and self-parodying. "This must be where that awful vampire lives. I'll bet that if I drive this big piece of wood through his heart, he'll stop making pathetic attempts to screw me. Well, it's sure worth a try."

Her little speech given, the woman lifted the coffin lid.

Tyler thought about trying to defend himself – leaping at her, scratching at her eyes, trying to grab the stake – but repeated batterings and a deep sense of fatalism left him so weak and demoralized that even trying to visualize moving left him exhausted. He tried to console himself with the knowledge that the bizarre circumstances of his death virtually assured him national news coverage, but it wasn't much help.

Fortunately, luck was on his side for once that evening. In throwing open the coffin lid, the woman made the same mistake Tyler had – the lid was open just long enough to rebound and come right back at him.

In the brief flash of light, Tyler saw two things – the woman with the pendant, teeth bared and incisors at full vampiric extension, standing over him holding a broom handle that had been broken to a sharp point like a dagger, and, just visible over her shoulder, a man watching the proceedings with a playful smile.

"Christ," the woman yelled at the lid's slam.

Tyler could hear her scrambling to lift it again when the man spoke. "Lucy, wait," he said, his voice so commanding that Tyler felt compelled to stillness even though he hadn't been doing anything but watching his life flash by.

"Luke," the woman said, obviously surprised. "What are you–"

"It is I, Dr. Van Helsing. I know your fascination for the thing in the box and I have come to see that you do not fall under his spell."

"I didn't think –" She hesitated. "I thought I'd never see you again."

"There is no room for 'never' in a timeless love, my darling. I was wrong to deny you your appetite, and I believe we may become stronger by satisfying it together."

Sitting in the dark with the couple's voices all around him, Tyler felt like he was listening to an old radio soap opera while recuperating from twelve rounds with the heavyweight champ. He was having trouble following the plot, but decided that at this point anything that didn't involve him being skewered was first-class entertainment.

"So what happens now, Doctor?" the woman asked.

"The monster has fed from you twice; once more and he

would have stolen your very soul. You stand at the brink, and only the creature's death can restore what you have already lost."

A renewed feeling of certain doom filled Tyler when the woman said, "Do what must be done." It became a scream in his head when the coffin lid rose and he saw the man standing over him, a nicely lathed stake upraised in one hand, a mallet in the other.

The man was youthful with olive skin and dark hair. He wore a gray suit with a pendant matching the woman's in place of a tie, and his grin of determination revealed teeth that matched his mate's in every disturbing particular.

Tyler didn't have a chance to move before the stake plunged toward and through his chest. The man with the pendant hadn't even bothered to use the mallet.

Screaming felt like drowning as blood poured into Tyler's lungs. He was on fire with pain for a moment and then peace overtook him, as if his brain realized his body was a loss and had cut it off. In the instant before oblivion, Tyler heard the close of the little play at which he'd briefly been the center.

"It is done, my darling."

"Oh, Dr. Van Helsing, you were *so* brave. How can I ever repay you?"

"You are all that I desire, my Lucy. And your love is the greatest of rewards."

The final sound Tyler heard was a low moan over tearing lace.

After dying, the last thing Tyler expected to do was wake up. There was no sense of passing from darkness to light, just sudden awareness of being. He felt no pain.

Tyler was still in the coffin. Its lid was open, and the man with the pendant stood looking down at him.

"Feeling better?" the man asked, as if he were inquiring

whether a nap had relieved a headache.

Tyler just nodded.

"Good. Look, I'm sorry about the stake thing. And I apologize for biting you while you were unconscious – I had to do that to take care of the damage. A bite makes you pretty much invulnerable for twenty-four hours the first two times; the third time it becomes permanent and other stuff happens. Is this all making sense?"

Another nod.

"So no harm done and no hard feelings, okay?" The man looked around, perhaps making sure the woman wasn't within earshot before he leaned closer and began to whisper. "Frankly, man to man, Rachel and I've been having some hard times over her wanting to do this 'playing human' thing, but if I'd known how wild it would drive her, believe me, I would have been encouraging her all the way. Having you squirting blood and all really helped, too – got the whole sex-and-death thing going."

He stood up straight again and looked far away for a moment as Tyler lay in silence, sure that anything he said would be wrong and/or fatal.

"So, here's the deal," the man continued in a normal tone. "I think it would be a good bonding thing if Rachel and I could do this again, but we can't go revealing our natures all over the place for obvious reasons. Since she's already cut you into the game, as it were, I thought we – the three of us – could do this same deal a couple of more nights, next weekend and then again on Halloween night, for the mood. That'd make three times I have to bite you – you see where this is going, right?"

Tyler nodded, slowly, as if the motion was being tempered by the realization of what was being offered.

"So it's up to you. Either two more sessions or I stake you again to keep you quiet, only this time I aim for the heart instead of a lung. If you agree, then after the third time you'll have to disappear to everyone you know and love, but we'll give you a couple million to get you started and one of these," he touched the pendant, "so others will know you're part of the club. What do you say? You'd be doing the two of us a big favor."

Tyler thought of his failing finances, his ruined family and love life, and his faceless future. He weighed death against everlasting life, a dramatic change in diet, and no more sunburns. It wasn't much of a choice, really, although he couldn't honestly say that he looked forward to the conversion process.

"Sounds good to me," Tyler said. He started to sit up, but the man's hand on his chest arrested him just as he caught a glimpse of the woman lying on the ground, asleep, and wearing nothing but her pendant.

"Hang on," the man said, pressing Tyler back down. "Rachel's not decent. And by the way, I don't know what the relationship between the two of you has been or what she promised it would be, but if you think any of this means you can make a play for her before or after, forget it. You touch her and I kill you, got it?"

"No problem," Tyler said, working a smile.

The man nodded mutual understanding and moved out of Tyler's view.

Tyler settled back and waited for the sound of his two new acquaintances leaving. The coffin was uncomfortable and it was tempting to try and catch a glimpse of the gorgeous vampire, but Tyler kept his wits about him – no woman was worth dying for. At least, he thought with a smile, not until now.

The boy didn't feed on Judith every time he visited, but he always hugged her, as if he drew strength from her body warmth. She disregarded the drained sensation she felt after his visits, for his touch gave her a languorous pleasure she blushed to contemplate.

The Pale Hill's Side

Margaret L. Carter

Do elves feel the cold on chilly nights? Judith McCrae tugged her thin shawl tighter around her shoulders. She'd forgotten how cool the Yorkshire downs could become after sunset on the last day of April. Critically examining her sketch of the beehive-shaped mound some fifty yards distant, she smiled at the fancy that a faerie lord might emerge from beneath the earth to carry her off. Even the country people who still called these prehistoric structures "elf-mounds" knew better; after all, the dawn of the twentieth century was only three years away.

Nevertheless, none of the locals approached this part of the moor after dark. Too many cattle had been found dead here, with no visible wounds. The rumors reminded Judith of the folk belief that elves drained milk from cows by night.

As an avid reader of Mr. Yeats' collections of Irish fairy tales, she couldn't resist making a detour in her holiday to investigate this reputedly elf-haunted site. Especially on May Eve, a very appropriate night. Now, though, the chill was quenching her enthusiasm.

The boy who'd guided her here had long since run home to bed. Judith was almost ready to do the same; she would have a tedious hike back to the village. Sketching the mound by moonlight had certainly filled her mind with enough "atmosphere" to render an intriguing article on north country superstitions that might earn her a few pounds.

The boy, Robbie – sadness shadowed her at the memory of his thin, pale face. Only fourteen years old, and unlikely to live to fifteen. As a doctor's daughter, Judith recognized the early signs of consumption in his pallor and his constant cough. His eyes had glimmered with tears and longing when he'd told her how he'd wandered here just two nights before. An elven lord, he said, had appeared on the moor and bespelled him. When Judith had asked Robbie to describe this being, the boy had stammered into awed silence. "Silver fire," was all he could say. He'd yearned to follow the elf-lord into the mound, but the creature had given him one burning touch and sent him away.

"He said I was too sickly, Miss." Robbie longed to see the creature again and would have lingered with Judith if she hadn't given him a handful of coins and ordered him to go home.

Suppressing a shiver from a gust of wind, Judith closed her sketchpad and picked up the electric torch that lay beside her on the blanket. Time to start back. As she stood up, stretching her stiff limbs, a movement caught her eye. A flicker of shadow between her and the mound.

She took a deep breath to tame the racing of her heart. What nonsense – she didn't believe in fairies. These barrows were nothing but the desolate tombs of prehistoric men. She scanned the dark slopes of the hilly moor, broken by outcroppings of rock barely visible in the moonlight. *Next I'll be seeing the ghost of Heathcliff. No more Bronte romances at bedtime, Miss Judith!*

Her fingers tightened on the torch. The sooner she returned to the inn, the better. While supernatural menaces sprang from over-fertile imagination, the real danger of robbers – or worse – might stalk here.

Having an attack of the vapors, now? she chided herself. She turned her back on the barrow and knelt to fold the blanket.

A man appeared in front of her.

He didn't appear out of thin air! It's impossible! She didn't waste time arguing with herself. Dropping everything she held, she made a sideways dash.

And nearly collided with him.

She looked up – looked upward forever, it seemed; she'd never seen so tall a man – into eyes that gleamed silver. He didn't let her run again. Cold fingers closed on her wrist.

Her attempt to struggle died stillborn. She felt dizzy. *So Robbie wasn't spinning an idle tale.* A line from Coleridge came into her head: "His flashing eyes, his floating hair –"

She was floating, and the man's – the elf's – face floated above her. *Of course, he's carrying me.* By the time she realized this fact, they had passed into the mound. Her panic flowed away like ice melting in a spring thaw. Instead, she accepted her helplessness with a dreamy languor. "Though I am old with wandering, through hollow lands and hilly lands –" That was Yeats. Judith felt a drowsy satisfaction at finding herself immersed in an adventure one of the foremost poets of the decade could only imagine.

When she forced her eyes away from the elf's to look at the tunnel around her, it seemed the walls shimmered as if made of water rather than rock. Or living jewels. She was carried through rainbow-hued curtains. Whether they parted before her captor, or he slipped through like a ghost, she couldn't tell.

After an immeasurable time, he set her on her feet. "You can walk from here, I trust." His voice made her diaphragm quiver, as the bass note of an organ might. Yet she heard something less unearthly behind it, a hint of a Scottish burr.

Hearing him speak cleared her head a little. She let him take her hand and lead her along the path between the glowing walls. Did his touch chill or burn? She couldn't focus clearly enough to decide. "What do you want with me?"

"My sister's child was wounded by one of your people's weapons. You are here for healing."

Elves can be hurt? Why don't they just work a bit of magic? she wondered muzzily. "Then you need a doctor, not me." Dimly she recalled Robbie's tale of rejection. "I won't be much more use than that boy you met the other night."

"That isn't the kind of help we require." She felt his eyes upon her. "Have you never heard that the Fair Folk abduct human nurses to feed their children?"

That doesn't make sense. I'm not a mother. Never even –

Led by the elf-lord, she emerged into a vaulted chamber whose walls glittered from the flames of numerous candles. "Is this sufficient light for you?" he asked. "It's far more than we need."

Judith nodded. Her eyes took in a confused impression of hundreds of books, silken wall hangings, and a wide bed with a tall, slender woman standing next to it.

"Fiona, I've brought you one that should serve well enough." As he led Judith toward the bed, the elven woman stepped to meet them. For the first time Judith paused for a good look at her captor. His long hair made a dark halo around his pale, sharp-featured face. His sister had the same silver eyes, glowing with pinpoints of red at the centers, and the same hair so black it gleamed, except that hers hung to her waist and seemed to ripple in an unfelt breeze when she moved. Both wore shining garments with capes that fanned behind them at every step.

In a moment of clarity Judith thought, *It's too perfect, too much like the poets' tales and my own daydreams.*

Renewed dizziness overcame her when the elf-lady's nails

grazed her chin. "A fine choice, Tammas," said the woman. "Shall we get on with it?"

Tammas? Fiona? These are Faerie names?

As if Judith had spoken her doubts aloud, the male elf said, "We borrow names from the folk we dwell among. Come, we've no time to waste." He drew her to the bedside.

She gazed down at a pale, thin child of ten or twelve, by human reckoning. The unconscious body was covered to the waist, the exposed parts naked. From the flat chest, delicate features, and wispy, golden red, shoulder-length hair, Judith couldn't tell whether the creature was male or female. But her gaze didn't linger on the sharp nose and chin or the feathery lashes of the closed eyes. She stifled a gasp at the sight of the unbandaged bullet wound on the left side of the ribcage.

"Shot? When?"

"Two nights ago." Tammas didn't look at her as he answered. He was leaning over the child, his hands stroking the temples.

More than half-awake now, Judith contemplated the injury. In two nights, without treatment, how could the wound have closed so far already? On the other hand, considering how bad it must have been when it was fresh, how could the child have survived at all? What could elves – she was aware enough now to realize the incongruity, the impossibility, of this situation – know of medicine? Had they even removed the bullet?

Again answering her unspoken thoughts, the elf-lord said, "We performed what – surgery – was required. The rest only you, or someone like you, can provide." His fingertips resting on the child's forehead, he crooned, "Wake. You are safe."

Violet-gray eyes fluttered open. They drifted to Judith's face. The floating sensation washed over her again. She faintly heard Tammas' voice saying, "She is for you, Liam." She felt Tammas' chill grasp as he guided her hand to the center of the child's chest.

Liam? It's a boy, then. Though she felt no heartbeat, she knew from the awakening glow in the creature's eyes that life smoldered in him. The glow lured her closer. She stretched out on the bed and wrapped her arms around the elf-child. Icy fingers explored her hair and the nape of her neck. Enfolded in darkness, she heard inside her head the crashing of waves on a stony shore. Their rhythm lulled her into nothingness.

◆

The glow. It's still here. When her eyes focused, Judith realized she was staring, not at eyes of unearthly beauty, but at a kerosene lantern. *Merciful Heaven, what a dream!*

When she sat up, she groaned aloud at the aches in her stiff limbs. Beneath her lay a pallet on a smooth rock surface. Bare rock walls surrounded her. *Oh, God, not a dream!* Some of the night's strangeness, at least, had been real; she was a prisoner underground.

Shivering, her eyes gritty from sleep, she surveyed her cell. The chamber was about ten feet in diameter, its entrance covered by a heavy scarlet drape. Beside her "bed" sat a neat stack of objects – blanket, sketchpad, pencils – all the possessions she'd left on the moor, even the electric torch. A few feet away she saw a tall pitcher, basin, and tumbler of earthenware, a plate, and a chamberpot. The atmosphere was musty but not suffocating; crevices overhead must admit some air.

Fighting both her fear and the pain in her chilled muscles, she got up to examine the objects more closely. The pitcher contained cold water, the plate a loaf of bread, a chunk of cheese, and a knife. "Bloody confident, aren't you?" she said aloud.

A glance showed her that the curtain was all the "door" this room had. God willing, she'd find her way out of this place. But not without fortifying herself for the quest. She washed, grimacing at her wrinkled, sweaty clothes, then ate and drank. She had fleeting doubts about the food, for wasn't eating anything in the realm of Faerie supposed to trap the victim forever? She decided, though, that the bread and cheese were commonplace country fare, doubtless stolen from a nearby farm. *What do elves eat, anyway?* Glancing around at the walls, she wondered what had happened to the jewels and rainbows. *They cast a glamour on me, I daresay. Isn't that what fairies are supposed to do?*

Well, they wouldn't get another chance. Bundling up in her shawl, she switched on the torch, clutched the bread knife, and stepped into the tunnel.

The clammy darkness seemed to grip her by the throat. She concentrated on the circle of light from the torch. Picking her way step by step over the smooth tunnel floor, she muttered reassurances to herself. The walls were *not* contracting around her. The light guiding her feet was real; all else was delusion born of her own fear.

The flaw in her plan struck her the first time the tunnel split into three. She did not know the way to the entrance. She had been in a trance when Tammas had carried her into the mound. She couldn't even hope to find the chamber where she'd met the child, for she'd been brought away from there unconscious.

Still, Judith didn't consider giving up. How far could these tunnels extend? If she walked long enough without doubling back on her path, she had to stumble upon the exit. Choosing at random, she took the right-most fork.

Several turns later, she began to lose confidence. The labyrinth showed no signs of coming to an end. She met neither of the elves and saw no rooms with opulent furnishings like the one she'd been taken to. Only a candle, now and then, burning in a wall sconce. Aside from that, she could almost believe she'd wandered below ground in some sort of brain fever and dreamed the rest. Soon she was breathing hard, her teeth chattering from the chill on her clammy skin. Fear rose like bile in her throat. Seized by panic, she began to run. Her own panting and the beat of her shoes against stone thundered in her ears.

She fell headlong on the floor, dropping the torch and the knife. She scrabbled for them in the undulating flame of a nearby candle. As she sat up, light in one hand and knife in the other, a curtain in the wall several yards away billowed and parted.

Tammas strode toward her.

Judith scrambled to her feet. When the light fell on the elf-lord's face, his eyes gleamed red. She brandished the knife, though a voice in the back of her mind told her the dull blade wouldn't kill a creature that could survive a bullet wound such as Liam had suffered. Surely the man was stronger than the child.

His burning eyes didn't flicker toward the weapon. Instead, he gazed steadily at her. As before, she felt lightheaded. A multicolored aura shimmered around the elf. Judith's fingers went slack. She hardly noticed when the knife slipped out of her grasp. When Tammas' cold fingers crept up her arms, a paradoxical rush of warmth swept over her.

"You can't attack us," he said in that clear, remote voice. "Don't waste your energy in the attempt. Liam needs you serene and whole."

She felt his arm around her waist. A sphere of light enfolded her. She thought she glimpsed fireflies dancing in alcoves in the rocky walls.

An instant later she found herself in the vaulted chamber with the wide bed. The boy Liam raised his arms to embrace her, and her head whirled with bright images whisked away before she could grasp them, like rose petals in a high wind.

Again Judith woke chilled and stiff. Her throat was sore, parched with thirst. After a drink and a hasty wash, she checked her cell. The torch and knife had been returned. She startled herself with a harsh laugh. Letting her keep the feeble weapon seemed a mockery; both she and the elves knew well that she couldn't harm them. In addition to her other supplies, she found oil for the lamp and a stack of folded clothes.

Simple cotton garments, she noticed. She wondered whether Tammas had stolen the clothes from some farm wife's bedroom or actually bought them. Judith washed more thoroughly, shivering, and dressed from the skin out. The skirt and bodice were a bit large for her but warmer than her own frock.

After another drink of water and a meal of the bread, sausage, and apples that had been left on the platter, she contemplated her prison. Her spirits drooped at the realization that no one would search for her. She had no living relatives; her few friends knew she often traveled for months at a time. At once she discarded the thought of another escape attempt. The terror of fleeing through the tunnels with no idea of her destination was still vivid. If she hoped to get out, she would have to persuade Tammas or Fiona to release her.

Oh, really? How?

To hold off the despair that threatened to swamp her, she picked up the sketchpad and pencil. Her drawing of the "elf-mound" faced her. Shaking her head, Judith flipped over to a clean sheet of paper. Almost without conscious volition, her pencil raced over one page, then another. When she paused to flex her cramped fingers, she had produced a rough sketch of the child Liam lying in his silk-draped bed and a pale imitation of Tammas' and Fiona's chill beauty. The dazzling luxury of their chamber as she'd seen it utterly eluded her.

How much was real? Had everything but the boy's embrace been part of the glamour? And what did he need her for, anyway? In legend the faerie folk kidnapped nursing mothers, not spinsters, to feed their children.

Inaction and stale air made her drowsy. Some time later, a rustle in the shadows woke her from a light doze. When she caught her breath, she saw the boy Liam standing over her.

Barefoot, he wore a loose silk shirt over a pair of short trousers. He rested one hand on the wall, as if unsteady on his feet.

"What are you doing here?" said Judith. Slowly she stood up, her cramped legs trembling. "Should you be out of bed? You don't look well." *Absurd, I don't know how he ought to look!*

"My mother and Tammas are still asleep, and I wanted you." His voice would have graced any cathedral's boys' choir. He lowered himself to the heap of blankets that served as Judith's bed and sat cross-legged, staring at her.

Cautiously she sat down near him, fascinated by the gleam of red at the centers of his silver eyes. "How did you find me?"

He looked mildly surprised at the question. "I felt you, of course. How could I miss you, when there are no others of your kind here? And I've touched you twice already."

"Touched? You mesmerized me, you and your – uncle." But no human practitioner could have controlled her mind so thoroughly. If this power wasn't magic, it was close enough. "What do you want?"

"I'm thirsty." He reached for her. She flinched at the touch of his cold fingers on her wrist. "Don't be afraid. I wouldn't hurt you."

The glow in his wide eyes drew her in. Submitting to the child's embrace, Judith lapsed into a delicious dizziness.

Some time later, she felt his cold lips leave her throat. Scanning his face, she gasped at what she saw.

His tongue flicked out to lick the blood from his lips. "Please don't be afraid. Your fear hurts me."

She sensed he was speaking of concrete physical pain.

Numbly she reached up to rub her neck. She stared at the red stain on her fingertips.

Liam's cool fingers stroked her forehead. "The bleeding will stop presently."

Lines from Keats flashed into her mind: "I saw pale kings, and princes too, pale warriors, death pale were they all...I saw their starved lips in the gloam..." She'd never understood "La Belle Dame Sans Merci" before, portraying the elven queen with horror as well as fascination. "You drink –"

"Why does that disturb you so much?" In spite of the revulsion she tried to cling to, his feathery caress and mild voice soothed her. "You eat the burned flesh of dead animals. The very thought sickens me!"

"That's different." Judith shivered. Liam handed her the shawl, then poured her a mug of water, which she automatically drank. Trying to steady herself, she considered what a sensational story this experience would make – if she ever saw the outside world again. "You're going to kill me."

A pained look passed over his face. "No, certainly not. We hardly ever kill human beings, only animals. That is how I got wounded."

Judith remembered the local rumors about this place. "The cattle."

Liam bent his knees and wrapped his arms around them, so like a human boy that Judith wondered again if she were dreaming. "I wasn't allowed to go near human dwellings. I'm supposed to take wild animals, or livestock wandering on the moors. But I was curious. Mother and Tammas never let me get close enough for a good look at those people. You're the first day person I have ever spoken to."

"A farmer caught you on his property and shot you?"

Liam nodded. "I fled for home, and Tammas found me when I collapsed on the way. I was unconscious most of the time until he brought you. I've never tasted human blood before – I'm really too young, but the wound –"

His casual reference to his diet made Judith cringe against the wall. To deflect her thoughts from the subject, she said, "How old are you?"

"Only twelve. I should not have started for, perhaps, another four years. Tammas will be surprised that I could bespell you without his help." Liam smiled with a disarmingly childlike air of pride. Judith almost felt like patting him on the head in congratulation.

Watch out, that's part of their glamour! He's still a wild beast.

"Tammas is your mother's brother? Don't you have a father?"

Liam looked puzzled. "Of course, didn't you? But I don't know who he was. Why should I?"

"My people would think it very odd not to know your father."

"Tammas has told me how your kind live, with both parents together all their lives. He says you can endure it because your lives are so short."

Judith almost laughed aloud at this cynical view of marriage. "And what about you? Your mother has to bring you up by herself?"

"She has my uncle's help, as you see. They are very close, because they are twins." He tilted his head as if listening. "Tammas has just awakened. It's sunset, and he is looking for me."

Forgetting her earlier horror of him, Judith grasped Liam's arm. "Listen, you have to help me get away. Tomorrow, when they're asleep, show me the way out."

"Oh, no, I cannot do that." He stroked her hand as if quieting a nervous kitten. "I need you. You brought me back from the void – I wouldn't have died, but I might have fallen into a living death and never awakened."

"All right," she whispered. "I'm glad I could help, but I can't stay –" She broke off, for now even her ears picked up approaching footsteps.

Tammas flung aside the curtain and glared down at the two of them. "Liam, you should not be out of bed."

The boy stood up to face his uncle. "I am strong enough to walk, and I awoke hungry. I didn't have any trouble with her."

"So I see." Tammas' eyes glided over Judith. "You appear unharmed."

She clenched her fists at her sides, too indignant to be properly frightened. "Let me go!"

"That isn't possible. Liam needs human prey, and he is both too weak and too inexperienced to forage outside, even with our help. You will be well cared for."

"Until I waste away and die, I suppose?" When he gazed at her coolly without answering, she went on, "I refuse to thank you for the clothes. You probably stole them anyway."

"In this case, yes. But we do occasionally walk among your kind and make purchases with honest coin." He leaned against the stone wall with his arms folded, eyebrows arched in what might have been amusement.

"You're not really elves, are you?"

Tammas shrugged. "What's in a name, as your poet says. In this region, that is what the people call us, and we've found it advantageous to play that role. We are nocturnal, we cloud men's minds with our 'magic,' and we live a very long time. Why not elves?" He turned to Liam. "Come along, you must rest."

From the threshold, Liam looked back at Judith. "I may come here again, mayn't I, Uncle? I don't need your help anymore, and I like talking to her."

After a moment's thought, Tammas gave a curt nod, then led the boy away.

Judith flung herself down on the bedroll and gave way to hysterical sobs.

After a while, exhausted into calm, she admitted to herself that she couldn't pretend she was delirious or dreaming. She was the captive of blood-drinking faerie folk. With no malice whatever, as casually as Judith might milk a cow, the "lord" would keep her here as nourishment for Liam until she died. Her only hope was to work on the boy's nascent fondness for her.

Well, I won't die anytime soon, that's certain! I'll show the bloody beasts!

To that end, she needed to maintain her physical health as long as possible. She forced herself to eat the rest of the food on the platter. After that, she performed a series of setting-up exercises in the limited confines of the chamber. Determined to cling to mental health as well, she sat down with her sketchpad and tried to ignore the darkness clustered around her.

◆

Judith passed uncounted hours drawing, pacing her cell, reading books brought to her by Liam, and talking with the boy. Ample though monotonous food filled the plate at frequent intervals. Her discarded clothes vanished, to reappear clean and folded. She wondered whether Tammas or Fiona mesmerized some local housewife into doing the laundry and forgetting about it.

Soon after their first meeting, Liam brought her a leather-bound copy of *A Tale of Two Cities* and insisted they read aloud to each other. He knew nothing about human life and wanted to know everything. Judith struggled with the double burden of trying to explain the customs of a foreign country a hundred years in the past.

The child seemed fascinated by Judith's own past and questioned her endlessly about her home, family, and work. Amused by his naivete, she couldn't remain repulsed or frightened by him. She went into detail about the pleasures of the outside world and her sadness at missing them, in hopes of awakening his sympathy. If he were capable of that emotion – she couldn't tell whether his fondness for her was anything more than a spoiled child's attachment to a favorite toy.

"I'm so tired of staying down here," he complained on one

occasion. "I miss the night. My mother and uncle say I'm not well enough to go out."

"I'd be glad to walk with you," said Judith, "just outside the mound for a few minutes."

Liam gave her a sly smile. "Yes, I know. So you could run away."

Judith suppressed a sigh. *He's ignorant but not stupid. I should have known.*

He nestled into her arms, as he often did. "I'm very glad you're here. Without you, I would be terribly bored. Besides, you taste good."

She couldn't suppress a wry smile at his outspokenness. Against her will, she'd actually grown to like this creature. *I suppose pet dogs like their masters, too. Doesn't mean I'd want to be a pet.* "I can't stay forever, Liam. I don't belong here, I need the sun." He listened with his usual air of bland incomprehension. "Listen, once when I was little I found a half-grown baby bird under a tree in our back garden. My father splinted its broken wing, and I fed it by hand, day and night. After a couple of weeks, it was well enough to fly. I wanted to keep it for a pet. Can you guess what Father did?" Liam gazed at her with his usual wide-eyed attention. "He made me let the bird go. He said a wild thing could never be happy in a cage. Animals have to live the way nature intended. I threw a crying fit, but he wouldn't give in."

Liam mulled over the anecdote in silence for a minute. "I see," he finally said. "But this is different. The bird could not understand. You can understand why I need you here."

Judith shook her head in exasperation. "I'll become ill, and then what good will I be to you?"

"I won't allow that to happen," he said. His fingers caressed her neck, sending shivers through her. "I wish you could *show* me what life in the day world is like. If you tasted my blood, you could – we could speak mind to mind. But Mother says it's too dangerous, especially at my age."

"Dangerous for you, you mean." Not likely that Fiona would waste a thought on Judith's welfare, except as it affected Liam. Repulsive as the thought of drinking blood was, Judith would almost welcome it to experience true telepathy.

"She thinks I depend too much on you already," said the boy. "She says that bond would place my life in your hands." His confiding embrace made it clear that he wasn't too worried about that risk. "She says I would become like an opium-eater craving the drug – whatever that means."

"If she's so concerned, she should let me go, and the problem would disappear."

Liam wrapped his arms around her neck. "I don't want you to go. And my mother says it is not safe to dispose of you until I'm completely recovered."

Dispose of me? Liam seemed oblivious to the implications. Judith, however, suspected that Fiona had meant something more final than turning her loose on the downs.

The boy didn't feed on Judith every time he visited, but he always hugged her, as if he drew strength from her body warmth. She disregarded the drained sensation she felt after his visits, for his touch gave her a languorous pleasure she blushed to contemplate. When he left her alone, she couldn't ignore the dampness, bare walls, and sour odor of her cell. Reading and sketching gradually lost the power to distract her from her monotonous existence. She couldn't tell day from night and quickly lost count of her sleep periods.

She felt at ease only when Liam came to her. His glamour, though nowhere near as powerful as his uncle's, softened the contours of the cell and veiled its walls in a shimmering glow. She was glad when he began to take his deathlike day-sleep in her chamber. His nearness, even in a trance so deep she couldn't tell whether he breathed, warded off loneliness and kept her fears remote and unreal.

The time came when he glided into her room with his eyes

aglow. "Judith, they're taking me above at last. They say I may be well enough to hunt!" She knew Tammas and Fiona had been bringing Liam rabbits and other small game all along, to supplement Judith's scant but frequent donations. She also knew how Liam had missed being allowed to chase his own prey. "Here, eat this, it's fresh. Isn't this wonderful news?" He handed her an apple.

Aware that he was watching anxiously, Judith bit into the fruit. More and more often, Liam had to remind her to eat. "Yes, it's wonderful that you're getting stronger. I'm happy for you. Enjoy your – excursion."

Liam hurried off without further conversation. His excitement made Judith's nerves tingle, too. If only she could go outside with him. After he'd left, she wished she had thought of following him. But no, Tammas and Fiona would have sensed her presence instantly.

Judith began languidly combing her hair with the silver comb Liam had brought her some time ago. She didn't bother with the mirror; who cared how she looked?

Tears gathered in her eyes at the thought of being shut down here while Liam ran free. And soon he wouldn't need her anymore –

Judith sat up straight and dropped the comb. The thought shocked her awake like cold water in the face. As soon as the boy ceased to need her, the adults would "dispose" of her. Judith got to her feet. For a few seconds, a surge of dizziness forced her to lean on the wall. Her legs felt stiff from the dampness. She realized this weakness had plagued her for a long time; Liam's constant presence had kept her from noticing.

She sank to her knees and rummaged in her small pile of possessions for the hand mirror. In the lantern's glow she examined her pale, thin face. She saw violet half-circles beneath her eyes. Stretching out one hand, she checked her fingernails. They were blue-tinged. *Anemia*

She had to escape. If Fiona didn't kill her, Judith knew she would die eventually anyway. With her health so impaired, it was a wonder she hadn't already developed pneumonia. *How long have I been down here, anyway? As long as a month?* Smiling bitterly to herself, she picked up the knife they had never bothered to take from her. The "weapon" mocked her helplessness. Her inability to find her way out of the underground labyrinth remained the major obstacle to her escape.

Judith paced the cell, forcing warmth into her weakened limbs, until Liam returned. He greeted her with a hard embrace. When his lips brushed her temple, she noticed they radiated heat instead of the usual chill. "If only you could have been with us! The moon is full, and –"

She gripped his shoulders. "Listen to me!" she whispered. "If you're well, your mother won't want me here anymore. She doesn't approve of my – influence – over you. She'll kill me."

Liam flinched, as if Judith's fear caused him pain. "No, she would not do that, after what you've given to me."

"Stop lying to yourself! She will. You have to guide me out, as soon as they're asleep."

Liam shook his head. "You excite yourself for nothing. I would never let them hurt you." He released her and reclined on his nest of cushions and blankets. "Now I want to rest. You promised to read me Mr. Dickens' *Christmas Carol.*"

Judith gave up the argument. Liam saw reality as he wanted to see it. *Don't we all?* she reminded herself. She tried to tame her tumultuous emotions as she picked up the book and read aloud: "Marley was dead, to begin with..."

Later Judith gnawed at futile escape plans while she watched Liam sleep. She knew she had to act before she drifted back into the nebulous dream state that had possessed her – how long? Several weeks, at least. She knew Tammas and Fiona spent each period from sunrise to sunset in a virtual coma, unlike Liam, who, since he was younger, needed less sleep. So during the day Judith could simply walk out, unhindered, if she knew the path. If only she could induce Liam to guide her. That prospect looked hopeless. The adults obviously thought so, or they wouldn't risk leaving Judith free to move about.

She wished she could pluck the facts from Liam's mind as easily as he sensed every nuance of her emotions. Something nibbled at the edges of her thoughts – something she ought to remember. Suddenly it came to her. *Maybe I can read his mind!* What had Liam said about sharing blood? If she tasted his blood, it would forge a bond between them. Their minds would lie open to each other.

But he wouldn't do that. His mother's prohibition had frightened him into abandoning the idea.

Why can't I just take what I need from him? Judith fingered the hilt of the knife. What she was contemplating made her queasy. She had to act quickly or lose her nerve. First she paced up and down the chamber a few times to loosen her muscles for the hike ahead. She breathed deeply to calm her racing heart. Then she knelt beside Liam and picked up one of his limp arms.

As she'd expected, the mere touch didn't wake him. She had become too familiar a presence. If she hadn't known better, his cold flesh would have made her think him dead. Not giving herself time to falter, she nicked his wrist with the point of the blade. A bead of blood appeared.

It's red, like mine. Not the ichor of the gods. How much would she have to consume? She swallowed against a wave of nausea. *Hurry up, get on with it.*

She lifted his wrist to her mouth and licked the drops oozing from the cut. No special taste, just a lukewarm fluid like her own blood.

Liam's eyes opened. Their silver glow drew her into a web of dancing lights. Her head whirled. A moment later, she was staring up at her own face. A rosy aura haloed her disheveled hair. *I'm seeing through his eyes!*

The chamber looked so bright, like summer twilight even though a single candle shed the only illumination. Yet the colors in her frock and the bedding were muted to pastels. The musty smell, channeled through Liam's senses, stung her. At the same time, she picked up the metallic scent of his blood and a hot, sweet fragrance that she realized must be her own flesh. It stirred hunger. Instead of feeling revulsion, she caught herself trembling with eagerness.

No! She didn't cry aloud. She knew, somehow, that she didn't need her voice to make him hear her.

She wrenched herself back into her own body. Liam's face contorted with pain as if she had slapped him. *Judith, don't, that hurts. Why are you treating me this way?*

Tell me the way out, now, or I'll gouge it out of your brain with my fingernails if I have to.

Don't leave me, please – would you give this up now that we have it?

His pain twisted inside her, too, but she armored herself against it. She wouldn't throw away her only chance.

Now, before your mother and uncle wake up. She felt his resistance, as if shoving against a door he was holding shut. She flung her loneliness and fear at the closed door. She felt Liam's resistance buckle under the strain. She battered him with the chill, the aches, the fatigue, the weakness she'd suffered from his feeding. A soundless cry from Liam shrieked inside her head.

I'm dying down here, you God-forgotten little beast!

Stop – please – cruel –

Judith turned her thoughts to her father's death and the desolation she'd felt after the funeral, finding herself alone in the world. When she poured out that anguish, Liam curled up inside himself, wailing.

Let me out, or I'll blast you with pain you've never imagined!

Very well – stop – I never wanted to hurt you –

She withdrew inside the boundaries of her own skull. For an instant the room spun. She groped in panic for support, afraid she had lost herself forever. Her senses came back into focus, though, allowing her to see normally again. Liam was holding her hands in a crushing grasp.

"I'm sorry I had to do that," she whispered. She realized she was shaking. "But I'll do it again if you don't keep your word."

"I will." He sank down on his pillow. "Now I understand why this bond is dangerous. To lose ourselves in a victim's – donor's – consciousness –" His voice was barely audible. He switched back to silent speech. *Go quickly. I shall guide you with my thoughts.*

Before she could weaken, she wrapped herself in her shawl and gathered up the electric torch and her sketchbook. Without the latter, she feared she would think this whole experience had been a delusion. At the last moment she ripped out one page, the best of her portraits of Liam. *A keepsake for you.*

Step into the corridor and take the left-most fork – Liam's whisper in her mind began. Mechanically she followed the directions, using the light only where no candles shone on the walls. Her legs ached from the strain long before she reached the exit. After some immeasurable time, however, she did reach it. Liam told her, *You have several hours until sunset. If you hurry to the nearest town, you'll be in no danger from my mother and Tammas.* He directed her to climb a flight of crude stone stairs and pull a lever that moved a delicately balanced rock door. She stepped through the portal and found herself inside the barrow tomb. *They use their mind-power to keep anyone from examining this mound too closely,* said Liam. *Now go, or I might try to lure you back. I could make you forget all that pain, make you happy with us – I know I could.*

A chill seized her at the memory of long hours during which she actually had been content as a pet confined in his lair. *Not the kind of happiness I want. Tell Tammas and Fiona not to worry, I won't talk about this place. Who would believe me? Goodbye, Liam.*

Afraid her own weakness would entice her back, with no help from him, she hastily stepped out of the barrow into the afternoon sun. It dazzled her eyes. She fell to her knees, gasping in the strange, brisk air of the open moor. Thinking of the Keats poem again, she murmured, "And I awoke and found me here –"

When her eyes adjusted, she scanned the deserted downs. The sun wasn't so bright after all, but overcast with clouds. The wind carried an unexpected chill. She had entered the mound on May Eve, and now the bleakness of autumn met her eyes.

"And I awoke and found me here," she recited aloud, "on the pale hill's side."

When I brought my fingers to my lips, I could still taste Belle's blood in my mouth. I sat at my computer and tried to remember everything about that first taste of the blood of another. I started to type.

Friends

Christine DeLong Miller

You really want to know about this, huh?

To the best of my recollection, the change began about five years ago. I was just beginning to get serious about my writing career and an acquaintance of mine had been relating an occurrence that had happened in her youth to a group of us as we sat having coffee one bright afternoon. We sat at the one and only sidewalk table at Le Cafe, down on Main Street. There was Belle, with her ever-burning cigarette and her 'regular' cup of coffee. Monica, dressed completely in black on this beautiful spring day, with a double latte. Then, there was me, Carrie, with the largest espresso that Le Cafe served. I had a major caffeine addiction at the time.

"It happened when I was about seven, maybe eight," Belle began. "I swear that it's true. The neighbor man should have never fooled around with that girl who lived down the road. For one, he was already married. And two, the girl was crazy as a loon and we all knew it. Anyway, he took her as a lover and of course, she got pregnant." Belle waved her hand in the air. "And, *of course,* he denied it. Well, that angered the girl. To make a long story short, the girl miscarried the baby. It being the south, and the girl not knowing much better, she took care of the matter at home.

"She put the poor dead baby in a jar."

"You're kidding," I said. This was wild. Of course, Belle was known to be a bit wild with her storytelling.

Belle shook her head, her dark hair bouncing. "I'm not. Some things are done a might different down south," she said with a thicker than normal southern accent.

"So, what happened?" I asked. I couldn't wait to hear.

Belle sipped her coffee, pausing for effect, I think. She was quite a bit older than the rest of us. Close to fifty at the time. But her mind still worked at about the age of twenty. I think that's why we got along so well. Belle looked me in the eye. "The girl took the dead baby in the jar and put it on the neighbor man's front porch so his wife would find it."

"I don't believe it," Monica said, leaning back in her chair. Monica never believed anything.

"It's the God's honest truth." Belle couldn't be swayed. Her sense of drama kicked in. "I swear on a stack of –" Belle swung her arm wide and as she brought her hand up to place it on her heart for the swear, (which she always did), her hand caught Monica's water glass. Belle made a move to catch it as it started over the edge of the table. She caught it alright. All she managed to do was to smash it against the edge of the table. The glass shattered.

"Son of a bitch!" Belle said. She laid her hand on the table. A shard of broken glass was protruding from her palm.

Monica shoved herself away for the table to go inside for help.

Belle grasped her injured hand by the wrist. "Damn, look at that bleed."

Blood dripped from the glistening cut onto the table, the

drops making lovely florets on the napkin beside Belle's cup.

I reached across and took Belle's injured hand. "Let me see," I said. Gingerly, I pulled the piece of glass from the wound.

"Oh, Jesus. I think I'm going to pass out," Belle said, raising her good hand to her forehead.

The sun seemed too hot on the top of my head as I gazed at the fresh blood that welled up from the wound. I don't know what came over me. Everything else around me blurred in my vision except the cut on Belle's hand. My eyes were glued to it, the blood in such sharp focus that my heart started to change its rhythm to beat in sync with the pulse of the stream that throbbed out of Belle's flesh. At the moment when the beats of my heart meshed with the steady pulse of the blood I raised Belle's hand to my mouth and –

I tasted.

I licked the rivulet of blood from her palm.

The sunlight intensified and I closed my eyes against it, feeling the warmth of Belle's blood wash over my tongue. It had the full-bodied, salty taste of a lonesome tear fallen from the eye of the broken hearted. Feelings of sorrow and loss, a wrenching ache in my heart, filled me. I wanted to cry. Then, Belle's tale about the baby in the jar entered my mind like so much babble. Suddenly, an idea for a story crashed through my brain like an angry ocean wave against a jagged, rocky shore.

"Carrie," Monica said.

My eyes snapped open. Monica looked at me strangely then handed me a damp cloth. I took the cloth from her and dabbed at the cut on Belle's palm. The cut didn't seem as large now, though I still had all of those strange feelings coursing through me.

"Is it bad?" Belle asked.

"I don't think that you'll need stitches," I said, "Here. Look." And it really wasn't that bad. Monica was still looking at me strangely but didn't say anything. "Listen, I have to go." I rose to leave. A wave of dizziness washed over me. I grabbed the back of my chair to steady myself and took a breath. It almost felt as if I'd been drinking alcohol instead of espresso.

"Are you alright?" Monica asked.

I smiled and shook my head. "No. I think I've had my limit of caffeine for the day. I'll see you guys later."

And I left.

◆

I arrived at my apartment and locked the door behind me. When I brought my fingers to my lips, I could still taste Belle's blood in my mouth. I sat at my computer and tried to remember everything about that first taste of the blood of another. I started to type.

It wasn't the flavor of the blood that I was desperate to capture. It was the mood, the source of the emotions that I had drawn from it.

The story.

My fingers flew over the keyboard as I coupled the experience of drawing blood from Belle and the onslaught of insight that I received from it with the story of the baby in the jar. I actually caught myself laughing from the joy of writing – the words coming so easily for the first time – even though the story that I crafted was tragic. The emotional rush from the infusion of Belle's blood was the most intense thing I had ever felt.

I finished the story in less than two hours.

I sent the story to a magazine that I had been trying to break into. Two months later, the story was accepted. My first piece that had been accepted. I was so excited. Four months after that, I received a copy of the magazine with my story printed inside. I had just become a publisher writer! I raced to Belle's to show her.

Belle read the story, her brow furrowed, while I paced the floor waiting for her reaction. Finally, she closed the magazine. She looked at me and grinned, sending the wrinkles on her face into a dance. "Where in the world did you ever come up with an idea like that?" she asked.

"What do you mean?" I asked, confused. Belle, herself, had given me the seeds to that story.

"A dead baby in a jar. God, how beautifully awful. Your mind makes up the weirdest stuff, Carrie." Belle laid the magazine on the end table and lit a cigarette, blowing smoke into the air.

I sat down across from her. "Belle – you told me that story yourself."

She let out a laugh. "I most certainly didn't. What ever gave you that idea?"

The sun shone through the window and I looked at her through dust motes and blue cigarette haze. "You don't recognize the story? It was the one that you told all of us that day at the coffee shop. The day you cut your hand." It wasn't the first time I had thought about that day. The day I had tasted Belle's blood. "You said it happened when you were a child. And it happened to your neighbor."

Belle looked at me out of the corner of her eye. "I don't know what you're talking about," she said, flicking her ash.

I didn't bring the subject of the story up again.

A couple of months passed and although I wrote steadily, like clockwork – everyday – I couldn't get another story accepted anywhere. I secretly pondered the question of whether the tasting of Belle's blood had anything to do with how well I had written that story of the baby jar.

I had actually dreamed about the taste of blood, the emotional high I had gotten from it. Twice, I had awakened drenched in sweat with the fear of having a major mental problem or of becoming some sort of sick, faux vampire.

Everyday that passed after I had written the baby-jar story,

I sat at the computer and everyday, I wrote. But the words came harder and harder, slower and slower. I received rejection after rejection. I began to question whether I had what it took to become a writer, whether that first story was just a fluke. I still didn't understand why Belle couldn't remember telling the story about the baby-jar. Could it have been that the story had flowed out of her with the tiny amount of blood that had coursed down my throat?

Surely not.

That fall, I went to Monica's house to help her strip the ancient wallpaper from her living room walls. Monica lived in an old turn-of-the-century home, in the historic district of town. To look at her – always dressed in black with her pierced nose – you could tell that the house didn't suit her lifestyle. But Monica wasn't one to turn down an inheritance from her grandmother and that was how the house fell into her possession. She would make it her own one way or another.

So, she and I set about stripping the wallpaper so that she could paint the living room walls the most sickly shade of gray that I had ever seen. It would suit her perfectly but it reminded me of moldy mausoleums.

We jabbered back and forth as we scraped with our putty knives. We must have talked of a million things as we battled the stubborn wallpaper. Finally, we ended up talking about sex.

"Do you remember your first time?" I asked.

"Oh most definitely," Monica replied, scraping a piece of paper from the wall and flinging it into the trash can that sat next to her ladder. "He had the most beautiful golden hair. Angel-like, you know. That's what I was attracted to. *Then,* anyway. But it was good, let me tell you..."

And Monica proceeded to tell me in detail what happened that night, the first time that she had had sex. I listened and I scraped, trying to remember my first sexual experience. My memories weren't as fond as Monica's. I remembered an awkward evening that I swore at that time would have been best forgotten.

"Judas!"

"What happened?" I asked, hearing Monica's swear.

Monica climbed down from her ladder. "I stabbed my finger. Look." She held up the middle finger of her right hand. There was a tiny drop of blood welling up from the tip of it.

I took her finger in my hand. "It's just a tiny poke."

Monica let out a giggle. "Maybe I'll pierce it."

The story about Monica's first experience with sex entered my mind. I needed a good story. Something publishable. The drop of blood on the tip of Monica's finger was almost ready to fall. Time to experiment.

I put Monica's bleeding finger in my mouth.

Oh, there it was again. That pungent flavor of life. There was so much emotion in that one drop of blood that I wanted more. I looked into Monica's eyes. There was a spark of something there but she didn't attempt to pull away.

I started to suck lightly at her finger.

Monica's blood caressed my tongue. Such heat, such lust. I almost couldn't take it. I closed my eyes and drank the emotion from her finger. When I felt myself reach the edge of ecstasy – pleasure like I have never known – I opened my eyes to find Monica smiling at me.

I started to pull away.

"No," Monica whispered, "don't be a priss." She cradled the back of my head in her other hand, lacing her fingers in my hair.

I felt a moan rise up in my throat.

Monica chuckled. "That's it. It's just blood sport, Carrie. There's nothing wrong with it. I've been tested." I felt her injured finger wiggle deeper into my mouth as she brought her lips to my ear. "Take as much as you want," she whispered, her breath hot and close. "Suck it, Carrie. *Drink my blood.*"

The moan escaped my lips and I suckled her finger, feeling

the throb of her heart pump down my throat. My knees went weak.

Monica and I sank to the floor. After a few moments, she withdrew her finger from my mouth.

I felt like a part of my soul had been excised from my being. "Please," I whispered.

"Shhh," Monica said, "There's more."

I watched as she unbuttoned her black gauze blouse, feeling as if I was in a different dimension. The hoard of emotions that made up the elixir of Monica's blood rushed through me, transporting me to some unknown place that was made only for the sake of lust. I was drunk with it, my mind racing to note all of the nuances of the sexual intricacies of her potion. I had to remember this. Had to remember everything I was feeling.

Monica's blouse now lay fully open and I was amazed at how aroused I was. I had never felt this way about a woman. My senses were heightened to the point of actual pain. She reached for the tiny dagger that dangled from a chain around her neck. I had always thought the dagger was only a piece of jewelry but now I knew its purpose.

Monica drew the dagger across the mound of her left breast.

Blood welled up in the dagger's trail. A cut, about three inches long. My mouth started to water and I wondered vaguely if I had finally lost my mind. We lay on the chilled wood floor, side by side. Monica's dark brown eyes met mine and she smiled.

"Come. Drink," she beckoned.

I couldn't help myself. It was as if I had never before felt anything, any of my senses, any emotions. Not like I was feeling now. Slowly, I moved toward the place from which the fountain of blood sprung at her breast. As I moved closer, I felt heat course through me and then, whatever caution my mind had warned me of flew away.

My tongue traced the trail of blood across her moist skin.

"Yesss..." Monica breathed as she guided me to nurse at her breast.

I drank, fully and deep.

Visions of a younger Monica flitted through my mind. Monica, locked in a sexual embrace with a golden haired boy. Sex, painful and sweet. Exquisite.

I wanted more as I sucked hard and long, Monica's fingers tangled in my hair, holding me close. Her moans of pleasure urged me on.

I wanted to drain her blood-dry.

It seemed like hours passed but it could only have been moments, then I heard the voice.

'What are you doing?' it asked, the voice clanging loudly inside my skull. I blinked. The voice was my own. The voice of reality.

I dragged myself away from Monica.

Monica's hands fell from my hair and she sighed, eyes closed, fully sated.

My God, what had I done. I'm heterosexual, no questions asked. Had it come this far? My thirst for the blood of a story?

I scrambled to my feet and left before Monica could even realize that I was gone.

◆

I arrived home with a cacophony in my brain. I raced to the computer, my fingers aching for the touch of the keys. Within an hour, I had written the most erotic story of a first sexual encounter that I could dream up. My breath came in gasps as I stumbled to my bed and fell upon it. Drugged with Monica's blood, I fell into a sated sleep, totally exhausted and more fulfilled than I had ever been.

Within five days of sending the story of a first sexual encounter between two lovers to an underground magazine, it was eagerly accepted. It was published that next month and when I received my contributor's copy, the editor had included a note pleading to see more of my work.

In the time between the incident with Monica and the time I got the copy of the magazine, I had run into Monica twice. Each time, I felt as if I could feel her blood pulsing inside me. Monica never mentioned what had happened between us. Neither did I. It was as if it had never happened.

But now that I had the story in print, I wanted to show it to her. Let her read it. See if she had forgotten about her first stab at intercourse, the one she had told me about that day, for that is what the story was about. See if Monica forgot it just as Belle had forgotten the baby in the jar when I had taken the story from her while I had taken her blood.

I invited Monica to my apartment for coffee.

"Hmm," she said after reading the story. "Good. Hot stuff." She sipped her coffee.

"Do you remember the first time you had sex?" I asked, looking at my dark reflection in my coffee cup.

"You know," she hesitated, "isn't this weird. I don't remember it at all."

I looked up to search her face. She was serious. I could tell by the confused look in her eyes that she honestly didn't remember. I sipped my coffee and thought about how important it was to me to have a writing career.

◆

Well, that's how it began. My writing career. And considering what I've gone through to achieve my success, I'd say that it's been worth it.

Have you ever wanted something so badly that you'd sell your soul to accomplish your goal? I'm sure that you know what I mean. Writers do tend to sacrifice a few things for their craft. How much you're willing to give up depends on how much you want the dream.

Listen, I've got the rest of the day free. I know you're probably a busy person but, I'd like to get to know you better. Why don't you stay for dinner? Maybe we could watch some videos later. Or, if you'd rather...

We could just sit around and talk.

All she saw was a dark shape. A hand lifted towards her and a voice said, "Hush, my dear." A woman's voice. Then Shahla saw a woman dressed all in black, with a sharp, pale face; the eyes hidden in shadow she could not see.

Blood Feud

C.W. Johnson

Twilight swooped down upon the city, as the soldiers had swooped down the year before. Now only the soldiers strolled the streets without fear, their laughter cracking the winter air. With rifles slung over their shoulders and pistols on their hips, they talked carelessly, even cheerfully as they waved cigarette embers in the gloom.

In the shadows, pressed against a wall, Shahla tensed. Though her pulse thudded in her ears she tried to make no sound at all, taking only the smallest sips of air until the soldiers passed. She still waited many minutes longer; then, as twilight deepened, hurried over stained cobblestones, hoping to outrun the night and the soldiers and reach safety. As if there were any safety.

At a corner Shahla paused to spy for soldiers. Cold fingers curled around her heart – she knew this street, her mother's cousin had lived here. Shahla remembered it full of sunlight, and men whitewashing the walls or standing in doorways smoking, and women leaning out of second-story windows to catch the latest gossip from passers-by. Now the street was empty, the windows boarded up and the walls scarred with bullet holes. Shahla's mother was dead; so was the cousin.

Shahla tightened her shawl about her head as she crossed the street. Her limbs filled with ice, not from the winter air but from terror: terror that at any moment a soldier might see her, a voice would call her to halt, hands would grasp her and move over her clothes and her body while she squeezed shut her eyes and bottled up the scream inside her...

Every shadow she passed she feared and every boarded-up window she resented. Once she had loved living in this city. She had loved shopping the marketplace in the carsija, holding the hand of her son Kerim as they strolled among the stalls containing row after row of bright peppers and fruits and brown eggs and fresh-caught fish, pausing to inhale the drifting odor of spices and roasting lamb. In the evening her husband Nasir would return and when he kissed her she could taste the coffee he had drunk all day and he would lift their son high into the air as Kerim laughed with delight. Now there was no food, the stalls in the carsija were empty and shattered, and Nasir was in the mountains with the other men fighting a futile war – if he were still alive, that is. Just a month ago they had news that Zaran, the fiancè of her younger sister Azrah, was dead. Azrah and Kerim were all the family Shahla had left in the city. Shahla hated the city and longed to be far away from it. They had hoped to leave it – but now night had fallen, it was too late and getting too dark, and they would have to spend another agonizing night trapped.

Shahla rounded a corner without slowing, without thinking, and immediately saw four soldiers walking towards her. Shahla backed around the corner and stood against the wall, not breathing. If they came for her she would run. Let them shoot her, that would be better than their hands on her again. But then Kerim –

No voices shouted and no figures loomed in the dark, and Shahla had to take a breath, and then another. She inched along the wall to the corner to glance up the street. The darkness was so thick she could see nothing clearly. Still looking up the street, Shahla stepped away from the wall, and into someone behind her.

Shahla jumped away, nearly crying out. All she saw was a dark shape. A hand lifted towards her and a voice said, "Hush, my dear." A woman's voice. Then Shahla saw a woman dressed all in black, with a sharp, pale face; the eyes hidden in shadow she could not see.

"You gave me a start," Shahla whispered, relieved. "I saw soldiers, and –"

"You are afraid of the soldiers," the woman said. She had a foreign accent, not the accent of the invaders, but from farther away, north and east.

"Of course," said Shahla, "everyone is – it's not safe here, I have to go. So should you."

The woman in black reached out and put a hand on Shahla's face. "They've hurt you, haven't they? They've... touched you." The words were gentle but Shahla flinched and started to deny it until the woman hushed her again. Without taking her hand from Shahla's face the woman moved closer. "I'm so sorry."

Shahla said, "It isn't safe out here. For either of us." Turning her face from the hand she added, "I must go. We're going to leave the city – there are convoys to take women and children to safety this week, they say the soldiers promised not to stop them." Moved by the other's compassion, Shahla added, "You could come with us."

The woman let her hand drop and shook her head. "It'll be no better."

"Oh, but it will..."

"No." She turned away and looked up into the night sky. "There is no safety." She spoke with a great, lethargic sadness that touched Shahla. "No matter where you go they'll hurt you – us – they've taken so much away and given so much pain..."

"You?" Shahla asked hoarsely.

Still staring up into the sky, the woman said, "I can take away your fear."

"Who are you?"

A sigh. "Once I was called Téodora, but that is only a word. Promises are made of words; words are worthless."

Then she turned back to Shahla and added, "Do you hate them?" She spoke softly but her voice suddenly had a knife's edge to it, something so cold and sharp it hurt Shahla. "Do you ever think about vengeance?"

"No," said Shahla, the word thick on her tongue.

"With all they've done to this city, to the women – to you – don't you wish to see them dead?"

Shahla recoiled, but her back was already against the wall. "I–"

"Vengeance," said Téodora, so close her face almost touched Shahla's. "Don't you thirst for their blood?"

Shahla's legs began to shake uncontrollably and she said, "I have to go," but she had troubled getting out the words; her chest felt constricted and she could barely breathe. She slid along the wall, not looking at the woman, and then she ran away down the street. Behind her she felt Téodora's presence like a cold void at her back.

◆

Night had wrapped the city in a thick web of gloom by the time Shahla reached the back door to a house. Glancing over her shoulder, she knocked *tap-tap, tap-tap, tap.* A moment later the door opened.

The hiding place was a room half-buried in rubble. Candles flickered feebly against the shadows, and the air, little warmer than outside, smelt stale. In the yellow light a dozen women and children, sitting on broken timbers or the buckled floor, turned to Shahla. She looked around the room at all of them, at the faces lined with hunger, cold, and fear, their eyes dull but their mouths open with expectation. With a great weight in her chest she shook her head.

Twelve-year-old Kerim, his limbs thin for a boy his age, ran up and hugged her. For a moment his embrace stoked joy in her; for a moment his deep brown eyes reminded her of Nasir. A long time ago Nasir could make her melt inside just by looking at her with his eyes, and she felt a near-forgotten tug deep within... But those days were long past and she pushed aside all thoughts of her husband, for the thought that she might never again hear the rumble of his voice or feel the heat of his skin against hers was too much to bear.

Behind Kerim stood Shahla's younger sister, Azrah. "We were so worried for you," Azrah said, clasping Shahla's hands, "when you didn't return."

Shahla looked around the room again. "There were too many soldiers. I had to hide and wait for them to move. Most of them are gone now, but now it's dark. Maybe in the morning they will still be gone."

"The morning!" said Azrah.

"It's too dangerous now..."

"When is it never dangerous?" Azrah asked, releasing Shahla's hands. "At least at night we have a chance of slipping through the city unseen by soldiers. And we have no food. Little Yovanka is coughing." She turned to face the other women. "There is only death here if we wait, holed up like rats."

"But the soldiers..." said Shahla.

Azrah whirled to face her sister. "Kill the bastards!" she said, and she spat on the ground. "If we cannot leave, then give me a knife so I can kill one of them!"

"They would just kill you –"

"Let them!" cried Azrah, lifting up her hands. "Let them!

They would as soon kill us anyway!" She turned again to the other women. "They've killed our fathers – our sons – our husbands –"

Shahla put her hands on Azrah's arms, slowly lowering them. "Shh," she hushed. "In the morning, we will go."

"It will be no better then," Azrah said, pleading in her face.

"She is right," said one of the elderly women, struggling to stand upright. Old Amela, wrinkled and with blackened teeth, addressed the women. "We have had no food for two days. The convoy may not wait for us. It would be death for us to stay."

Shahla looked at Amela, then went and knelt by the other elder, Suneda, who sat cross-legged on the frigid floor and nodded to herself. "What do you say," she asked Suneda.

"Nothing here, nothing here, nothing here," Suneda muttered, staring at the ground. Then she looked up and the reflection of candles danced in her eyes. "Better to die swiftly, with Allah's grace, let us go, let us go, let us go."

Slowly Shahla stood up. She turned her palms up in resignation. "Then we go now."

Outside the night air seemed even more bitter than before. Shahla watched anxiously as everyone filed out of the house. The last to come was Mejra, who kept her daughter very close to her and away from the others. Shahla felt a stab seeing Mejra, who had said nothing in two days. And no one had said anything to Mejra – everyone knew what the soldiers had done to her – but behind her they whispered about her and speculated about her husband. *Look how they set us against each other, Shahla thought. And even seeing that I still do not have the courage to speak out, to let Mejra know she is not alone...*

◆

The silent, cold march across the city took two hours. Each moment, as they threaded through back alleys and skirted deep mortar craters, was steeped in fear. Fortunately the streets were empty of soldiers and the shadows thick. Without incident they crossed the river on an ancient stone bridge. On either side of the river the city lay in near-total darkness, with the black shoulder of the mountains behind them, the dome of the moonless sky above, the slosh of the river beneath – and ahead, open lowlands and the convoy to safety.

Months of sporadic bombardment had reduced a third of all buildings in this part of the city to rubble. Walls lay tumbled in the street like drunks. It tore Shahla's heart to see her once-beautiful city in ruins.

"Will we see Papa?" Kerim suddenly asked. His voice sounded unnaturally loud in the quiet, and Shahla put a finger to her lips. "Will we?" Kerim persisted, whispering. After a moment of hesitation, Shahla nodded.

"Is he dead?" Kerim whispered.

"No!" Shahla said. She leaned close to him. "We'll see him soon."

"The soldiers might have killed him."

"We'll find him," Shahla answered. "And together we'll go someplace far from the war."

"Mama?" Kerim said. "When you were gone, I prayed to Allah to send an avenger." Shahla squeezed his hand in reply. Suddenly Azrah, in the vanguard, halted and reached back with a hand. Shahla looked up. At the next corner, illumined by starlight, stood a soldier with a rifle.

Frantic, Shahla looked around. The buildings to either side were demolished, nothing more than piles of snapped lumber and smashed bricks. They were out in the open, visible – vulnerable.

Behind Shahla the others also stopped. No one spoke; but seven-year-old Yovanka coughed twice. The soldier looked up.

Shahla reached out for Kerim and pushed the boy behind her. The soldier had unslung his rifle and was looking at them. Shahla's heart squeezed tight and her mind raced: they could run, but the older women would not get far, and –

The soldier took a step towards them. "You shouldn't be here," he said. His voice was hesitant, uncertain. When he came a little closer Shahla could see he was young, hardly more than a boy with a round face and close-cropped hair.

Azrah boldly stepped forward. "We're going to the convoy."

The soldier shook his head. "You can't go any farther. There's a curfew. Go home."

"We don't have a home any more!" Azrah said sharply.

"Azrah!" Shahla warned.

But her sister persisted. "You want us gone – fine! We're leaving." And she took another step forward.

"You can't go any farther," the young man repeated. "My orders – "

"Are you going to shoot all of us?" Azrah demanded.

"No," said the soldier. Looking over his shoulder he added, "But the others will. Please. Go back. Go home. It's not safe here."

Shahla came forward and tugged on Azrah's arm. Azrah spit at the soldier. "Bastard!" she hissed. "You're all murdering, thieving, raping bastards!"

"Please go! I could get in trouble for not –" Once again he glanced around, then looked back at the women and children. "Go!"

Shahla pulled on Azrah's arm until her sister retreated with the rest of them, back down the street. Once out of sight of the soldier, Azrah started down a side alley.

"Azrah!" Shahla said in a harsh whisper.

"We can't turn around," Azrah said, stopping to face her sister. "Now that we've come this far. To turn back..."

"It's not safe! There must be soldiers everywhere between us and the convoy."

"We don't know that, we don't know!" Azrah put her hands on her sister's arms.

"We must go back," insisted Shahla. She signaled to the other women, who gathered their children. Tightening her resolve and her shawl, Shahla began to march back. Some of the children were crying now, despite their mothers' attempts to hush them. Frustration stiffened inside of Shahla, ready to burst her skin. Next to Shahla, Azrah muttered to herself under her breath. Shahla only wrapped her arms tighter about herself and, as the web of shadows spun around her, thick and suffocating, hurried on.

Hurried through the streets until the squad of soldiers descended on them, like jackals at a kill.

◆

Crying and calling out for Kerim, Shahla was shoved through a doorway and down stone steps. The cellar room had a musty smell and she remembered all of this from before. "Just kill me, just kill me instead!" she begged, hysterical. She couldn't even see their faces – there were at least three of them – despite the lit lantern hanging from a nail in a pillar. Hands pressed Shahla to the cold floor. She looked around at anything but them, at the dirt floor and the wood beams in the ceiling and the boxes stacked against the walls as they lifted her dress above her waist.

Shahla looked away and held her breath as long as she could so as not to smell their sour breath; she tried to angle her face away so as not to feel the scrape of their stubbly beards. When two had finished raping her, the third stood over her unbuckling his belt. "Hey, where you going?" he asked. "It's my turn."

"Ludvo's waiting," said one of the other two men.

"I'll catch up," the man said, kneeling down by Shahla. The sound of shoes on stone steps, a wave of cold air, and then a door closing. With a grunt the last man leaned against Shahla. His meaty face pushed against her neck.

"Kill me, please," Shahla whispered. "Kill me –"

"Shut up."

Shahla turned her head away. She felt another wave of cold air, and heard another voice say, "Why don't you try me instead?" A woman's voice, a foreign accent.

"What –" began the soldier, angling his head around. "Get out of here!" he rumbled.

But Shahla could see her: the foreign woman dressed in black, Téodora. In the lantern-light she pulled the shawl from her head, revealing her pale, sharp features, long black hair, and narrow dark eyes.

"I'm the one you really want," she said, moving towards them, swaying slightly, her voice high and musical. "You don't want her."

"Goddammit," said the soldier. "Tomas! Dravan!" he roared. His twisted around and groped for his pants down around his hairy thighs.

"You don't need her," said Téodora. "You can have me..."

Grunting, the soldier yanked his pistol out of his belt and fired twice. The shots boomed in Shahla's ears, mixing with Téodora's shriek; the foreigner spun around and crashed against the wall, into a stack of boxes that splintered as she fell, her limbs flailing. Shahla threw up her arm to shield herself, jamming the knuckles of her hand into her mouth.

For a moment there was only the ringing echo of the shots and the soldier's panting. Then, still clutching his pistol, he turned back to Shahla and, putting a heavy hand on her shoulder, rested his weight on her.

Shahla had her eyes closed. *Oh Kerim,* she thought; she wished to die and she wished to see him again. *Mama I love you* she imagined his voice, and then she imagined Téodora's voice, *Now you've made me angry –*

Shahla opened her eyes. Above them stood Téodora, her face distant and dispassionate. The soldier swung his pistol around, his other elbow digging into Shahla's breast. With one hand Téodora caught his wrist. Something snapped; the soldier's meaty face went pale and started streaming sweat. He grunted, dropped the pistol, and cradled his arm against his body. "Dravan!" he shouted. "Christ, get away from me!" he added in near hysteria as Téodora slid her hands around his neck. Taking a step back, she yanked him off Shahla and to his knees as easily as if he were a rag doll.

"Don't tell me you like her better than me!" Téodora said, laughing, but the laugh was colder than the night. One hand she slipped behind his head and the other gripped his one good arm. Inexorably she pulled him closer, even though he bucked and tossed his head, accompanied by a grinding, crunching sound. The soldier began screaming. "Don't you like me?" she asked, and laughed. "Won't you dance with me?" she said, swaying to an imaginary waltz.

In desperation the soldier heaved himself to his feet and lunged against her. The two of them crashed into the pillar, knocking the lantern to the floor. The sudden darkness snapped Shahla from her stunned state and she started to crawl across the dirt floor. The soldier started begging for mercy, then abruptly screamed again, accompanied by wet tearing sounds. Her heart pounding, Shahla scrambled blindly until she put her hand on the cold stone of the steps. Feeling her way to the door she tumbled into the cold night air. From the cellar the sounds of the soldier cut off. Shahla pulled her dress back down and staggered up the street, her only thought to get as far away as possible.

◆

Shahla paused to lean against a wall, panting. Her entire body ached with each breath, and her ears rang in the silence. She limped from one block to the next, pausing to look up at the wheeling stars and wonder when the dawn would come.

Her heart tightened at the sight of a small figure standing

in the middle of the street, but then recognition took hold – "Kerim!" Shahla called out. At first the boy cringed in fear, then cried, "Mama!" as she swept him up in her embrace.

"Are you all right?" she asked, kissing his bruised and swollen face. "I thought I'd never see you again, I was so afraid –"

He was trembling in her arms; he pointed, saying, "Azrah."

Shahla looked. Only a few meters away Azrah lay in the street, her dress above her waist, her arms outflung. Shahla ran to her. Azrah's open eyes stared unseeing at the frozen night sky. Shahla knelt down by her sister's body and pulled down the dress, while the story spilled out of Kerim. The soldiers had beaten them both and then, then they had pushed her to the ground and they had held Kerim tight and made him watch.

"We're all going to die, aren't we?" the boy said solemnly. "And Papa? He must be dead, too."

Shahla kissed Azrah on the forehead and closed the eyes. Kneeling there, she felt a gust of cold wind and looked up. At the far end of the street she saw another shadowy figure, a woman in black coming toward her, and the sight hit her like a blow. Her heart hammered in her chest. Standing she said, "No," and grabbed Kerim's hand. "Forgive me," she whispered to Azrah's body.

Walking swiftly away down the street she said to Kerim, "We're not going to die, I promise you. We're going to get on the convoy and be safe and live." Kerim glanced over his shoulder at Azrah. "Don't look back," Shahla said sharply. Softening her tone she added, "That'll be our watchword from now on: don't look back."

"Yes, Mama," the boy said, as Shahla took his hand and they ran over the cobblestones.

◆

The street sloped downwards, the final stretch before the

flatlands. "Look!" Shahla said, pointing to flickering lights ahead. "That must be where the convoy is. Look, Kerim!" The sight gave Shahla new strength despite the exhaustion that tore her muscles, despite the stabbing pain when she breathed hard. Maybe they would find Nasir waiting for them somewhere far away, or even in the camp. Shahla already imagined holding him, kissing him, the joy in his face when he would hug Kerim...

And then she slowed. Kerim pulled at her arm, tugging her forward. But she pulled him back sharply and against her; stopping, she wrapped her arms around his head and pushed his face against her dress. She could see trucks all right, about a hundred yards away, and men with pale, alien faces, wearing blue berets and foreign uniforms, standing by. But between her and the trucks was a roadblock. A trio of ragged sawhorses manned by the invading soldiers, smoking cigarettes. "Oh, Kerim," she breathed.

Kerim yanked himself away. "Come on, Mama," he said.

"Kerim, we can't, there are soldiers."

Panting, Kerim stood and looked at the soldiers at the roadblock. The boy's breath came out in the cold night air as steam. Shahla put her arms around him. His muscles were taut to her touch. "I don't care about the soldiers," he said firmly. "You promised..."

Shahla swallowed, straightened, and looked again at the roadblock. "All right," she said, and she took Kerim's hand. The fifty yards to the road block felt like fifty miles, and when they came out of the shadows into the light, and the soldiers saw them and one turned towards them, Shahla, her heart pounding, felt cold and naked despite the shawl wrapped tight around her head.

One soldier with a thick black mustache and small dark eyes watched closely as Shahla and Kerim approached. He cradled his rifle in his arms as if it were a baby. Shahla nearly stumbled, her legs felt so weak, as she approached; but she kept up her stride. "Go back," thick black mustache said.

Without stopping Shahla lifted a hand and pointed to the trucks. "We are leaving."

Thick black mustache took a step to block their way with his rifle. "You can't. No one is to leave the city."

"Please," whispered Shahla, her voice cracking and hating herself for showing her weakness, "just let us go."

He just gestured with his rifle butt.

"Then let my son go," Shahla pleaded.

"I won't go without you!" Kerim said.

"No one goes."

Shahla saw some of the men at the trucks looking curiously at them. "Please!" she called out to them. "We just want to leave with you!"

"Quiet!" Thick black mustache prodded them with the stock of his rifle.

"Don't touch us!" Kerim exclaimed. Shahla pulled him away. "You bastards!" Kerim cried out. "You're stealing our country!"

The soldier flushed. "You piss-mouthed little...this is our land, it was ours for millennia, it was you people who invaded us!"

"That was centuries ago!" Shahla said sharply.

"We have long memories!" thick black mustache roared as Shahla dragged Kerim up the street, despite his resistance.

"You killed Azrah!" Kerim shouted. "You killed my father!"

As tears ran down Shahla's cheek, stinging her bruises, she tried to hush Kerim. "It won't do any good..."

But the boy kept shouting hoarsely until his face turned red. "I'll kill you! Someday I'll kill you all! I'll take *your* land and rape *your* women and –"

And then he wrenched himself from Shahla's grasp.

Running down the street, Kerim stooped to pick up a rock and throw it at the soldiers. It fell short but they unslung their rifles. "Kerim!" Shahla screamed. She started to run for him but her ankle twisted and she tumbled to the street. Shahla looked up as Kerim picked up another rock to throw. "Kerim!"

The shots one-two-three! cracked the air. Shahla shuddered as if pierced herself. Kerim immediately fell to the ground. Screaming his name Shahla scrambled over the cobblestones to where he lay face down. She turned him over; there was blood on his face where he hit the street. For a moment he looked at her, then his eyes rolled back in his head and he convulsed. "Kerim? KERIM!" Shahla looked around desperately. The soldiers at the roadblock watched her dispassionately. Beyond some of the men in the blue berets from the convoy were talking heatedly to a soldier and pointing towards her; but the soldier kept gesturing with a rifle.

Looking down Shahla held Kerim tight as his whole body shook in her arms. "Soon this will all be over," she crooned to him, "soon this terrible night will be over, Kerim, and there will be a new day for us." As she caressed his face, his mouth moved wordlessly, then filled up with dark fluid. "Kerim? Just think, soon we'll see your father, we'll all be together again. Kerim, can you hear me? Kerim!"

The boy shuddered once more; then he was still.

◆

On a rooftop, underneath the stars glittering like fragments of ice, Shahla found Téodora looking out over the darkened city. "I was afraid you wouldn't come," Téodora said.

"He's dead," Shahla said. The words had been bottled up deep inside her chest, but they rushed out of her mouth with a ragged edge: "Dead...dead...they're all dead!" As Téodora came to her, Shahla turned away, toward the edge of the roof with her arms folded. She had wandered a long time on the broken-backed streets, numb with such cold that her soul felt frozen. "Azrah and even Kerim. Oh, Kerim," said Shahla. She wished to cry but she could not, not with the sea of ice inside her.

"Kerim?"

"My son..."

Téodora bowed her head. "Kerim," she repeated. "I can't even remember my own son's name, it was so long ago." She looked up. "They killed him, too." She put her hands on Shahla's. "I'm sorry I couldn't save them." Gently, she turned Shahla around and gestured to a corner of the roof. "But I collected these for you, my dear."

Stacked like cordwood were the bodies of a half-dozen soldiers. Téodora smiled at Shahla as if offering her a bouquet of flowers.

"Who are you?" Shahla whispered. "You're not one of us."

Not looking at her, Téodora said, "Your men and my men have fought for many, many centuries. Our men have killed each other...and they raped and killed us and slaughtered our children." Now turning to Shahla, she said, "Do you want vengeance for your men, or for...?"

Shahla swayed, as if dizzy, in the cold wind. "I don't know anymore," she said. "All I feel is pain and all I want is revenge."

"I can take away the pain," the other woman said, stepping closer. "I can make you feel nothing. I can give you everything you want." She pulled back the fringe of her shawl. In the starlight her face might have been porcelain – it might have been stone – and her eyes were as dark as Kerim's had been when he died. She took Shahla's right hand in her left and put her other hand on Shahla's hip and moved her in a silent waltz on the rooftop. "We'll dance on their graves!" she cried out, laughing coldly and throwing back her head.

"Vengeance," breathed Shahla.

"Yes, vengeance!" Téodora replied, her eyes shining.

"Vengeance!" cried Shahla.

"Yes," said Téodora, "yes, I see the blood lust in your eyes!...But there is a cost."

"I would pay anything," Shahla said, "but – I have no money."

"I do not want money. What are you willing to pay?"

"Anything. Everything. There is nothing left for me."

"Nothing. Not even your life? No one you love?"

Wearily, Shahla said, "Once there was a man I loved, but that seems so long ago, I can barely remember his name. Oh, I wish I were dead," said Shahla, sighing. "I wish them dead. I hate them."

Téodora nodded, and leaned out over the edge. "I can give you that." She swept back Shahla's shawl. "It is a blood feud," she whispered in Shahla's ear, "between us and them." Her arms slid around Shahla to pull her close and her cold lips grazed Shahla's cheek.

Shahla pulled back a fraction and asked in a frightened voice, "What...things will you do to me?"

Téodora laughed. "What perversions you mean? Tell me, my dear, do you care about your soul anymore?"

Tears rolled down Shahla's face. "No," she whispered, "no." She added, "Oh, Kerim!"

"Good," said Téodora, pulling Shahla close into her embrace. "Remember always: vengeance," she whispered into Shahla's ear.

"Vengeance," whispered Shahla, thinking of Mejra and imagining her with a cold, stone face.

"Vengeance," said Téodora, her lips touching Shahla's earlobes, "vengeance," and then her cheek.

And then her neck.

◆

Two nights later, or a hundred – it does not matter – soldiers hustled Shahla into a crumbling, abandoned building and tore away the black veil that covered her face. "I remember this one," said one of the soldiers, a big, beefy man with a graveled voice. "Unfortunately Bodin here was across the city and missed the chance to have fun with you." He draped an arm around a young man, little more than a boy, really, with a round face and close-cropped hair. Shahla said nothing, stood stone-faced. "Strip her," he snapped to his men; to Shahla he added, "Some women have been taking it into their minds to hide knives and to cut our throats – not very hospitable." The soldiers pulled Shahla's dress up and over her head, leaving her standing naked before them. She did not move, did not even shiver in the biting cold. She only stared straight ahead.

"There she is, ready and willing," said the beefy soldier, playfully tapping Bodin in the groin. The young soldier flinched. "Just be sure to leave some for us!" he laughed. And he walked to the other end of the room with the two other soldiers where they lit cigarettes and started telling jokes.

Not looking Shahla in the face, the young soldier put his hands on her cold body and lowered her, almost gently, to the ground. She lay there impassively while he tugged at his belt and – he hesitated for a moment, glancing over at the other soldiers – knelt down over her.

The other soldiers were laughing hard at a joke their leader was telling, and they did not pay much attention to the noises Bodin was making. Only suddenly they noticed that Bodin was rolled over on his back, thrashing like a fish on the bank, with only a ragged red hole where his throat had been.

Shahla stood in a pool of blood, her naked back to the soldiers. The big soldier cursed and as he ran at her pulled his pistol from his holster. Shahla twisted suddenly, knocked the pistol out of his hand, and grabbed him by the front of his fatigues. "Goddamn!" he shouted as he struggled to free himself. *"Shoot her!"* he shouted to his two colleagues. "Shoot her!" They raised their weapons but did not fire for fear of hitting him.

Shahla pulled his red, sweating face close to hers, pale and dispassionate, and held him there for a moment as he struggled. "For Christ's sake, shoot!" he shouted. He struck at her face with his left hand. She did not even flinch. "Bitch!" he roared at Shahla. Shahla put a hand on the back of his head and with one swift motion jerked his head backwards–he screamed like an animal at the slaughterhouse–and tore out his throat with her teeth.

The body slid to the ground as she faced the last two soldiers. As they stared at her she opened her mouth and shrieked. She stood there, frail and naked and splashed with gore, and this sound, this inhuman shriek, rolled out of her, a scream of sorrow and pain and fury that shook the ceiling beams and rattled the basement window. Dropping his gun, one soldier clapped his hands over his ears and ran out of the basement. The other soldier, blinking and trembling, kept his gun aimed at her. "Oh God!" he sobbed as Shahla advanced, fear seizing his guts like a wolf; he fired; she staggered back but then whirled around on one foot, like a dancer, to face him again. "You can't hurt me anymore," she said when she seized him with a wild, hungry look in her eyes. "I'm already dead!" She threw her head back and laughed, like a celebrant at a party.

Then she bent her head to his neck and drained the life from his body.

◆

In the city women are no safer than they ever were. Sometimes a nervous soldier will abruptly shoot a woman he sees walking down the street. "She showed her teeth to me!" he protests to his comrades as they cautiously poke at the body. But now they are equal, if not in life, then in death; the men have joined the women at the feast of fear, eating the bread of suspicion and drinking the wine of terror.

And blood runs rivers in the streets.

"Zara, I love you," Jared said. "If you want" – it was an effort, but he made it – "a baby, that's fine with me."

She turned to him, her face lit up like a birthday candle. "You darling! Really?"

Winding The Clock

Deborah Markus

A night or two after their third fiftieth anniversary (flowers, champagne bath, three-layer golden ring as seen in a *New Yorker* advertisement), Zara interrupted Jared just as he was about to doze off on the couch over his day-old Sunday paper.

"I miss motherhood," she said in a wistful tone he'd learned never to trust.

"How can you miss something you never had?" he asked reasonably but tactlessly.

Zara slapped shut the book she'd been reading just to keep him company and glared. "All right. I missed motherhood. Is that better?"

Jared sighed. It had been such a wonderful weekend. So peaceful. In fact, Zara hadn't gotten a bee in her bonnet in the better part of a year, and Jared couldn't say he missed the commotion.

Well. No point in postponing the inevitable. "All right.

You missed motherhood. Now would you mind telling me exactly what that means?"

"It means I want a baby."

"That's ridiculous."

"It is not!" She threw her book at him – *The Scarlet Letter,* Jared noticed as he ducked – and stood up in a full snit. "My biological clock is ticking!"

"Honey, you stopped having a biological clock close to two centuries ago, remember?"

"I don't care," Zara said stubbornly. "I still want a baby. I want to be a mother."

Though he knew that the best and quickest way out of Zara's enthusiasm was a course of smiling, nodding patience, Jared felt a prickle of pure irritation. He didn't need this, he really didn't. Damn it, he worked hard all week and then came home and did the dishes. (Well, the glasses.) He busted his butt making a living for the two of them – and if Zara thought it was easy finding good night work, maybe she could take over the financial side of their partnership for a decade or two – so she could pursue her "art", whatever it was this week. He was caring and nurturing and all he asked in return was a little peace before bed every morning. Was that so much?

Apparently. He sighed again, tried again. "Darling, listen to me. We have a beautiful home. We have a wonderful relationship. That's pretty amazing all by itself, you know. How many people could stand to be together even half as long as we have, much less enjoy it the way we do?"

Zara gave him what Jared thought of as "the look". "It sounds so romantic when you put it that way."

"You know what I mean. I'm trying to tell you how lucky we are, how much we already have. A hot tub in the bedroom, the beach just outside our door..." She continued to look unconvinced, and Jared steered away from the material and started in on the intangibles. "We have our health and each other, you're doing so well with your painting –"

"It's sculpting, damn it!" Reflexively, Jared ducked again, but she didn't throw anything else. Yet. "How can you say you care about me when you won't even pay attention to the most important thing in my life?"

Oh, Lord. "I do care about you, honey." He stood up and risked taking Zara in his arms. She looked pouty – and gorgeous, maybe even more than usual with her lips like that, and he thought she probably knew it – but she didn't shrug him off, and he kissed her. She half responded, and Jared felt hopeful and did it again, harder. Maybe they could do a little belated anniversary celebrating, and she'd forget this crazy notion. "How can you think I don't care?" he murmured close to her ear.

"Then show me."

"I intend to."

Zara leaned back in his arms and arched her neck, reminiscent of their first date. "Let me have this, then," she whispered, brushing against him with body and hands. "Let me have a baby. I want one so much."

Jared groaned and pulled away. "Why not?" Zara asked winningly, putting her arms around him and pressing close enough to break certain laws of physics. "It would be so sweet. Our own little family –"

"I like our family the way it is now," Jared said. "Just the two of us."

"But don't you ever get lonely?" Zara asked. "Don't you ever wish we could take someone with us when we move?"

Yes, of course he got lonely. Or had. That was why he'd chosen her for a companion. No matter how annoying Zara could be at times, Jared had never regretted his choice.

He looked at her with mingled exasperation and affection. True, it had been her beauty that attracted him at first, but her staying power as far as he was concerned was her constant sense of the new. She was never bored and never boring, and had come into Jared's life at a time when he was beginning to despair that eternity wasn't worth it. As his wife, she gave him a good jolt whenever he felt himself starting to slide back into complacency or ennui. Or even when he didn't. A little preventive medicine.

"You're all I need," he said now, and Zara scowled as if he'd insulted her.

"I want more," she snapped. "I want a family."

During the next few weeks, the atmosphere in their home had all the charm and warmth of a demilitarized zone. Jared worked longer hours than he had to, and Zara barricaded herself in her studio, often staying in it overday. They hunted separately, and were polite – just – when they had to speak to each other at all.

Predictably, Jared caved in first. After his initial miff was over – so she wanted to play it that way, did she? fine. let her enjoy herself, by herself – he found himself missing her terribly, and worrying when she showed no signs of thawing. Sure, she'd get over this eventually, but how long would it take?

And what if she *didn't* get over it? What if this meant so much to her that she was willing to leave him over it?

Jared felt a shiver of real fear. She could, he knew. As much as he liked to think at times that Zara wouldn't last two nights, never mind days, by herself – not the way she liked her comforts – he knew deep in his heart that she could do without him far better than he could without her. She had a streak of wildness that would get her through anything, and a sense of adventure that would make lean times look like fun. And with her passion and beauty, she wouldn't be alone long if she didn't want to be.

Whereas he – how could Jared ever find anyone else like her? He wouldn't want to even if he could. Zara was all he'd ever wanted.

So, all right. If the price of keeping her in his life was letting someone else in as well, so be it.

Besides, maybe he wouldn't have to. Maybe she just wanted him to agree to it, to *any*thing; to say that he'd do whatever she wanted him to. She'd done that before. Remember the tigers?

Jared looked for her on his very next night off and found her in her studio. The door was shut, but not locked, and he opened it and wasn't surprised to find he couldn't enter. "Zara?" he said timidly.

"Go away," she said, not looking around. He was heartened to see that, though she stood before clay and wax and marble, there were no signs that she'd been working recently. Her hands were motionless before her, clenched into fists.

"Zara, I love you," Jared said. "If you want"– it was an effort, but he made it – "a baby, that's fine with me."

She turned to him, her face lit up like a birthday candle. "You darling! Really?"

"Really." Jared was feeling qualms now along with his relief, and hoped they didn't show. From the beaming smile on Zara's face, he felt it safe to assume they didn't.

"Oh, come in!" Zara opened her arms, and Jared moved to and into them, swallowing his misgivings as best he could as Zara fluttered kisses over his face.

"You mean it?" she asked.

"Absolutely." Oh, boy. She sounded serious. Well, he'd called her bluff and she'd ended up calling his. "You're going to have to handle it, though," he warned. "The whole thing. I don't know anything about –"

"Oh, I will! I promise! I'll love it!"

"So go ahead and call a lawyer or an adoption agency or whatever," he went on resignedly. "I wonder if we can do this over the Net?"

Zara's face clouded up and she gave him a wounded look. "What do you mean?"

Jared stared back. "What do *you* mean? You said you wanted –"

"But not like that," she said. "I want it to be *ours.*"

He gaped at her. "What?" he managed after a few gulping moments.

"Ours. Yours and mine. Of our blood – well, our kin. You know what I mean." She pressed her hand against her flat belly in an age-old gesture. "Our baby."

"But – how?"

Zara smiled at him. "You know how."

"No, I mean – Zara, come on. Are you joking? Is this whole thing –"

"Of course I'm not joking. I'd never joke about something this serious."

Jared wondered. "But then how can we – Zara, look," he said awkwardly, a trace of old prudishness asserting itself. "If it were possible, if we could – just by – well, we'd have a dozen children by now. A hundred."

"Wouldn't we, though."

He looked down at her shining face and saw only earnest desire. "Then how?"

"I don't know. There must be a way."

"There can't be! Honey, we're not alive anymore, remember? We can't even be alive ourselves, much less make life."

Zara rolled her eyes. "Seriously," Jared said. "How could it work? What would the baby of two vampires even be like?"

"Like us, of course. Beautiful and –"

"And immortal?"

"Of course." Dismissively. She was probably spending more time thinking about whose eyes it would have.

"But then how would it develop? How would it grow up? I mean, *we* don't age. So why would our baby?"

"That's different."

"How? Why?"

"It's a baby. That's a special case." She was talking about the baby as if it already existed. Also as if she'd made a long and extensive study of vampire reproduction habits. Which was maybe what she'd been doing while they were avoiding one another, but Jared didn't think so. It had sounded more like heavy-duty sulking to him.

"If it was conceived and born and growing," he said doggedly, citing his own non-existent study, "it would have to be human. The way we were when we were alive. It would *have* to be alive. That's kind of the point. You know, bringing another life into the world?" And another mouth to feed, which was something else to think about. What on earth would it eat? Could Zara nurse it?

Now there was a distracting thought, just when he needed his wits about him.

"Well, maybe it would be human in that sense," Zara admitted grudgingly. "Just until it grew up."

"And then what? Then it bites its senior prom date and we know it's one of us? I don't think so."

She glared at him. "Honey, come on," Jared said. "I agreed to this. So let's do it. We'll do what other people do who can't have children of their own. We'll adopt a beautiful baby, any age you want, any sex. We can get a little girl you can sew cute outfits for, or –"

"If I wanted that, I could buy a Barbie doll," Zara said angrily. "I don't want to adopt."

"Why not? What's wrong with it?" Jared could hardly believe he was defending something he didn't even particularly want, but at least what he was talking about was on the same planet of possibility as they were living in. "We can pick what we want that way. We can even get one that's already housebroken."

"Oh!" She stepped away from him and her hands

clenched furiously at each other, as if restraining themselves from slapping him. "You're talking about our baby as if it were a pet dog!"

"I'm just trying to be practical. If we're going to have a baby around, that's something we'd better learn to do, don't you think?"

"That's exactly it. We're *having* a baby. We're not taking someone else's, we're not waiting in line for a million years and having a bunch of social workers look at our house and our records and –"

"I bet it doesn't have to be like that," Jared interrupted. "I don't want to sound crude or anything, but a little money cuts through a lot of red tape."

"This isn't a shopping trip!" Zara almost shouted. "And even if you're right, there'd still be so much explaining to do. To the baby. Why he's different from us. That he can't tell anybody else about his family. Can you imagine how he'll react the first time he goes to a friend's house to play and sees that not everybody sleeps in coffins?" She snorted. "Try keeping *that* a secret on show-and-tell day. We'd be moving every *week*."

"But –"

"And what about all the nagging we'll get about when he gets to convert?" she bulldozed on obliviously. "'Why do I have to wait? I'm old enough now.' The way most teenagers bug their parents about borrowing the car keys, only a million times worse."

He saw her point, sort of. "Or, worse yet," she went on, "what if he has some kind of Van Helsing complex?"

"Oh, come on."

"I'm serious! All teenagers rebel against their parents. They have to. I've been reading about it. So our baby grows up a little and decides to go all moral on us, and the next thing we know there's crosses all over the house, garlic in the kitchen, every time we have an argument he starts talking about stakes..."

"Okay, okay," Jared said. "I get the point. But you know, the stuff you were talking about before, about not telling people and realizing how different we are from everyone else and all – we'd go through that kind of thing with our child no matter what." Jared felt a momentary surge of hope. "If you're not up to it, maybe we'd better just –"

"It wouldn't be that way with *our* child, though," Zara insisted. "We could raise him as one of us, even if he was physically human for a while. And we wouldn't have *two* major things to explain to him, about being different *and* about being adopted. We wouldn't have to worry about his going off on a quest to find out who his people *really* were. He'd already know."

Jared rubbed the bridge of his nose tiredly. "All right," he said. "So we don't adopt a human baby. But you know, I'll bet there's a young vampire out there somewhere who really needs a good home."

"Oh, please," Zara snorted. "Young as in fifty and looks twenty? Or twenty and looks five? I don't want a permanent baby, and I don't want some leeching moocher. I *want* a child."

Leeching moocher? Jared was too worn out by the whole discussion to even ask. Zara was standing before him, arms akimbo, clearly braced for his next question, and he evaded her for a moment by pulling up one of the studio's rickety stools and settling gratefully on it.

"All right," he said again. "So we don't adopt. But I'm telling you, I don't think we're equipped to make babies anymore. I think that's one of the things we gave up. You know we've never used birth control, and I've never heard of a vampire who got pregnant."

"You've never heard of a vampire who's been married for as long as we have, either," Zara pointed out.

Jared sighed and shut his eyes. He tried to cheer himself

up by thinking that Zara now wanted something impossible, but that only meant that instead of having to put up with a baby, he'd have to watch Zara go into hot pursuit of a solution. And she'd be at it forever, unless she got bored. And Zara never got bored.

◆

The next few weeks were a litter of books and thermometers and varying positions at varying times, and those last bits might have been fun except for Zara's businesslike attitude. She wasn't in the mood for anything but the basic act, and snapped at Jared every time he forgot and began to enjoy himself.

At last one night she pushed away from him and sighed. "This isn't any use," she said. "These are all standards and methods for human parents. Who knows how they apply to us, or if."

Jared thought that might be an end to it, and prepared himself to go into heavy-cheering-up mode. But Zara didn't require that, at least not yet. Instead, she switched to a different set of books. Biology and metaphysics and supernatural fiction. And she started hogging the computer. Jared never got to play his favorite games anymore, because Zara was always online: following leads, exchanging letters with God knew who, searching and still not finding. She had so little time and inclination for lovemaking that Jared found himself missing even the chart-and-eggtimer nights. When he offered to help with her work however he could, she just glared at him.

This too passed, though it took longer. One night that Jared had off from work, Zara came out and joined Jared glumly on the couch, where he'd just sat down to watch television. It was some old movie.

"Hi," he said cautiously. He wanted to ask if she'd had any

luck, but he didn't dare.

"It's no use," Zara said, answering his unspoken question. She sagged against him and he gladly put his arm around her, spirits rising guiltily. Maybe now their lives could go back to normal, such as it was.

"Everyone I've tried talking to thinks I must be joking or crazy," Zara added. "And the ones who don't, don't know any more about this than I do."

Jared didn't risk saying anything. He only stroked her hair.

"If we could just figure it out!" she burst out after a moment. "It doesn't make any sense!"

"What doesn't, honey?"

"Us. How we work. Or don't work. I mean, we're perfect, right? That's why we're immortal."

Jared didn't argue. "Perfect in the sense that either everything works perfectly," Zara went on, "or it keeps regenerating perfectly, and that's why we don't age or die. So why shouldn't *that* part of us be functioning? I mean, if we couldn't have sex at all I could understand it –"

"God forbid," Jared said. Zara didn't smile.

"But to have that part of us be just fine in some respects and missing parts or whatever in others..." She trailed off for a moment. "I just don't get it," she finished sullenly, shrugging Jared's arm off and flopping back against the couch as she stared at the television with unseeing eyes.

"Honey," Jared ventured, "I don't know if what you're saying is quite right. I don't think it's exactly that we work perfectly. I think it's more like we *stopped* working. I mean, we died, so we can't die *again,* but for some reason we're still able to move and talk and think and all that. Like the guy in the old joke who's been dead for twenty years but is too dumb to lie down. Call it the spark of death or something."

Jared wasn't really that interested in the answer to the question of his own continuing existence, truth be told. He never had been, even when he'd first converted. He wasn't the analytic type. He was only grateful to be what he was. But Zara was staring at him wide-eyed, as if his every word was fascinating.

"That's it," she breathed. "Jared, that's it!"

"What is?"

"The spark. Oh, Jared, look!"

She was pointing at the television. Puzzled, he glanced over at it, but all he saw was the old black-and-white flick that had been on the first channel he'd switched on, and that he'd been too lazy to do anything but mindlessly watch.

"What about it?" he asked.

"That's *Frankenstein,* Jared! Don't you see?"

He thought he might be beginning to, and he didn't like it. "Now, wait a minute, Zara."

She didn't even hear him. "Oh, Jared, that must have been what gave you the whole idea – the spark! The spark of life!"

"Zara, I wasn't even watching the damned thing!"

"And you saw it and thought of it on just the night that I was ready to give up the whole idea! That's got to be more than just a coincidence – it's a sign!"

She looked at him, eyes shining, face determined.

"You were right," she said. "You were right all along. We *are* dead. We can't make life – not as we are. We'd need to be alive for that. At least for a moment. Just the right moment. We'd need a spark of *life.*"

She looked back at the television. Jared's eyes followed hers and, yes, there was the good doctor, about to throw all the switches and make everything happen. Jared couldn't remember a scene like that in the original story, but then he hadn't read the book since it had first come out. The movie's was definitely more of a twentieth-century idea anyway – channeling electricity in a mighty burst through a patiently waiting body.

"Zara, listen," Jared said uneasily.

She didn't. She was too caught up in her own inspiration. "I wonder if it really has to be lightning," she mused half to herself.

As a matter of fact, it did.

...Emily had tried several times to ask him the question...Who was Jane Dalotz?...but every time she broached the subject, a bitter cold wind seemed to pass through the house, and the chill of it left Emily speechless; her lips frozen together in a petrified silence.

Who Was Jane Dalotz?

Sukie de la Croix

Emily had always been puzzled by the photograph of Jane Dalotz. Was the gray-eyed young girl, posing coquettishly before the camera, beautiful or not? Emily had to know; at 10 years old the pursuit of beauty and the flight from ugliness were the two most important things in the world. But with Jane Dalotz, it was impossible to judge her comeliness, as the girl's lips had been neatly cut away from the photograph.

◆

Alone in the attic, Emily drummed her fingertips on the wall, then pressed her palms flat against the plaster and pushed as hard as she could. She was searching for the door leading into the secret room, or to a magical world, or to the place where all of her questions would be answered. All attics had at least one secret room.

Her favorite storybook – which she had found in Jane

Dalotz's trunk – was called *The Doctor And The Secret Room.* In the story, every morning after breakfast, the white-haired Dr. Caxton climbed the rickety stairs into his attic, pulled a hidden lever and then disappeared into a secret room, where he prepared potent medicines from mysterious powders and frothing liquids.

In the two years since Emily had first discovered the attic, she had probed and groped its dark recesses searching for the hidden door: she had tapped the walls for hollow sounds, concocted potions from dandelions and burdock leaves, and recited incantations...*Ab-ra-ca-da-bra...rump tee tump tee, rump tee tump tee, open the hidden door for E...mily...* but she had yet to locate the trigger that would gain her entry into the secret room.

Emily brushed the cobwebs away from the dormer window and peered out through the diamonds of tinted glass. She watched her mother skip girlishly down the path through the herb garden, wearing a simple yellow cotton dress and a wide-brimmed straw hat, adorned with moon daisies and bright red poppies. Even three floors up, with the windows closed. Emily could still hear her mother's sweet voice, singing... *Drink to me only with thine eyes.*

Suddenly Emily gasped and cupped her hands to her mouth, as her mother tripped and fell face down into the oregano. For a moment she lay there motionless, before rolling over onto her back, giggling and thrashing her arms and legs in the air like an upturned beetle. *Drink to me only with thine eyes. And I will pledge with mine. The thirst that from the soul doth rise, doth ask a drink divine. But might I of Jove's nectar sup, I would not change for thine...*she finished the song, then hauled herself up onto her feet and brushed down her clothes.

Emily breathed an exaggerated sign of relief, then turned her attention to the wooden trunk, which she dragged across the floor and into the swathe of sunlight cutting through the window. Throwing open the lid, she snatched up the photograph of Jane Dalotz and held it to her breast; Emily's heart pounded, her pulse raced, as she and the desecrated image of the young girl clung to each other like castaways on a raft; two lovers adrift in uncharted seas.

After a minute or so, Emily detached herself from the photograph and propped it up against the wall. Then, with a reverence reserved only for the possessions of the dead, she began unpacking the rest of the trunk, laying each item out on the floor: the purple velvet dress with the lace collar, the string of jet beads, the much-loved storybook *The Doctor And The Secret Room,* and the letter tied up in a blue ribbon.

With the shrine spread out before her, Emily again picked up the photograph, this time holding it at arms length, thereby resisting the strange power it held over her. Emily studied Jane's face; the girl was turning away from the camera, head slightly bowed, though her seductive gray eyes looked directly into the lens, flirting with it, or perhaps with the man standing behind it. Or perhaps...Emily's heart pounded again...or perhaps Jane's sensual gaze was for her. Emily turned the photograph over and read the label on the back: Jane Dalotz, photographed by Charles Dodgson.

Emily had once asked her mother about Jane Dalotz. It was the day that she had first discovered the attic; she remembered it was a bitter cold February night, a storm had blown in from the North, and the house and garden were covered with a blanket of snow. Emily had been sitting near the fire, threading her embroidery hoop, when she had related to her mother the events of the day; how she had found the attic, the trunk and the photograph of Jane, and how Jane's lips had been cut away from the picture. But when Emily asked the question...'Who Was Jane Dalotz?'...her mother had only sighed, gazed up at the cracks in the ceiling, and replied, 'Oh Emily, that's a very sad story. Ask your father about it when he returns from his travels. He knows more about it than I do.'

But Emily's father hardly ever returned from his travels. He was a diplomat. Emily wasn't quite sure what a diplomat was, only that it meant her father was abroad for 10 months of the year. She would receive letters from him, postmarked Bombay, or Cairo, or Katmandu. Then once a year, at the beginning of December, Emily and her mother would shiver on the platform of the local railway station, waiting for his train to arrive. The procedure would be reversed at the end of January, when they shivered and waved him off on his travels again.

The day after Emily's mother had avoided answering the question about Jane Dalotz, Emily decided to ask the cook; the rosy-cheeked old woman – whose breasts swelled to twice their normal size during her regular bouts of laughter – had been working at the house since long before Emily and her parents had moved in. She was as much a part of its structure as the foundations, the walls, the roof itself, and as settled in as the clusters of swallows' nests that clung to the eaves, long after the fledglings had upped and flown south for the winter.

The cook was busy chopping onions for soup, when Emily had climbed up onto a stool next to her and asked her the question outright...'Who was Jane Dalotz?'

'Ah! Now there's a story,' cook had said, laying her knife aside. 'That was before you moved here. Mrs. Dalotz was a wonderful woman, very grand, married to an army officer. Jane was their only child. She was as happy and as healthy as a child could be, until one day, while Jane was playing in the garden, she was bitten on the lip by a snake. the doctor was called in, but he couldn't do anything for her. She just withered away to nothing, the poor little lamb. Her mother sat with her during those long painful days that followed, and Mr. Dodgson, a friend of the family who was visiting at the time, sat with her through the long sleepness nights. But Jane's life just seemed to drain away from her, and some people say..."

Emily was never to learn what 'some people say', as the

cook's story was cut short by Emily's mother, coming in from the garden, carrying a basket of newly harvested vegetables.

'Beatrice!' Emily's mother had said, 'Now don't go filling the girl's head with rumors and nonsense. Take no notice of her Emily..."

And that was the end of it.

When Emily's father did return home from his travels that following winter, Emily had tried several times to ask him the question...Who was Jane Dalotz?...but every time she broached the subject, a bitter cold wind seemed to pass through the house, and the chill of it left Emily speechless; her lips frozen together in a petrified silence. The name of Jane Dalotz was never spoken of in the house again.

Following closely the rules of the ritual, Emily stretched out her hands over the shrine laid out before her on the attic floor. Her fingers twitched nervously, as she picked up the letter, untied the blue ribbon, then slid the single sheet of paper out of the envelope. The letter was addressed to Jane Dalotz, and was signed by her father, Captain Andrew Dalotz.

> *My dearest Jane,*
>
> *My heart is saddened by the news that reaches me. I pray for you every night, that you will recover from this terrible thing that has happened to you. Your mother and my dear friend, Charles Dodgson, have both written to me of your nightmares and visitations from demons. Your mother tells me that you writhe in agony, while she and the doctor stand by, helplessly watching over you...*

As always, when Emily read the letter, she wept over the tragic death of the young girl; the girl she had never met, and would never meet. She also wept for herself, cursing the wicked twist of fate that had trapped her here in this dark place, alone with her secret morbid desires.

When the daily ritual was completed, Emily was suddenly struck by an idea. Leaping to her feet, she kicked off her shoes and tore at her clothes, until she stood naked before the shrine. Then she picked up Jane's plum-colored dress, slipped it over her head, and smoothed it down around her body. It fitted perfectly. Emily closed her eyes, lifted her arms to the skies and danced a trance-like ballerina dance, until she finally collapsed to the floor, breathless and dizzy from the pirouettes.

When the room stopped spinning, Emily opened the storybook, *The Doctor And The Secret Room,* and began reading it out loud, *Once upon a time, there was a good and kind doctor...*At the point where Dr. Caxton goes up into his attic and opens the door to his secret room, Emily fell silent; out of the corner of her eye, she glanced a movement, and she turned to see a door opening in the wall.

With slow, even steps she walked through the open doorway and into the room beyond. She expected to see Dr. Caxton's strange medicines for colds, and flu, and gout, but what she found there was very different. The room was lit by a row of black candles, their flickering flames casting ungodly shadows over the walls; walls exhibiting a single row of framed photographs. On a table at the far end of the room, someone had placed a bowl of cherries, and next to it a sign that read EAT ME.

Like a General inspecting his troops, Emily paraded past the gallery of captured images on the wall, stopping to examine each of them in turn. The photographs were all of young girls, each of them wearing Jane's velvet dress, and, most disturbing of all, each of them with their lips neatly cut away from their faces. Beneath the pictures hung brass plaques, reading: Alice Liddell – photographed by Charles Dodgson, Margaret Hatch, Charlotte Webster, Amy Hughes, Florence Terry – all of them photographed in the studio of the ubiquitous Charles Dodgson.

After studying the photographs, Emily focused her attention on the bowl of cherries and the intriguing sign: EAT

ME. She picked the largest cherry from the bowl, examined it for bruises, and when satisfied that it was clean, she popped it into her mouth. For a while she rolled it around aimlessly on her tongue, then when she finally bit into its smooth, shiny skin, something unexpected happened; instead of the familiar tang of cherry, her mouth filled with the foul, coppery taste of blood. Emily gagged and spat out the fruit. It was then that she heard the voice...'Eat me. Eat me.'

About three feet in front of Emily's face, a pair of moist lips hovered in the air, parting slightly to repeat the words over and over again. Then more lips appeared, until the walls of the room bowed outwards, bursting at the seams with a chorus of voices...'Eat me. Eat me.'

Emily closed her eyes and covered her ears, but unable to escape the rising crescendo of voices, she ran from the room, stumbling down the stairs, through the kitchen and out into the garden. Her heart pounded as she continued to run: past her mother, who was asleep on a bench, cradling an empty bottle of whisky, down the path dissecting the vegetable garden, through a gap in the fence, and into the wild woods beyond; all the time hearing the voices growing fainter, the further she distanced herself from the house...'Eat me. Eat me.'

On and on she ran, through thickets of brambles, skidding on silky patches of ferns, and leaping over shallow streams, until the voices were left far behind. Taking refuge under the branches of a hazel tree, she listened hard, but all she could hear now was the singing of birds and the occasional rustle of a small animal scampering through the undergrowth. She sat down and leaned back against the tree, and she stretched out her arms, her hand touched something cold. And there it was, lying in the grass next to her, the photograph of Jane Dalotz; the only love she had ever known.

Emily picked up the picture, her eyes brimming with tears; whatever demons she had unleashed back there in the attic, the purpose of it all was now clear to her; for Jane's lips had been restored to the photograph. Lips that were so seductive, that even the snake could not resist taking that one fatal poisonous bite. Never again would Emily have to ask the question...'Who Was Jane Dalotz?'...because she now held the answer in her hand. Quite simply, Jane Dalotz was the most beautiful person who ever lived.

As the warm tears trickled down Emily's face, she sensed that familiar magnetic pull from the photograph, and she leaned forward to kiss the lips of her lover; and as her lips grazed the cold glass, she felt a tongue pressing into her mouth, and her own tongue responding to the warm embrace.

And then she felt the bite; a sharp pain in her lower lip. She tried to pull away, but the picture melted into the contours of her face, then wrapped itself around her head and clamped tightly shut. She struggled for breath, but instead of the sweet woodland air, her mouth filled with the bitter taste of sour cherries. Her fingers tore at the frame, as she tried to release herself from its iron grip. But it was no use; Emily's young body shuddered one last time, and then drifted away, to the magical world, to the place where all of her questions would be answered.

◆

Two weeks after the funeral, an old man stood at the foot of Emily's grave. In his hand he held a copy of *The Doctor And The Secret Room,* which he began to read out loud. "Once upon a time, there was a good and kind doctor"...When he had finished reading, he closed the book and listened. Somewhere in the distance, Emily's mother was singing. *Drink to me only, with thine eyes. And I will pledge with mine. The thirst that from the soul doth rise, doth ask a drink divine. But might I of Jove's nectar sup. I would not change for thine...*

The old man waited until the song had ended, then he pulled a brown paper bag from his pocket, took out a bright red cherry and popped it into his mouth. As he savored the taste of Emily's warm blood, Charles Dodgson reverted to his familiar shape and form, then slithered away down the path and disappeared into the brushes.

Week after week Bobbie sat up on that chair buck naked, and at the end of every class all she ever saw were rows of canvases splattered and splashed with muddied paint, all of them seeming to ignore the fact there had been a completely nude model freezing her ass off for five bucks a night right in front of their easels. But then, Bobbie didn't know much about painting, just how to sit very still and very naked...

Bongo Bobbie's Bel Air

Kyle Marffin

Bobbie just closed her eyes and thought about Dad's Bel Air.

It was easier like that. As good a way as any to handle sitting up on this rickety platform, cramping on a hard backed chair with just this ratty gray sheet draped over it, a 500 watt spot glaring right overhead and frighteningly close to her hair.

It was awkward. A whole room full of people huddled behind their easels, furiously darting their heads around their canvases every few seconds to stare at her – scrutinizing every inch of her in a disquieting way that was all the more embarrassing because it was so dismissive – only to dive back behind their paintings to dab on a few more brushstrokes.

Awkward enough, not that Bobbie was what you'd call shy. Though sitting up here in front of everyone, completely naked, did its share to enhance the humiliation. But there were those that said Bongo Bobbie had elevated humiliation to an art form the very day she stepped off the Greyhound from Eau Claire.

So Bobbie pretended she *wasn't* sitting here.

Instead she just went on picturing herself in Dad's Bel Air, that brand new shiny-sleek two-tone teal and white '59. She pictured herself sprawled across the huge backseat with an Archie comic on her lap and the Wisconsin breezes ruffling her hair as they headed down US 51 to the Dells or up north for a week of fishing and swimming whenever Dad snatched a few days off from the mill and Mom could get someone to take her place at the diner. Bobbie pictured the Wisconsin River whizzing by, the pines blurring into blue-green velvet along the highway when Dad gave that two-tone rocket a kick and greased it up to seventy, smiling quietly to himself because even though they couldn't spring for the 409, that Bel Air's stovebolt six ate up asphalt like a roadcrew hopped up on bennies. Bobbie pictured all that, and smiled to herself, just like Dad always did.

She just kept her eyes closed, even though clenching them shut kind of hurt tonight, seeing as how she'd gotten popped good last night, and she'd used up half a jar of Max Factor Pale Fawn Mist foundation to try to cover the purply-blue shiner *that* left her with.

Bobbie sniffed away an itch on her nose, determined not to move. The artists hated when she moved, practically hissed sometimes, as if a perfectly still model mattered one damn bit for what most of them were painting. She twitched and sniffed, noticing how that 500 watt spot was brewing up a telltale odor of just-starting-to-toast hair. Finally she couldn't help herself. Quick as she could, Bobbie scratched one nostril and brushed her hair back over her face. But the long bangs and cascade of shoulder length brown barely covered last night's shiner.

Cecil had clobbered her but good this time.

Bobbie closed her eyes and tried to ignore the furious scrubbing sound all those Grumbacher bristles made on the canvases. She tried to ignore the chit-chat murmuring from behind the stretched canvases about the latest 'isms from NYC and who'd sold out to take an illustrator job at an agency and where the best spots in Chicago were for stretching a dime cup of coffee into an hour of refills and polemics. She tried to ignore Sackville, the huge and age-unknown modern painting instructor imperiously strolling between the easels in her multi-colored muumuu and prodding one Rothko-wannabe after another to *'free themselves'* and to *'see past the false reality of plastic third dimensions to the core of the painting'.*

Sacks had a lot of good supposed-Sorbonne lines like that, and just now it sounded to Bobbie like she was ladling a bunch more onto a fresh victim who'd been foolish enough to argue back. To Bobbie's ears he sounded like a sincere enough fellow with a continental accent – no, for real on *this* cat – till Sacks finally stomped away from his easel muttering something about his rigid academism being 'positively fascist'.

Whatever that meant.

So Bobbie tried to ignore all that, along with the tangy turpentine odors and the almost-wholesome linseed oil scent. She just closed that good eye and the sharply smarting one too and did her best to dream herself somewhere else, back into that showroom-smell new Bel Air hitting the highway, back to good times and fun times and on-the-road adventures. Back to better times before the cancer got Dad and Dad's death got Mom, back before Eau Claire stopped feeling like home anymore.

"All right, that's time folks," Sackville called.

Bobbie blinked her brown eyes open, and the Bel Air and the highway and Dad all vanished. The third floor walkup Monday evening painting class stared back at her in all its bohemian best: goatee'd boys and steam-iron-straight haired girls, resplendent in their carefully paint-spattered chino's, their berets and black turtlenecks. But they only stared at Bobbie for a second. That's how long it took her to wrap the gray sheet around herself, click off the spotlight and scoot behind the portable screen.

"Let's clean up quick tonight," Sacks hollered. "The Old Town Triangle Actors Cooperative will be up in five."

Behind the screen, Bobbie immediately treated herself to a long overdue Viceroy. She stretched out cramps and climbed back into her clothes, trying to get the scent of that Bel Air's interior back into her head, trying to bring back Mom and Dad's happy chatter. But the smoke tickled her nose and all she could hear were paint boxes snapping shut, canvases stacking along the walls, feet shuffling out of the studio. She checked her Bulova, bit her lip when she saw it was almost eight, and wiggled the black tights over her hips all crooked, the waistband snapping into place with an audible *pop.* With a second hand shop London Fog tossed over her shoulder, Bobbie was still yanking on her wrinkled plaid skirt's side zipper as she stepped out from behind the screen.

"God, will you just look at this crap, Bongo?" Sackville whined as she stacked a pile of still-wet paintings behind the door. "What would Pablo say if he could see me now?"

One shoe on and the other still in hand, Bobbie hopped over Sackville's way. The word around the Old Town art world was that Sackville actually *knew* Picasso in her younger days, though Bobbie always figured that was just in the biblical sense, and most likely at twenty pesos a pop or whatever the going rate for a cheap fuck in Franco's Spain had been. "C'mon, Sacks. He'd say 'take the money and run'." Which is precisely what Bobbie wanted to do. A fast exit from 'Job No. 1' so she could be at 'Job No. 2' by 8:00 had been the plan, seeing how beatnik coffeehouse waitresses were a dime a dozen up and down Wells Street.

"Uhm, Sacks?"

Sackville stared at a canvas, shaking her head. "Hmmm?"

"Sacks, I really have to go." Bobbie eased her other foot into an imitation black Capezio flat.

"Uh-huh. Bongo, will you look at this? What's the world

coming to? Dylan's gone electric, WDPR won't even play Coltrane anymore. And now my own damn students think they're going to go Lichtenstein on me? In *my* class?" She spun a canvas around to reveal a 20" x 24" nude Bobbie, painted in DC comics Mars Black contour lines and dabbed dots of bright process colors, a cartoon balloon above her head: *blank.* Perhaps the artist was making "a statement", but Bobbie didn't catch it.

She didn't catch a lot of things.

"Yeah, uhm...pretty silly Sacks. Look, could we just settle up and –"

"Bongo, the world's been going to hell in a handbasket since JFK lost his head in Dallas."

Bobbie checked her watch again. It was a block down North Avenue and two more down Wells to *The Unseemly Bean* and she was damned sure going to be late now.

"And *this* – just look at this, Bongo." Sackville held up another painting, the canvas' wooden stretchers and blank white back facing Bobbie. "Damn Limeys."

"Sacks, I –"

"This one's from that British guy. Did you hear me light into him? No? Well, he was a real cockney cock sucker, that one. British invasion, my ass. Goddamn pinup painter, that's what he was." She spun the canvas around. "Look."

Week after week Bobbie sat up on that chair buck naked, and at the end of every class all she ever saw were rows of canvases splattered and splashed with muddied paint, all of them seeming to ignore the fact there had been a completely nude model freezing her ass off for five bucks a night right in front of their easels. But then, Bobbie didn't know much about painting, just how to sit very still and very naked, a skill that she'd honed to another art all her own with her really-just-when-the-rent-was-overdue 'Job No. 3'. The only thing she really liked about modern art was the hopeful feeling it sometimes gave her that things couldn't really be as bad as they were painted.

Bobbie's eye for detail may have developed a sudden squint, but to her the painting looked fine. No, it was better than 'fine'.

It was darn good. But as good as it was...

It was goddamned scary.

"Gee, Sacks, that painting, it's...it's –"

"I know, Bongo. Can you believe this representational crap? Good Lord, cheesecake in *my* class." Sackville carried the painting over to the others stacked by the door just as a fresh group of beats and 'niks started to wander into the studio and shove the squeaky wheeled easels aside. The 8:00 Actors Cooperative.

"Well, I...I kind of like it, Sacks." Bobbie couldn't help but stare at the painting. "I think."

"You do?" Sackville sidestepped a threesome with their heads buried in their Albee scenes and hustled the painting right back over to Bobbie. "Then it's yours. I insist."

"Sacks, I couldn't, I –"

Sackville shoved the painting into Bobbie's hands.

"Sacks, thanks. I think." Her fingers smudged wet paint along the edge of the stapled canvas. "This one's really pretty, not like all the other...well, you know what I mean. But what I realy need is to get paid. Like, with money."

"Sorry, Bongo, but hardly anyone paid up tonight." Sackville was already on her way out the door while another bucks 'n berets clique ambled in. "Keep the painting instead. Maybe you can sell it to a dirty book store."

"Sacks, I need my money." *I can't eat paintings,* she thought, and the well-placed shiner winced all by itself.

But Sackville was gone, a couple hundred pounds in a swirling muumuu vanishing like a fairy. A fairy up five bucks for the night, at any rate.

Bobbie wiped her paint smeared fingers clean on her skirt, briefly proud of the stain like it was some kind of membership badge. She adjusted her black beret on top of her head, slung her bag over her shoulder and carried the painting with her. And she stared at it all the way down the three flights of stairs and out onto North Avenue.

Outside, she had to set the painting down to button up her trenchcoat. It was one of those dreary November nights, thick with a damp Chicago cold that Bobbie never could manage to describe any way other than 'icky' and not at all like the crisp winter nights back in Eau Claire. At least it wasn't snowing. The breeze buffeted the canvas as she headed east towards Wells, but she held it out in front of her, still staring at the painting as she negotiated her way through shivering crowds ducking in and out of the coffeehouses and bookstores and storefront folk clubs. She stared at it all the way to The Unseemly Bean.

Unable to take her eyes off of it, actually.

Because whoever the Brit with the flair for paint had been, he'd whipped up a perfectly realistic and perfectly naked Bobbie with an obvious black eye peeking out from under her bangs.

A perfectly naked Bobbie sitting on the front fender of a perfectly two-tone teal and white '59 Bel Air, in fact.

◆

Bobbie stuck the painting on the shelf behind the bar, peeking at it all night.

That the Unseemly Bean had a bar was no surprise. Long before the Pollock-wannabe's and the Ginsburg-wannabe's and the Dylan-wannabe's and the Kerouac-wannabe's and the Brando-wannabe's and the don't-know-what-yet-but-it'll-be-something-vaguely-artistic-wannabe's had taken over Old Town, the dark little storefront sized spot on North Wells Street had been a cozy shot & beer tavern. Since, it had gone through a dozen different incarnations in as many months, but the liquor license hadn't been intact for most of them. And thus, *The Unseemly Bean.*

A folk duo wound down their set of Pete Seeger and Simon & Garfunkel knock-off's while a couple of poets furiously scribbled revisions on their tattered black and white Composition Notebooks, ready to take the stage.

And Bobbie?

Bobbie plunged into 'Job No. 2' and hustled trays of espressos and cappuccinos and just-plain-coffees to the tables, picking up snatches of weighty intellectual exchanges and pocketing the occasional dime and quarter tip along the way. She added the coins up in her head as she tucked them into her skirt pocket, hoping to make enough at 'Job No. 2' tonight to be able to skip 'Job No. 3'. It was cold out, and there was talk of snow now, and she didn't relish sloshing up and down Wells through wet mush till some gray flannel type worked up the courage to ask her 'how much' before he scooted back to the safety of the burbs.

Usually she didn't think about Dad's Bel Air when she worked the tables at the Unseemly Bean. Usually didn't think about Dad or Mom or Eau Claire. Usually she listened to the singers wail their thinly veiled protest songs and the poets raging against the oligarchy, whatever that was.

Usually.

But tonight she kept glancing over her shoulder at the painting, perched there on the bar between the espresso machine and the eight burner Bun-O-Matic, and she saw herself in the wet oil paint, lounging against the two-tone teal and white fender, saw herself there all naked and showing off that shiner like it wasn't a secret at all, saw all that and shivered each time she did, wondering how the hell the guy who painted it *knew* she had a shiner under all that makeup and *knew* about the Bel Air, and *knew...*

"C'mon, Bongo!"

"Yoh, Bongo!"

"Bongo-Bongo-Bongo," the coffeehouse crowd took up the chant as the folk duo slinked off the stage. The first poet waded through the crowded tables and the self-styled disaffected types brewing up a thick fog of cigarette smoke and even thicker layers of even more affected pipe smoke. The poet hopped up on the stool. He held his notebook in one hand and a pair of bongo drums in the other.

He waved the drum set at Bobbie.

"Bongo-Bongo-Bongo," the crowd continued, and Bobbie smiled in spite of herself.

It was a regular routine and Bobbie practically lived for it. Maybe she didn't know that she couldn't keep a beat for her life, and maybe she didn't know that the Unseemly Bean's crowd wanted her up there pounding the drums because they thought it was funny. And maybe she didn't write and couldn't strum a Silvertone and hadn't studied with Strasberg and wasn't even something uncreative but respectable like a social worker. And maybe she didn't know that so many of the girls she thought were her friends usually went double catty on her when she wasn't around just because it pissed them off royal that Bobbie was so damn cute, even if she didn't have a clue. And maybe Bobbie didn't even know that most of the guys managed to lose their well rehearsed intellectual veneers long enough to go all high-school-locker-room and nudge one another and joke about how they'd like to get their mitts on *her* bongos. Which they *could* if they only had an extra twenty...ten in a lean week...five if the rent was overdue.

Maybe she didn't know any of that.

So Bongo Bobbie set her tray down, bowed to the crowd and headed for the stage where she took the stool behind tonight's first poet. She hiked her plaid skirt up high and clutched the drums between her thighs as the "Bongo-Bongo-Bongo" chant finally died down.

By the time the third poet took the stage and launched into a twisted potpourri of part standup-part poetics, even

Bongo recognized she was having trouble finding the beat. It could have been the scraggly bearded poet's rhythmless pastiche of Lenny Bruce meets Greg Corso.

Could've been that.

But more likely it could have been the steely eyed glare from the mysterious guy sitting far in the back of the smoke filled shadows cloaking the Unseemly Bean.

The disarmingly handsome guy – black haired, mop-topped and so damn handsome he was almost pretty – who locked eyes with her and made her shiver right down to her toes inside the Capezios, made her freeze right in mid-beat and make the poet lose his place (as if anyone could tell). Because that dark eyed gaze sliced right through the smoky haze, right into *her* and made her *see* things.

Bobbie dropped the bongos and bolted off the little stage.

◆

"Yoh, Bongo! Wait up."

Bobbie tightened her grip on the painting and stepped up her pace. It had started to snow, just a sickly dribble of slushy gray flakes, but enough to slick the sidewalk along Wells.

"Bongo, come on!"

A hand slammed down on her shoulder and Bobbie almost dropped the canvas when she spun around. "Leave me alone, Cecil. I'm still recuperating from *last* night."

Cecil stuffed his hands in the pockets of his wool overcoat; just another of the many hangers-on the Unseemly Bean and Wells Street and the rest of Old Town attracted like a magnet: The just plain curious from the bungalow belt, the English Lit prof's from DePaul and Loyola, the occasional strays from the secretarial pool ogling the skinny cute guys with their sideburns and beards, the Ivy Leaguers and the ad men who slummed for cappuccinos and chianti's in the galleries and the jazz joints and coffeehouses, looking for some easy snatch before they took the last trains out of the city and back to their cozy *Evergreen Park's* and *Oak Forest's* and *Willow Springs* and all the other places where they bulldozed away the trees and then named the streets after them.

Cecil was a card-carrying member of the latter, mixing roguish Beatle Boots with his Brooks Brother suits, a dog-eared copy of *On The Road* always cracked open for show on the 7:57 or the 11:42 back to Shirley and the kids and the dog and wherever. "Yeah, last night, Bongo. Sorry about that. I never made good last night."

Bobbie flicked the bangs off her forehead and the streetlight caught the shiner now that the Pale Fawn Mist had pretty much worn off. "Meaning that love tap, or that you never paid me?"

"Both, I guess. I was kind of drunk."

"Well, I'm kind of tired, so beat it, okay?" Bobbie started off down Wells again, but he followed along.

"So what was with the am-scray routine back there?"

Bobbie didn't answer.

"Oh come on, I'll help you carry your art treasure home. What's the matter, Sackville stiff you again?"

"Buzz off, Cecil."

"Come on, Bongo. Won't take long. My train leaves in an hour."

"So what, you'd only need a minute anyway."

Cecil grabbed her harder this time and spun Bobbie around again. She yelped, one hand smudging the edge of the painting but good. "Now look what you did!"

"Bongo, we both know your rent's due Monday. So lets not fuck around and...well...go fuck around."

They crossed the street by the old Dr. Scholl's factory, vanishing into the shadows of an unlighted block of tenement rows.

And never noticing the shadow that wasn't a shadow following half a block behind.

Cecil was still panting from the four flight hike up to Bobbie's 'atelier'. Actually, it was a one bedroom flat. A cold water flat at that, and there weren't many left in Chicago, not even in the tired old blocks that clung to the fringes of Old Town. But Bobbie had managed to find one for herself.

"You know Cecil, you could let me get undressed first. Maybe once?"

"Mmmm...no time, Bongo," he murmured in something vaguely resembling passion as he shoved her back to the bedroom, shoved her down on the bed, shoved his tongue in her mouth and shoved his hand under her skirt. "My – mmmm – train..."

All in all it didn't take any longer than one of the Saturday morning cereal commercials Cecil worked on. Thirty seconds to a hard-on, thirty more of desultory humping and a final and prolonged thirty of grunts and spurts. Cecil rolled off and leaned back on the creaky old iron frame bed, hands folded behind his head and an unusually self satisfied smirk on his face.

Bobbie finished unraveling the black tights off her feet, glancing at her watch as she did. *Yep, ninety seconds.* She hoped it wouldn't take much longer than that to get him to leave. "What about your train?" She tossed the balled up tights more or less by the closet door and tugged her blouse out of her skirt.

"There's time." Cecil stared at the painting perched on the dresser. "So what's with the car?"

"I wouldn't know. Maybe the artist saw something you can't." Bobbie slid off the bed and carefully hung up her skirt and blouse in the closet. She picked up the tights and tossed them in the hamper, then stood there at the closet door in her slip, checking and rechecking her watch. "Cecil, your train?"

"Fuck the train." He leaned across the bed to the

nightstand and grabbed Bobbie's purse. "Oh, I get it," he said, lighting one of Bobbie's Viceroys and then glancing back at the painting. "The shiner, you mean? The artist could see it, so what?"

"Have a cigarette, why don't you?" Bobbie crossed her arms over her chest. "And no, I didn't mean the shiner."

"I didn't know anyone who bothered with that fat old broad's class could actually paint." Cecil still held Bobbie's purse. "But this guy's pretty good. I still don't get the car, though."

"Yeah, well you don't have to get it. Now is there anything else you want in there? Got a bulletin for you, but the way this works is *you* pay *me.* Rent money, remember?"

"Well, as it happens, precious, I'm a little short for cab fare to Union Station."

"So – walk. And you better get going or you'll miss your –"

"Actually, I'm a little short on train fare too." Cecil looked up and smiled.

"Why, you son of a –"

Bobbie dove at him. But Cecil flung the purse aside, dodged Bobbie and had her wrists held tight in a blink. His other hand balled into a fist. He swung it in an arc and right for her face.

It halted an inch from her unbruised eye.

"You want a matched pair, Bongo?" He still clenched the Viceroy in his lips, the hot orange glow at the tip hovering just a breath of smoke away from her cheek.

"That's better, Bongo. Now, you're a fucking waitress. Hey – get it? A *fucking* waitress?" Cecil let her hands go. "So where's all those tips you waitresses shake your ass for all night, huh?"

"'All those tips' rolled under the bed."

They had, so Cecil did too, at least until he'd scooped up a buck or two of dimes and quarters. He stuffed the change in his pocket as he zipped up, then headed for the parlor where he slipped back into his gray flannel suit jacket. "Look, I'll catch up next time, okay?" Cecil tossed his coat over his shoulder and pecked her on the cheek.

When the door slammed shut, Bobbie felt the tears boiling up behind her eyes, but she fought them back, the same way she did when she used to get a fish hook jabbed in her finger and didn't want Dad to see. She lit herself a Viceroy and stood by the big parlor window. Opening it a crack, she ignored the damp chill that immediately dribbled in, ignored the way it clung to her bare arms and wormed its way under her slip just like Cecil's hands. She ignored all that and just watched the blue smoke glide out of her lips and out the window till it vanished in the moonless darkness and the anemic snowflakes. She ignored it all, not even bothering to glance down through the rusted fire escape to the street below, not the least interested in Cecil appearing on the front stoop down there, buttoning his coat and turning his collar up.

Bobbie ignored all that, absentmindedly watched the cigarette smoke hovering outside the window and thought about sleek two-tone cars that beckoned with open doors and on-the-road adventures. She just thought about wide whitewalls chewing up the asphalt and clean, brisk breezes blowing in her hair and that teal and white Bel Air.

Not Dad's.

The Bel Air in that painting on her dresser.

She thought about that car and the guy who might have painted it and how he might have seen her – seen *her* – for real.

Shiner, shaky dreams and all.

She thought about all that till the Viceroy was smoked down to the cork papered filter. She flung that out the window and turned away and to bed, never watching the little cork tip flutter in the darkness to the street below, never watching how it fell right at the feet of the beautiful dark haired shadow lurking beside her building's front stairs. Never seeing that shadow bleed out of the darkness and onto the street, where a face turned up to peer through the fire escape grates at Bobbie's window.

Stared.

Sighed.

And then disappeared into the darkness.

◆

"Sorry, Bongo," Sackville said as she unlocked the door to the third floor studio. "He hasn't been back since Monday night. Speaking of which, where have *you* been the past two nights? I like a good still life as much as the next person, but something tells me this bunch isn't showing up just to use the easels." Sacks swirled into the studio and flicked on the overheads. "Anyway, good riddance, I say. I'm not doing that whole Royal Academy thing here, you know. It's 1964, for Chrissakes."

"Well, don't you know his name or anything, Sacks?"

Sackville shrugged and proceeded to arrange the easels around the studio. "What's the big deal, Bongo? Now get undressed, will you?"

But Bobbie still hovered in the studio doorway.

"Something up, Bongo?"

Bobbie shook her head, staring into the empty studio, trying to place that mysterious painter's easel and paint box from Monday night, trying to remember his face. "I don't think I'll work tonight, Sacks."

"Finally landed a millionaire, did you?"

"Sacks, you haven't actually paid me in a month."

"Yes...well, like I've been telling you, a lot of the students, they don't always –"

"It's okay, Sacks." Bobbie backed out of the doorway. "I mean, it's *not* okay, but...well, you know what I mean."

"Actually, I don't have a clue, Bongo. Say, are you really okay?"

"Sure." Bobbie forced a smile. "Like always." She cinched up the belt on her tattered trenchcoat. "Sacks, if he shows up tonight, maybe you could mention I was looking for him. Maybe mention that I'll be at the 'Bean?"

"What, that Brit?" Sackville shivered, her entire muumuu quivering like multi-colored jello. "That cat was a little on the creepy side, didn't you think?"

"I never really got a look at him, Sacks. Well, not here in the studio, only later...well, I *think* I saw..."

"Bongo, what's going on? Don't tell me you've got a thing for the Limey that painted that awful...Bobbie – a painter? You know, fucking artists won't make you one, kiddo. Anyway, I thought I always told you...you have to fuck *up.*"

But Bobbie didn't answer, unless her brief smirk counted. 'Fucking *up'* still eluded her. Just plain fucking up – *that* she'd mastered, all right. She adjusted her beret and headed down the stairs, leaving Sackville reluctantly surveying still life props.

The last few nights' flurries had finally brewed up into a real November snow earlier in the afternoon. Bobbie sidestepped drifts and dirty gray slush puddles all the way to The Unseemly Bean. It was only 6:00, but the usual crowd of jobless dilettantes nursed their coffees and listened to some long haired blond girl warble through Peter, Paul & Mary songs up on the stage.

Thursday night was Bobbie's only weeknight off at the 'Bean, so she took a table in a dark corner and let herself be waited on by another coffeehouse waitress twin in snug knee length plaid and the regulation black turtleneck, black tights, black flats and beret. Bobbie paid for her coffee and planted an extra dollar bill in the waitress' palm, then ripped open a fresh pack of Viceroys. Tonight's largess came compliments of her last stash of wadded singles hidden in the Chase & Sanborn can in the kitchen. That well-hidden stash was one way to keep the Cecils and the rest of them from treating her purse like it was the Community Chest. And if she carried the money with her, she'd only blow it on another doomed-to-remain-unused sketchpad or some seemingly irresistible used bookstore poetry paperback or a new gotta-have folk LP – none of which ever managed to pay the elusive entrance fees to Old Town's aesthete cliques anyway.

Lulled by a steady stream of earnest debates wafting up from the tables along with the foggy cigarette haze and the acoustic six string soundtrack from the stage, she'd foolishly paid for each of her refills and worked her way through half her pack of Viceroys when the empty chair on the other side of her little table suddenly slid away.

And there he was.

Tall. Thin. No, not thin. *Lean.* Like he was one with his blue denims and his black T-shirt and the scruffy motorcycle jacket. A long angular face with a long angular nose, but it worked somehow. It was classic, angelic, half hidden under bushy black brows that almost merged with his shiny, dark mop top of hair.

"May I?"

It was *him.* There was no mistaking it once he spoke. He sounded just like one of the Beatles – Bobbie knew – she'd stayed home sick from the 'Bean one night just to hear them do an interview on WLS when they hit town to play The Amphitheater. Just those two words and she recognized the voice she'd heard arguing with Sacks Monday night. British, but not foppish-faggy. Just kind of cool. Kind of *very* cool.

"Sure." Bobbie nodded. "Free country."

He nodded back with a wink and a smile and Bobbie felt herself go weak in the legs and was damn glad she was sitting down. It was him all right, she knew it by the way his dark eyes smoldered under those bushy brows and locked with hers and spoke volumes without even saying a word, and she felt – no, she *knew* – this thin, dark stranger with the keen accent saw right inside her. Knew her. Knew her as good as if he'd grown up next door in Eau Claire.

He ordered an espresso and sniffed the steam when it came, but just set the little cup back onto the saucer without a sip.

He gladly took one of Bobbie's Viceroys and let his hand linger on hers when she held out the match to light it. The touch of his fingers made Bobbie's legs go more than weak, it made them clench together to halt an unfamiliar and uncontrollable and not at all unappealing trembling in her thighs that tried to capture the moist heat warming up between them. All the same, those long lingering fingers sent a strange shiver right down her own and straight up her arm to her heart.

He finally pulled his hand away and toyed with the cigarette. "Bit nippy out."

Bobbie nodded, suddenly tongue-tied.

He turned around and gestured towards the little stage. A guitar and stringbass duo was stepping down while an emaciated looking fellow with the heebie-jeebies stepped up, shuffling sheaves of homage-to-heroin poems. "Not performing tonight, Bongo?"

Her tongue untied. "Don't call me Bongo."

"No. You don't like being called Bongo, do you?" He nodded, his eyes locking tight with hers. "No, you don't. I promise I'll never call you Bongo again."

"Thanks." Bobbie lit up a fresh Viceroy, noticing he never bothered to drag on his anymore than he drank his espresso. "It's Roberta, actually."

"Rob – Oh, I see. Roberta. Well, Bobbie suits you very nicely, I'd say."

"Me too. My folks always called me Bobbie."

"Back in Eau Claire?"

"Yeah, they – Look, how do you know that?"

But before he could answer, the coffeehouse crowd started up the nightly 'Bongo-Bongo-Bongo' chant. Even the junkie flunky up on the stage managed a giggle and chimed in, dropping all his papers when he started to clap along.

"You don't really want to play your drums tonight, do you?"

Bobbie shook her head.

'Bongo-Bongo-Bongo...'

"You always liked it before. Why not tonight?"

Bobbie shrugged her shoulders. "Yeah, I loved to play those drums, and everyone always likes it when...but then, that night..."

"Monday night?"

'Bongo-Bongo-Bongo...'

"Yes, Monday night," Bobbie said. "I was up there playing, like always. And then I looked out from the stage and I saw...something."

"Me?"

She dragged hard on her cigarette. Raised her coffee to her lips and pretended to sip from the empty cup, her eyes peering over the rim to stare back at his. Bobbie nodded. "You."

'Bongo-Bongo-Bongo...'

"You saw me out there in the shadows Monday night, Bobbie. So?"

"I saw you looking at me and all of a sudden I knew...I knew that..."

"You knew that they'd all been laughing at you all along?"

Bobbie set her cup down, stared at the table, but finally raised her eyes to look through her bangs at him. Her head never moved, but her eyes said a 'yes'.

'Bongo-Bongo-Bongo...'

"You listen to me, Bobbie from Eau Claire. You don't ever have to feel bad, don't ever have to feel ashamed, don't ever have to envy this jaded lot." He leaned across the rickety little table till his lips nearly brushed her hair. "Whatever you think they are and whatever you think they know and whatever you think they have is all nothing...compared to you."

Bobbie would have melted right onto the floor when he whispered that in her ear. But just then he stood up, took her hand and she rose too.

The *Bongo-Bongo-Bongo* chant stopped. The jerky jointed

junkie on the stage didn't catch on right away and kept on clapping.

Bobbie's fingers tightened on the cold hand. "Who *are* you?"

"Some call me Flynn." He reached for her trenchcoat, and though Bobbie felt disappointment flood through her the moment he let go of her had, she couldn't help but smile when he held out her coat for her and gracefully laid it over her shoulders.

"Yeah? And what should *I* call you?"

"Well, you can call me Ghandi if it will get us out of here quicker." She mulled that over for half a second, but then he laughed, Bobbie laughed and they both turned to the 'Bean's watchful crowd. Flynn glared at the stage and the junkie poet finally stopped clapping.

"Ladies and gentlemen," Flynn announced. "Bobbie sends you her apologies, but we're afraid she'll be unable to perform for your...*pleasure*...tonight." Murmurs wafted up from the smoke circled tables. "Now-now, Bobbie's very sorry, we simply can't have the intellectual elite begging now, can we?" Flynn paused, surveyed the room, which was as quiet as a church all of a sudden. "No, I don't suppose we'll have to worry about that *here,* will we, chaps?"

And with that, Flynn and Bobbie scampered out of The Unseemly Bean, laughing hysterically all the way out into the snow and the darkness on Wells.

◆

It grew colder as it grew later, finally freezing the snow from gooey slush into icy crystals that powdered their shoulders and clung to Flynn's boots and Bobbie's flats.

They wandered down Wells, past the storefront galleries and the dirty book stores and the look-alike coffeehouses. Bobbie's Bulova told them it was just shy of ten when they crossed the Wells Street bridge over the murky Chicago River. It told them it was just past midnight when they circled back through the Loop and let the skyscraper canyons shelter them from the freezing wind and snow for awhile. It was past three when they ambled down Michigan Avenue with its boulevard traffic and the horse-n-carriages and the Chanel and Tiffany salons. But they ignored that and just walked along at a slow-motion-slow pace with Flynn's arm wrapped tight around Bobbie, talking non-stop the entire time. Talking about Eau Claire and Bobbie's parents and eking by in a big bad beat city neighborhood full of trends Bobbie just couldn't keep up with. Talking about cold dark nights just like this in Liverpool and Manchester and London, snowy nights on tramp freighters to the States, sooty snowy nights in Greenwich Village and Phillie and Boston and places Bobbie'd never been.

"What time is it now, Bobbie?" he asked when they crossed Division at State, where even the jazz clubs were finally closing for the night.

She pulled up her trenchcoat sleeve, shivered, and glanced at her watch. "You have a curfew or something?"

"No. Just curious. A fellow could lose track of time in your company."

"4:15. *A.M.* Pretty late, huh?"

"Pretty late, yes."

"You have to be somewhere?"

He shook his head.

"Sure? No wife waiting at home, wondering where you are?"

"No, Bobbie. No wife. Once..."

"Divorced, huh? That's okay." She sounded hopeful. Late night revelations had a way of making dreams vanish like melting snow.

"No, I'm not divorced, Bobbie." Flynn guided her down Division, jogging aside as a group of drunks giggled their way out of greasy a spoon and into a cab. "She died, Bobbie. But that was a long time ago."

"Back in England?"

He nodded. "Yes. Back in England. But a different sort of England, I imagine. I'm not really sure what England's like anymore."

She punched him playfully on the shoulder. "Oh, come on. How different can it be? Merry ol' missed out on this whole 'beat' thing, the Mods beat the Rockers and that's that, right?"

Flynn smiled, more to himself than to her. But then he held her tighter and ushered them both along. "Yes, that's that, Bobbie."

They continued walking till their path led them back to Old Town and Wells Street and the shadows bleeding through the snow off the old Dr. Scholl's factory. It was five A.M. on the dot when they halted in front of Bobbie's building.

She pressed herself close to him. "You'll come up, right?"

"It's pretty late, Bobbie."

"Well, I won't tell." She laughed and dragged him up the stairs. "Anyway, might as well enjoy the place while I have it. I don't come up with the rent money Monday, I'm going to be sleeping on tables at the 'Bean."

Inside her apartment they both brushed snow off their coats and hair and Bobbie's beret, and she kicked off her flats, slush flying off the soles and across the well-worn hardwood floor.

"Can I get you something?" she asked, tentative and unused to the accommodating hostess routine; Bobbie's guests usually got *her* the moment the door closed and the deadbolt clicked shut. "You must be freezing."

"I am cold. But no, nothing for me."

"Well, I need something to warm me up." She shuffled off to the kitchen and left Flynn to wander the parlor.

"So, are you going to tell me about the painting?" she called from the other room.

He smiled and nodded to himself as he ran his fingers over her portable record player and the stack of albums beside it: Dylans and Barry Sadlers mixed in with hidden Beach Boys and the Beatles and Jan & Dean. "What about it?"

"Like how you knew about...well, all about..."

He drew lines in the dust on her 12" Philco with the Giacometti sculpture of twisted coat hanger antennas. He eased onto the sofa, or more correctly, the strange lumps of barely upholstered springs and stuffing that filled up most of the little room. Flynn sat there and gazed around the parlor and out the window where the snow built up dirty gray-white crests on the fire escape grates. There on the sill, he saw it, and his smile warmed and widened. "I painted what I saw, Bobbie."

A plastic toy car gathered dust there on the sill. A carefully glued and painted plastic Bel Air.

"I painted your dreams."

But his smile faded when he noticed the faint traces of purple light drifting in through the window, painting the toy car a threatening shade of violet.

"So, what are you, some kind of magic man? You are, aren't you?" Bobbie's feet swish-swished across the floor. "You sure you don't want something to take away the chill?"

"No, really. It's awfully late, Bobbie. Maybe I should –"

She glided into the parlor with a juice glass of red wine in one hand. Plopped down on the sofa and sniffed as the dust exploded from the cushions, then pawed through her trenchcoat for her Viceroys. Bobbie dug through her purse and then under the sofa cushions for a match. "Flynn, you're really sure you don't want something?" She lifted a cushion, sneered, and dropped it back into place. "Go ahead, take a sip." Bobbie started to hop off the sofa.

But his hand locked on hers. "Nothing, Bobbie." He stood up and wrapped her in his arms. "Nothing but you."

Bobbie's Viceroy fell to the floor when he kissed her. She

forgot about the chianti in the juice glass. Forgot about everything.

Forgot about the 'Bean and all the beats and 'niks and hangers-on and the laughing-laughing-laughing at her, and forgot about Sackville and the studio and sitting there red-faced naked night after night and the leers and the jeers and the rejections and the way Chicago and Old Town could ruthlessly crush a body's hopes. She forgot about it all and just surrendered to his kiss, his cool chilled-from-the-snowy-night kiss, soft like velvet frost on her lips.

No beer and nicotine stink stung her nostrils, no java and junk laced tongue slammed against her teeth. No effete fingers ripped the seams on her sweater or tugged at her skirt.

Instead, Flynn lifted Bobbie up into his arms and carried her into the bedroom.

He lay her down on the bed so gently the cast iron frame never uttered a squeak. He lowered himself over her – paused – glanced at the window, at the purple haze breaking through the snow and the city darkness, then lowered the yellowed venetian blinds and drew the yellower drapes closed tight over them.

Bongo Bobbie had been fucked from one end of Old Town to the other, every frenzied, clutching, groping embrace a desperate plea for acceptance even when it was sometimes just for the rent. She thought she'd seen it all, even for a girl fresh from Eau Claire and just on the legal side of her twenties.

But even Bobbie wasn't prepared for Flynn's touch.

It was delicacy that was almost reverence. It was satin snowball kisses. It was soft icicle fingers, gracefully undressing her, slowly removing her black turtleneck in a shower of static sparks that lit up the darkened room. It was frozen feather kisses on her shoulders as he undid her bra, it was tender cool touches lingering on her breasts like they each were an altar, shivery soft hands playing with the zipper at her waist, sliding, silky sliding skirt and slip off. It was glacial hands slowly unraveling black tights down her long legs, peeling panties away and planting kisses along every inch of skin.

"Look, I don't ask for much, Flynn." Bobbie sat up on the bed and looked across the room to the painting on the dresser, the perfectly naked and perfectly bruised Bobbie on the perfect '59 Bel Air. She reached out to Flynn, ran her fingers through his mop top of black hair. "Just say you love me. You don't have to mean it."

"But I do, Bobbie." He raised his eyes to her. "I love you." He glanced at the window again, then looked back to Bobbie. And for a moment – just a second – she shivered with a strange mix of fear and delicious desire, seeing something in his eyes that didn't make sense, something red and dark and burning with icy fire, saw something white and cold and glinting behind his pale lips.

But whatever she saw vanished when Flynn slowly lowered his head between her legs, and Bobbie just surrendered to it all, and then she was riding in a Bel Air, clean winds licking her hair and crisp moonlight bathing her skin and her own soft moans lilting like music from the dashboard radio, till even that image faded and Bobbie cried out with pleasures she'd never ever felt.

When it was over, when Bobbie caught her breath, she pulled Flynn up to kiss him and it was all ice and night and the taste of her.

Their lips parted. "I...I really should go, Bobbie."

"Are you nuts?" She wrapped her arms around him and spun Flynn around, back on the mattress. She had his black T-shirt off before he could answer. Her fingers were already at work on his belt and the denims.

"No, Bobbie. It's late. *Really* late. What time is it now?"

She started to glance at her watch – stopped – unbuckled the clasp and tossed the Bulova across the room. "No more questions. That was...special. I owe you."

"No, Bobbie, you don't owe –"

But the jeans were off already and Bobbie was on him, holding him and stroking him, guiding him into her.

Flynn looked at the window again. Looked back at Bobbie and saw the violet light only he could see stealing through the venetians and drapes and washing over her skin, saw the light growing pale, saw it burn from purple to pink and orange. "Bobbie, I –"

"Shhh." She lay a finger on his cool lips and held him tighter, rode him, her fingers clawing through her hair and raking over his pale chest, her legs digging furrows in the blankets and the mattress, rocked and buffeted until the old bedframe sang along, but she didn't hear it, not really, because she could only hear herself again, and it was as good as it had been a moment before. As good...as good...every bit as good...

Bobbie fell down on the mattress beside Flynn. She stared at the ceiling, a pinkish glow washing away the plaster cracks and cobwebs and mildew stains. "Wow." She brushed damp bangs off her forehead. "I never...I mean I've had a lot of – well, you know, but...wow."

Flynn said nothing.

She leaned over and pecked him on the lips. "I need a smoke." She hopped off the bed. "Cover up, why don't you? You're still freezing."

Bobbie scampered to the bedroom door. Halted there. Spun around and smiled. "Don't you go anywhere, now."

She was back in a flash, a Viceroy dangling from her lips, the juice glass of chianti in hand. "Jeez, it's freezing in here." She set the glass down, pulled a dirty ashtray from out of the nightstand drawer and plopped down on the bed. "Aren't you cold? Come on, let's get those blankets pulled up here, it's..."

He didn't answer.

Bobbie smiled, yanked the blanket out from under Flynn's legs and tugged till she covered them both up. She set the cigarette in the ashtray and turned back to him. Kissed him on the lips again.

But she realized he didn't kiss her back.

"Flynn?"

Bobbie nudged him.

Then she punched him in the ribs.

"Flynn?"

She wrapped her arms around him and kissed him hard on the mouth, lips crushing into his.

But there was...nothing.

Just cold skin. Still. Unmoving.

Bobbie leaned her head down to his chest. Pressed her ear against his flesh and listened.

That's when the tears started to trickle out of her eyes. They sprinkled across his pale skin and ran right down onto the blanket.

"Flynn? *Flynn?!* Oh God, Flynn..."

The Desk Sergeant's shift was over at 5:00 P.M. and he really didn't need to close out the day like this. He looked down at his half completed triple carbon form, then back up at Bobbie. "Miss, what do you say I let you talk to a detective?"

"No, you don't understand," Bobbie sobbed. "You have to send some cops over now. I mean, he's still there."

"We will, we will." The policeman stepped out from behind his desk and took Bobbie by the arm. He grabbed the form, guided her down a hallway and paused by a half opened door. "But let me just bring you in here for a moment to talk to someone else, okay?"

Bobbie nodded, wiping her eyes with a soaked Kleenex. She waited there by the door that read *Homicide* while the Desk Sergeant went inside.

He was back in a moment. "Detective O'Mara is going to talk to you, Miss."

"And then you'll send some men over to my apartment?"

He ushered Bobbie in and sat her down beside a cluttered desk. "Sure, but first you talk to the Detective." He left the half filled out form on the desk blotter and turned away. At the doorway he stopped a plain clothes cop in shirt sleeves and a shoulder holster, talked in hushed tones for a moment and then left with a relieved sigh.

"I'm Lieutenant O'Mara," the plainclothes detective said as he took his seat behind the desk. "The sergeant tells me you have a dead man in your flat?"

Bobbie nodded.

"And why didn't you just call the police right away? I mean, when you discovered the man was dead?"

"I – I didn't think he *was* dead. Flynn's a young guy. Well, I *think* he's a young guy. I mean, I *assume* he's a young guy, he *looks* young enough, but then you never know. I mean, he's kind of strange, he...well...he was kind of...we were just... he...and then he was just like...like not 'there' anymore."

"Not 'there'. Uh-huh."

"I know it sound crazy, officer, but it's like the light just went out in his eyes and he stopped breathing and went stiff as a board. And he was just...dead."

"So why didn't you call us then?"

"I don't have a phone."

"You don't have a...where exactly do you live?"

Bobbie told him. The detective sat back in his chair and mulled over the address, trying to picture the block, the building.

"The super has a phone. But I didn't want to call from there. I mean, I don't have the rent money ready for Monday and like I'm going to call from there with him listening to me tell the cops I got a dead guy up in my bed, I mean..."

"Okay, okay. Now what were you and this...uhm –"

"Flynn."

"This Mr. Flynn, what were –"

"Not *Mr.* Flynn. Just Flynn."

"Okay, what were you and this Flynn doing when he just...'died'?

Bobbie's eyes dropped and she felt her cheeks go hot red.

"You can tell me. This is homicide, not vice." The detective opened his top drawer and pulled out a pack of cigarettes. He offered one to Bobbie, took one himself and lit both. "Look, I don't really care, see? You two were tootin' some Mary Jane, that's fine. You do a little hooking on the side to make the rent, that's fine too. Now, what were you and this Flynn –"

"We were fucking."

O'Mara nodded. "Well, that's to the point." He dragged long and hard on his cigarette. "Look, you seem like a nice kid. This guy was into some kinky stuff, maybe? Something got out of hand?"

Bobbie shook her head. "No, nothing like that. Flynn isn't...*wasn't* like that. Neither am I. We were just fucking." She stared at her own cigarette, watching it burn down in the ashtray. "I killed him."

"Okay, *now* we're getting somewhere." O'Mara grabbed a pencil and started to scribble on the form. "So, how exactly did it happen? He try to rape you? You fought back, hit him with something, maybe? You know, self defense is a good route to go, you can –"

"I think I fucked him to death."

O'Mara dropped his pencil. He tried to stifle the laugh, but didn't quite succeed.

"You think this is funny, Detective?"

"Well, I'm sorry, but...'fucked him to death'? I hear you beatnik broads are kooky, but *you* must be some lay."

"The hell with this." Bobbie stood up and started for the door. If you guys think this is just a big joke, then I'll just leave."

But O'Mara was out and around from behind the desk in

a flash. He grabbed her arm. "Hold on, miss." He was still chuckling, though. "Look, you say you got a dead guy in your apartment, I'll get a couple of uniforms and we'll go see, okay? But what do you say, maybe on the ride over you try to come up with something better than 'I fucked him to death', okay?"

They all stomped last night's snow off their shoes in the building's vestibule. Bobbie had walked to the police station faster than they drove her back, but Friday rush hour traffic always snarled the streets leading out of downtown.

6:00 PM and it was nearly dark as midnight already. Cold water phoneless apartment buildings didn't splurge on light bulbs either, so the cops – the detective and two uniforms – carefully negotiated the four flights of creaky stairs. Bobbie could take them two or three at a time in another mood, but this November evening the weight of the city and the last of her crushed hopes slowed her down. She shuffled along half a flight behind the three men, still rambling answers to the detective's questions like she had all the way over in the squad.

"I don't know, I was just freaked, you know? I just lay there beside him a long, long time. All morning, I guess. Lay there on the bed with the drapes and the blinds closed, like I didn't want to see him in the light, like that would just make it too real." The police huffed and puffed and waited for her on the landing by her apartment door.

"Look, what would you do, Officers? No, for real, what would you guys do? You meet this guy and he's like the best ever, and then he's just...just dead in your bed, I mean –"

"Just give me the key, Miss," O'Mara said. The two uniforms tried not to snicker.

The door squeaked open to a dark parlor. O'Mara stepped in first, sniffed and immediately wrinkled his nose. He leaned over to one of the uniforms. "Well, *something* died in here, that's for sure."

"No, it always smells like that," Bobbie said. "So, it's not the Ritz, okay?"

"Not the Ritz?" O'Mara said. "Jesus, kid. The only reason this joint's still standing is the termites are holding hands." He felt along the wall and flicked on the lights. "Okay, where's your bedroom?"

Bobbie'd heard that question enough times. She pointed down the dark hallway and let them go ahead of her. She didn't want to go back to that room. Didn't want to see it all again, to see Flynn, beautiful Flynn, lying there all cold and still on the bed. Not after laying beside him crying all morning, after sitting on the floor by the bed and crying all afternoon, didn't want to see, didn't...

"So, is there a light in here?"

"On the nightstand," Bobbie answered.

She listened to their thick soled broughans clomp across the floor and bump against the furniture. Saw the pale light suddenly leak out into the hallway where she hugged the wall.

She heard the drapes draw open, the blinds rise.

"Miss, would you please come in here?"

"No." Bobbie hugged the wall tighter. She started to back down the hallway. "No, I really don't want –"

"Get your ass in here," O'Mara growled. "Now!"

It was the longest walk she ever took. She didn't want to see Flynn again, not after he saw her dreams, not after he saw right inside her, touched her inside, in her heart, where she hadn't been touched since Mom and Dad and Eau Claire and glorious rides in two-tone Bel Airs. No, she didn't want to see him all cold and still and lying there, didn't want to see...

...The empty bed.

The two uniforms poked through her closet. O'Mara stood by the window, tapping his shoe on the hardwood floor. Loud.

"You know, we can put your beatnik butt in the clink for

filing a false police report just as easy as we can for 'fucking a guy to death'." O'Mara took a threatening step toward her, but Bobbie wasn't even looking at him. Her eyes were all wide and as round as her opened mouth and she stared at the empty bed.

"Nothing in here, detective." The uniforms stepped out of the closet. One looked out the window. The other peeked under the bed.

"Check the other rooms," O'Mara snarled. Then he turned back to Bobbie. "So, anything you want to tell me? You're really a co-ed, that it? Some sorority prank? You know we're getting tired of all you kids pulling..."

But Bobbie never heard a word.

Oh, they grilled her for another hour, but O'Mara and the two uniforms finally left.

Left her sitting on the empty bed, actually.

Sitting there, running her hands over the cold mattress and the rumpled sheets. Sitting there and staring across the bedroom at her Salvation Army reject dresser and all the dimestore perfume bottles and tangled scarves and plastic jewelry clutter.

Staring at the spot where the painting had been.

Had been, but wasn't now.

It was gone. The bed was empty and the painting was gone. And Bobbie realized it had all just been another silly dream, another pointless wish that never came true and vanished like melting snow. And that made her cry almost as hard as she did when she just thought Flynn was dead.

◆

Bobbie finally got off the bed.

She headed straight for her closet and stood up on tiptoe so she could reach the giant old suitcase tucked up on the top shelf. She popped it open and did her best not to notice how the smell reminded her of vacations with Mom and Dad and on-the-road breezes in her hair and rides in that goddamn Bel Air.

She had her clothes packed in a few minutes. Grabbed some essentials from the bathroom and the last of the stash in the Chase & Sanborn can in the kitchen and tossed that all in the suitcase too. She ran back to the parlor and started to collect her record albums and an armful of books, but stopped suddenly.

Bobbie just dropped them all on the floor.

She stumbled over to the parlor window and looked at the little plastic Bel Air sitting there on the sill. She picked it up and brought it close to her face. Looked over the tiny plastic details and the nifty two-tone paint job she'd done all by herself.

Then she opened the parlor window and lobbed the car out as hard and as far as she could.

Bobbie slammed the window shut and checked her watch. 8:30. She threw her trenchcoat on, flung the door open and ran out of the flat.

She was out of breath when she burst through the doors of The Unseemly Bean. The usual cloud of cigarette and pipe smoke strangled her. The usual gaggle of self-styled poets and Folk Guitar 101 Graduates lined up by the little stage, *sans* bongos tonight. The usual Friday night crowd filled the little tables. The usual touristy types from the downtown office canyons and the suburbs fidgeted uneasily in their chairs and their gray flannel suits and their wingtips and their prim secretarial Butterick pattern suits and their tortuous pumps and tried unsuccessfully to look like they belonged. And the usual beats and the 'niks huddled at *their* tables and sneered at the slummers and their rigid conformity and then turned back to their politics and art and poetry and painfully relevant social issues, too self-absorbed to notice their own Draconian uniform rules and coffeehouse etiquette.

No one banged tables tonight and no one called out *'Bongo-Bongo-Bongo'.* In fact, no one even seemed to notice

Bobbie bounce off the tables and head for the backroom, where she got another *'you miss one more night, Bongo and you're canned'* speech from the 'Bean's boss while he reluctantly counted out her forty dollar salary. And no one seemed to notice Bobbie recounting the bills on her way back out the front door.

No one except Cecil, that is.

"Yoh, Bongo!"

Bobbie paused on Wells, and her shoulders slumped, her whole body slumped when she heard that. "No, Cecil, not tonight. I really mean it."

But he caught up to her as she started walking again. "Hey, slow down, will you? So, where are you going so damn fast? And with all that cabbage?"

She didn't answer, but just stepped up her pace.

"Don't tell me you're still mad about Monday night?"

"And the night before that, Cecil?" She crossed Wells and started down her block, head down, staring at the sidewalk, refusing to even look at him. "Get lost, okay? I got places to go. I'm serious, I'm not in the mood tonight."

"And that would be a problem because...?"

"I mean it, Cecil. I'm out of here. So just buzz off."

"Out of here?" They reached her building and he followed Bobbie up the front stoop. Cecil paused on the cracked concrete, looked over his shoulder, looked at *something* parked there at the curb – shook his head – then traipsed after Bobbie. "So where the hell are you going?"

"Somewhere. Anywhere." She flew through the front door and started up the staircase.

"You're talking crazy, Bongo."

She halted on the second flight of stairs. Didn't turn around, but stood there with her back to him and said as clearly and carefully as she could, "Don't - call - me - Bongo."

And then she was flying up the stairs again, two steps at a time. But Cecil was right at her heels, and when they reached the top landing, he grabbed her arm, spun Bobbie around and slammed her hard against the wall. "I'll call you Bongo," he sneered, one hand already clawing like a snake under her skirt. "And I'll call you bitch, and I'll call you anything and anytime I fucking want."

He shoved her against the apartment door and it just flew open. Bobbie fell inside and onto the floor. Cecil stormed in right behind her.

And that's when Flynn's hand shot out of the darkness and grabbed Cecil by the throat.

◆

Those long and slender fingers that made magic with a brush and made cool velvet sighs on Bobbie's skin were hooked into gray-white claws right now, gripping Cecil's throat so hard that little red rivers of blood bubbled up from under the skin.

Cecil gurgled, choking out nonsense and a couple of barely recognizable 'God-damns'.

Flynn yanked him off his feet. "Here's a thought, mate," Flynn said in his Cockney best, his voice changing into more of a growl with each word. "When you're about to say your last words, blasphemy's really not the best approach."

"Flynn!" Bobbie started to get up off the floor. "Flynn, you – you're not –"

But the words froze in her throat when Flynn let go of Cecil and turned around to look at her. Because it was Flynn, but it wasn't, and it became less and less Flynn by the moment. His eyes scrolled through shades of black and red till they glowed like brakelights. His ears poked through his black hair, his nostrils flared and steamed. His lips twisted into a sneer and peeled back to reveal long, white fangs that were sliding right out of his gums.

They looked at each other, Flynn and Bobbie. She quickly decided this was one of those times when there wasn't much to say.

Flynn turned back to Cecil and couldn't help but chuckle – if that's what you could call the guttural sound that came out of that shiny fanged hellmouth. And Cecil? Cecil just whimpered – cried like a baby, actually – and naturally he wet his gray Brooks Brothers suit pants. He backed towards the door, eyes wide with terror and disbelief, glancing crazily back and forth from Bobbie on the floor to the nightmare thing standing there in the parlor darkness, glowing eyes and slavering fangs and clawed fingers reaching out for him.

One step, two steps, three – Cecil backed halfway to the door when Flynn lunged. And then Cecil was flat on his ass on the hardwood floor and Flynn was on top of him, red eyes burning holes into Cecil's, long horror-movie-sharp teeth descending towards Cecil's throat.

Flynn paused. Raised his head, stared deep into Cecil's eyes and leered. "Very well, you can go ahead and scream now."

Cecil started to, but then those fangs clamped down on his throat and there was just the sound of his loafers slamming the hardwood floor and his flesh ripping like fabric and wet, bubbly, oozing, puddling, slurping sounds.

Flynn stayed there a long time.

Finally he got up off of Cecil and turned back to Bobbie.

And he was just...just *Flynn* again. Just beautiful, magical Flynn with the bushy brows and the moptop hair and the motorcycle jacket and the jeans and the taut black T-shirt. He crawled over to Bobbie and cradled her in his arms.

"Flynn, you...you're not dead?"

"Well, I suppose that's something we'll have to talk about. But not right now, I think. In fact, I think getting out of here might be a grand idea."

"Sounds like a plan to me. As it happens, my bag's all packed."

Bobbie hefted herself up off the floor and started for her bedroom. But she paused at the dark hallway and turned back, as if she was afraid Flynn would be gone again.

But there he was, standing up in the parlor. Standing there and delicately licking the wet, red tip of one finger.

And there was Cecil on the floor by the door.

Bobbie ran into her bedroom.

She was back in a moment, lugging the overstuffed suitcase in one hand, adjusting the black beret on top of her head with the other. Flynn took the suitcase from her and guided her around Cecil and to the door.

"Flynn, is he...dead?" She looked down at Cecil, his legs twisted like pipe cleaners, his arms splayed at his sides, fingers clawed right into the hardwood, his eyes still flung wide open, glassy and rolled back in the sockets.

His throat half gone.

Bobbie gulped. "Well, I don't plan on getting close enough to feel his pulse, but I'd say he's dead."

Flynn shrugged his shoulders. "I'd imagine so, love."

They bounded down the stairs, arm in arm. "So, you were all packed, Bobbie. Were you going to just leave? Without me?"

"Flynn, I thought you were dead. You *were* dead."

"Well, yes, I was. In a way. Where were you going to go?

They made it to the front door and Flynn held it open for her. Bobbie sauntered out and stood on the stoop, cinching up the belt on her trenchcoat and giving her beret another tweak. "I didn't know, actually. Just away from here."

"Home?"

She shook her head.

"Well, what would you say to heading west?"

"Like where?"

"What would you say to California? That's more or less where I was headed when we...met. Sort of working my way west."

Bobbie smiled and locked eyes with him. "Oh? How long have you been doing that?"

"For a bit, Bobbie."

She mulled that over. "Okay, but how are we getting to California? I have exactly forty seven dollars."

"I have a little money."

"Still...California. That's a long –"

Flynn touched her lips with a finger and silenced her. He set down the suitcase, laid his hands on Bobbie's shoulders and gently turned her around. "Will that do?"

And if Bobbie had only believed a little harder, she'd have known all along what would be there.

Despite the last few days' flurries and snow, it looked washed and waxed to perfection, sitting there with an almost anxious stance at the curb.

A perfectly two-toned teal and white 1959 Bel Air. Just like Dad's. Just like...well, almost. Bobbie squinted and then read the chrome script on the twin checker flag emblem on the front fender: *409 V-8.*

"You don't miss a trick," she said, beaming. "So, are we going to have the cops tailing us all the way to California because of this thing?"

"For this? No. But I do think it's time to be off, love. What say we avoid explaining your gentleman caller back up there."

Flynn tossed the suitcase in the trunk and opened Bobbie's door for her. As she slid in, she looked in the back seat and saw the painting resting there. Flynn got in the driver's side and fired up that huge V-8. "Oh that. Well, it was smudged. Thought I might fix it before I came back for you."

She smiled, slid across the front seat and snuggled into him as the car roared away from the curb.

And as they made their way onto Ogden Avenue and passed the sign that read *Route 66 – Los Angeles: 1,989 Miles* the Bel Air's front window rolled down and a black beret flew out and blew into the gutter.

She could handle a human. If she was quick about it she could still accomplish her task this very night. She took a step forward, and reached out for him.

It was then that he clapped a pair of silver handcuffs on her.

Sixteen Candles

Kiel Stuart

One hour before midnight.

Candice Jevetta crouched outside the bungalow where she had died nearly thirty years ago, listening for the sounds of her father within.

Yes. He was there, bumbling around the living room, probably looking for his damned glasses.

The little brick house hadn't changed much. The porch screens were ventilated here and there with rips no one had bothered to mend; the pines had nearly overgrown the front yard. Huron Street backed up to a still-empty field that was not all that far from the graveyard.

Far enough in time, though. 1967. The summer of love, she thought bitterly.

Candice Jevetta was a prisoner of the night. Or, as she called it in the PC 90s, "daylight-impaired." Her father came first on her hit list. Then she was going to destroy the creature who had made her what she was. After that–

Well, it had been a long time since she'd seen a sunrise.

She glided forward and touched the doorknob.

"Can I help you, sweetie?"

She whirled. A man stood on the front walk. Taller than she, about six-one if he lost the slump, sharp lean face with a sneer welded to one corner of the mouth, eyes gray as stone.

For a single instant she was afraid. Then she knew he was human, and relaxed. She could handle a human. If she was quick about it she could still accomplish her task this very night. She took a step forward, and reached out for him.

It was then that he clapped a pair of silver handcuffs on her. "Let's move," he said.

◆

Candice did not scream. She had learned to be silent when worse things were being done to her. All during the ride in the front seat of his Jeep she'd sat quietly. From Port Hollister to Rowena wasn't quite fifteen minutes at worst, but the silver burning her wrists felt like hours under a blowtorch.

When they stopped, he'd dragged her into a building that she knew well. Then it was up three flights and into a suite of rooms.

He let the silver handcuffs off her, and stood waiting. "Talk," he said.

She turned away from him, looking at her hands. The burns on her wrists were already healing, the pain only a memory now. But memories could ache.

The room was long and narrow, sunken from the entrance, with deep green carpeting and an arched window at one end. Couch and chairs and television looked as if they'd been chosen for comfort, not appearance. There was a fireplace on the adjacent wall, and a lot of books, laid around almost haphazardly. It smelled like academia.

"Birchwood," she murmured. "I thought it burned ten

years ago."

"Nah," said her captor. "Just a small fire. I've stayed here ever since; no one else will."

Birchwood. On summer nights like these, she used to come here drinking with her friends. Used to. She moved to the window, her back to the man.

Birchwood was a miniature Gothic edifice overlooking Long Island Sound. The University owned it, used to house visiting faculty there, she remembered, gazing out the curtained window. The Sound glittered with moonlight. It mocked her. She could not escape the man's rooms; she knew it; felt it. Silver at the windows? Crosses, spells, scattered throughout? No matter. Trapped.

She turned to the human. "Who are you? What do you want?"

"My name is Wilson Grant Sedgwick." When she didn't react, his eyebrows shot up, surprised. "You know," he prodded. "Author of *A Werewolf's Tale?*" So. Author. It made sense; he looked like a man who spent his days slouched over esoterica. And that computer in the corner. She gave him nothing but her vampire's stare. But it wasn't working on him.

"And Lives of The Witches?"

Folding her arms, Candice perched in an armchair across from the couch. Her Chevy Suburban–the one with the safe box in the back–was still parked at the far end of Huron Street. Could she reach it before dawn? And if not... "You can call me Grant."

She didn't.

The sneer in the corner of his mouth turned to a frown. He sat on the couch and placed a tape recorder on the coffee table before it. "How did it happen?" he snapped.

"Ohh, I get it," she simpered, laying in a Deputy Dawg accent. "Ah done got me a Anne Rice wannabe."

"Just tell me." He clicked on the recorder.

"Not into one of those."

"Fine. I'll take notes." He turned off the machine, flipped open a reporter's notepad.

"No way."

"I see." He leaned back on the couch, rubbing his chin with a broad thumb. He almost smiled. "Well, let me put it this way. You looked like you were on a mission tonight. Wouldn't you like to complete that mission?"

Wouldn't she just. Wouldn't she just love to snake her hand around her father's neck, and look into his face as he realized who she was. And tell him why she was doing it. All about why she was doing it. For an instant she shut her nightseeing eyes. "Suppose you go straight to hell." His lip curled. "It's a good thing you're not bitter."

"It's a good thing you invested in silver."

He shrugged. "See this book?" It was on the coffee table next to the recorder, a glossy hardcover with a lurid picture of a werewolf. "And this?" Another one, with an equally lurid trio of semi-nude women.

She nodded.

"My two titles. Sold millions. I don't suppose you read, though."

Could that mouth do anything but smirk? "I read. Just not this stuff."

He leaned forward, eyes shining like toad's eggs. "Because you live it."

She shrugged. Still hours until dawn, but –

"How did it happen?"

"You're a writer. Make it up."

"Ah." He put his hands on his knees. "But that's the thing, you see."

So his mouth could do something besides sneer. "That's the crux, as it were," he continued, his voice softer. "I can't."

"Why not?"

"Ran dry. Blocked. Whatever you'd like to call it." He scrubbed at his face with the back of one hand. "It's been three years, and everyone is screaming. My agent, the publishers, even, for God's sake, my 'public.' So there you have it."

"I see. And they call me a vampire."

"Come on. Just a little info, and I might let you go."

She was thinking. Her stare – with which she controlled some, not all, humans – wasn't working on him; besides being hung with crosses, he might also be hung with other amulets, other spells. She couldn't get out of this room. She had her emergency bag of burial earth in a little suede pouch at her waist; he hadn't taken that from her. If she could find a safe place, a darkroom –

"Funny, you don't look like a vampire," Grant prodded, laying down the notebook. "Jeans, T-shirt, and a creamy peach complexion. How's a girl pull it off?"

She almost smiled. Maybe if she gave him that, everyone could call it a night. "It's a stain – Dy-O-Derm. It won't wash off. Bodybuilders use it to look tan for a contest. Doing the face is the hardest."

He nodded. "Clever touch. How'd you manage to go thirty years without anyone recognizing you, Candice?"

She forced herself not to react. "You know me, then. Why the games?"

"Saw you at the 7-11 last week. Got a good memory for faces."

Some quick calculations. He was forty-five or so; that made him around her age, maybe younger, maybe older, when she'd died. "So that was your hobby even back then. Collecting gruesome stories."

"You really don't recognize me, do you?" When she didn't answer, he looked back down at his notepad. "Tell me how it happened." There was a clock on the end table next to him; he turned it so she could see it.

She folded her arms. "Don't even try this. If I'm fried, you don't get your story. Ever. You're gonna have to make it up. And like you just told me, you can't."

"Look, maybe I can help you. I do have a good memory for faces. Whatever mission you're on –"

She flexed one hand in front of her face. The burns were already gone from her wrists. "I was visiting my sister's graveside when it happened," she murmured. "It was late. Past midnight."

He tensed, like a gun dog on a bird. "Your sister? How'd she die? Is she one too?"

"Laurie killed herself."

He was scribbling now, fast, not looking at her. "Teen suicide, boo-hoo. Why?"

"Because," she said, through clenched teeth, "my father – our father – had a case of the midnight creeps. *Comprende?*"

"Double boo-hoo." He scribbled faster.

A good backhand to the jaw, she thought, would do wonders for his attitude.

He shot her another glance. "And that's where the vampire got you?"

She didn't answer. If she escaped this human's trap, that was one vampire who wasn't going to "get" anyone else.

"Who was he?"

"I don't know. I never saw him."

"But you did see something."

Oh, yes. Something. As she'd lain dying on the chill wet ground, her eyes had been fixed on a gold button in her palm. Round. A shield and a bird on it – the bird not an eagle. "Give me that pad."

She sketched it for him, then handed it back. "I tore this off his coat. That's all I have to go on."

"I see." He frowned as he studied the sketch. "It isn't much, is it?"

"You asked."

He sat silent a while, writing, mumbling to himself.

Candice began to fidget.

"Well?"

"Well what?" He stopped his writing, looked up at her.

She pointed to the clock beside him.

He scratched his head, squinted. "Oh. I see. Right." He got up. "Come on."

She followed him to the door. He stopped. She waited, feeling the weight of the silver, the traps.

He didn't open the door. He turned to his left and pointed her through an archway. Beyond it was a little room with the windows locked and shuttered. In the middle of the room was a polished wood coffin. He went to it and tipped the lid open. She bared her teeth, furious, helpless. "You said you would let me go!"

"I lied." He backed out of the room, but paused, leaning against the archway. "Sweet dreams, Candice."

He was right by the coffin when she rose the next night, bending a little at the waist, looking at her. She shuddered; too much like the other nights, another man, standing over her bed. She stood quickly. "So you're not taking any chances with your meal ticket."

His mouth twitched. "And a good evening to you, too." He handed her a juice glass filled with dark red liquid. She took it gingerly; the smell told her what it was. "Where did you get this?"

"University hospital. You don't need to know how."

She turned away from him so he could not see her shudder as she drank.

There was a cast-off couch in the room; he perched on its arm. "Don't you want to know what I did with the rest of my day, dear?"

"No." This room was guarded, too. She glanced at the shuttered windows and the arched doorway.

"All right. Then I guess you're no longer interested in who made you what you are." He walked out of the room. "Not his name, not where he was buried. And certainly not the fact that I'm going to see him now."

She followed, despising him; he knew, she thought, he goddamn knew I would follow.

◆

The cuffs were on again. They drove in his Jeep to her Suburban and were careful switching cars. At least he was. The writer obviously didn't want her getting away – yet.

Pulling out into the street, he glanced at her. "So there's a way you can get them...er, vampires, when it's still night?"

She nodded. "A way to call a vampire to graveside, a way to destroy one then and there. That's if you didn't forget the sword, the chain, and the candle." She had the holly stake in her hands; it didn't hurt, and that surprised her. She supposed it would hurt when driven through the vampire's heart.

There was a reason for the holly stake. A gunshot – even a silenced shot – would draw too much attention, would leave a silver bullet, to be found by someone.

He laughed. "So how did you come to know this, and why would you tell me?"

She didn't address herself to his second question. "Do you think you're the only one who can use a library? I read about it." She tried to hold her wrists in a more comfortable position. "Now it's your turn. Who is he? How did you find him?"

"His name is Josiah Greenward. Dry-goods merchant, back in the 1700's, around when they founded this place. Port Hollister, I mean, not Rowena. Your button makes him a member of a secret society. The rest was a process of elimination."

"Secret society?"

"Yeah." When he grinned, his whole face changed. She almost liked it. "Sort of like the Masons."

Would it hurt her to laugh? But by the time she thought it over it was too late.

"They were called The Loyal Order of the Ravens," he went on, businesslike. "Get ready; we're almost there. He'll be in the mausoleum."

They parked almost on top of the cemetery and she stood listening. "Anyone?" he asked. She shook her head, and they walked to the mausoleum that lay on the crest of a low hill.

Inside, Grant lit the candle, holding the sword in his right hand. Candice grasped the holly stake and chanted the words as Grant laid the candle on top of the stone bier. This was where Josiah Greenward would take his daytime rest.

Slipping the chain into his free hand, Grant stood glancing nervously from Candice to the opening of the mausoleum.

The flame danced against her gaze. One candle. Sixteen candles. Then the old tune was echoing in her head, and it wouldn't leave. Where were tears when you really needed them?

She waited, breathing into the dark, repeating the chant silently now.

And the vampire was there.

He was about her height and plump, his cheeks looking as if he'd stuffed them with wads of chewing gum. Rosy, moist. Had he just come from feeding? The image shot bolts of anger through her.

The vampire saw them and drew back, but Grant tossed the silver chain around his shoulders. The creature hissed with pain. His fangs were longer than hers, sharper.

"Surprise," said Candice.

"Ahh," the vampire said, eyes lighting on her. "One of my own."

"More than you know," she said, and reached out with the stake.

The vampire's gaze fell on her handcuffs. His lips drew back in a sneer. "And he keeps you with silver bracelets, like a pet."

"Women have higher pain thresholds than men, asshole."

The vampire growled, writhing, but the chain held him fast.

She saw that Grant was afraid. The sword trembled in his hand. The vampire saw it, too. "Ah! You have never done this before, have you?"

Grant nodded. Don't tell him, she thought. Don't. He'll –

"Use the sword," the creature mocked. "Use it on her."

In the candlelight Grant's face went slack. The vampire held him in his gaze.

Don't look at him, Candice pleaded silently.

The sword raised again. Grant turned to her. His eyes were black disks, and she shrank back.

"Yes," said the vampire. "Now destroy her."

Grant hesitated.

The vampire snarled. "Destroy the girl. I command it!"

"Grant..." she said, her back pressed against the mausoleum wall. "Grant!"

He took a step toward her. His gaze wavered. "I –" Grant turned his head, and the chains went slack.

That was all the vampire needed. He twisted free of the chains and charged Grant.

"No!" Candice sprang forward with the stake. There was a dull crunch as she drove it home. The vampire howled, an echoing animal sound.

"Shut him up!" Ignoring the flames of agony, Candice reached for the silver chain.

Grant stood as if frozen.

She flung it around the vampire again. "Do it!"

Grant blinked then, seemed to come to life. He swung the sword in a flat arc and had the head off.

Candice watched, shaking, as the vampire melted into nothing. Then she bent to retrieve the stake. She had to grab for it twice, three times before her numbed fingers made contact.

She left the silver chain for Grant to pick up.

Done.

They were back in the car before Grant spoke again.

"Well," he said, "that's it, I guess. No, don't thank me, all in a day's work. I'll get my car back from Huron in the morning." His words were casual, but his voice cracked, and his face was far whiter than hers.

"Did you get the candle, too?"

He nodded, then fell silent. They drove back to Birchwood and he left her, cuffs on, with the remote for the TV. Then he went to take a shower.

Near his computer was a bowl of jelly beans. She snagged them and searched for something to watch.

When she found what she wanted she snuggled in the deep armchair, the bowl of jellybeans on her lap, riffling her fingers through them like they were jewels. She felt odd, like she was living in someone else's body. It had been good to see the vampire die. But now it was – like what? she asked herself. A letdown?

Grant came back inside, hair damp, dressed in clean clothes. "All right. Your car's parked, the objects are back where they belong, I'm...freshened up." He paused. "Looks like we got away clean."

She didn't laugh.

He came to stand at her shoulder. "What's that you're watching – 'Beach Blanket Bingo?'"

It was obvious. He stood in silence, watching along with her. When the credits rolled, he spoke. "Do you watch a lot of television?"

"The only way I can still see daylight."

"You can't eat the jellybeans."

"No, but...I look at them, and for a while I can convince myself I'm...still normal."

He took the remote and began surfing. He found a documentary about a teenage vampire club and left it there, glancing at Candice.

One of the girls, in a long black dress and white Kabuki make-up, was telling the reporter how she liked to have her boyfriend cut himself, how she would –

It was more than Candice could stand. She got up, striding to the window. "Stupid kids, stupid fucking kids. Why would they do this? Why do they think they want to be what I am? I can't shed tears, I can't see myself in a mirror, I can't cross running water, I can never see the sun again."

She heard him come up behind her. "Immortality?"

"This isn't living. It's more like purgatory."

He stood at her side now. She glanced at him, then at the cord that held the curtains back. She shut her eyes.

"Maybe they're after the power?"

"What power?"

"Well," he gestured, "Being able to turn into mist, a bat, to fly..." he trailed off, looking at her, a little helplessly.

"I can't do those things. I can barely do my hair without a mirror."

"You can't...fly, or...?" He looked shocked.

"Give me another 300 years. Or maybe you need another vampire to teach you how."

"What can you do?"

"Get this silver off me and I'll show you."

"Splendid. Why don't I just take the cross off, too? Here. Let me open my shirt; why make things difficult?" But he did remove the silver cuffs.

She gave one last glance at the curtain cord and walked away. "I'm going to bed."

"It's not dawn yet."

"Doesn't matter. I've had a busy day." She left the room

without looking at him.

The following night Candice agreed to talk. There was something biting at her and she had to keep her mouth and brain working or it would pounce and devour her.

He got his notepad out and began. "How did you do it? All those years ago? I mean, if you need another vampire to teach you...Where did you stay? Surely not in the car, not for thirty years."

"Not in the car, no." She told him as briefly as possible: about rising the night after her burial, panic-stricken, stealing a car, fleeing as far as it would take her that one night.

"But you had the presence of mind to take a bagful of dirt from the grave."

"It was just something I remember reading. Or hearing."

"How far did you get?"

"Massachusetts. I won't tell you the exact location."

"Fair enough."

She outlined the rest; that same night finding the old woman who spent her life taking in abused kids; her amazement when the woman treated her no differently.

"What made you come back?"

"She died."

"Did you kill her?"

She sprang up, hand drawn back to strike him. He flinched.

"Of course not," she said, settling into the chair again. She looked at her hands. "I never killed anyone, either."

"No?" His eyes went round.

"Not until last night."

"Go on," he said, his voice gentle.

She could have gone on at length. Told him what it felt like to hide for thirty years, to be furtive even in her research, lest she be caught reading a book on vampires.

Poor sweet old Betty Durston. "Miss Du – The old woman...She was good to me. I took her car, though."

"And drove here? And you've been around at least a week."

She shrugged.

"What will you do now?"

Do. Left undone. You left it undone. "I don't know." But she did. Had put it off long enough.

"Stay here, then. You took an incredible risk, coming down in the car, sleeping in it. Someone could have stolen it."

"And got himself a nice surprise after sunset." But she knew he was right.

The thing was hammering at her now. It wasn't the other vampire. That had been no more than putting down an animal with rabies. It was her father.

You left things undone.

She began to pace. "Stay here with the slave bracelets? No thanks."

"They're not on now."

"No," she said, "that's right." And sprang.

The cry was still in Grant's throat when she whipped the curtain cord around him. He was down on the couch and bound almost before the questions started sputtering.

"Be still," she told him. "I have a job to do."

"You can't," he gasped. "They'll catch you this time, they'll –"

"He's old, he's fat, he had a heart attack. That's what they'll think."

"Candice, please..."

"I don't have time for this now," she said, and went out.

She was at the bungalow in minutes. And he was still there, still inside, still hadn't cheated her by croaking off before she could do it herself.

Do it. The screen door still wasn't locked. The inside

door was. It gave way under her hand.

He was coming in from the kitchen. He looked up when she entered, thinner than she remembered, lots older, more frail. His thick reddish hair had turned to something resembling gray lichen. He moved with difficulty, opening his mouth, taking her in with wide eyes.

She was on him in one stride, grabbed him by the collar and threw him, not too hard, against the couch.

He propped himself up with one hand, wiping the other across his mouth. "C-c-c-c –" It was the only noise that came out of him.

"Hi, Dad," she said. "How's it going?"

He breathed at her for several minutes. "Candy. We put you in the ground," he said at last.

"Not deep enough, I guess. Isn't it a stitch?" She crossed to his side, hauled him to his feet again. He was so light in her grasp.

"What...how?"

"Wanna see? C'mon." She pulled him over to the big mirror that was above the piano, held him up, turned his head to face it. "Here. A nice father-and-daughter portrait."

He was alone in the mirror.

Sounds began to bubble from his lips. She cut him off by baring her fangs, in case he was a little slow on the uptake.

"Look what you made of us, Dad. The perfect little family. You and your habit."

There was a worn-copper glint of the old light in his eyes. "I never did nothing you didn't want me to."

She backhanded him casually. He spun across the room and she lifted him to his feet, set him on the couch.

"Don't even try that again. I'm your judge, jury and executioner. Right here, right now. And you thought you would get away with it." She walked to the foot of the stairs, put a hand on the banister. Big bad vampire, she thought, you can't even bring yourself to go up there now. "I used to lie in bed and listen for your footsteps. Now you know what it's like being trapped."

"Candy –"

"Don't ever call me that again." He didn't say, come off it, Candy, you wanted me to. He didn't have to; he never had to open his mouth again. His voice, his answers, his excuses, were lodged inside her own head now. For eternity.

She licked her lips. "Mom's gone?"

He nodded, wiping again and again at his mouth with the palm of one dry old hand. "Ten years."

"Too bad. I would have liked to ask her, 'What the hell did you think was going on? Why didn't you bother to stop him?'" Oh, Mom, she thought. "Well. Always was evasive, wasn't she?" The taste at the back of her throat was more bitter than blood.

"Please, look at me, can't you see? Can't you leave an old man in peace?"

"Yes. I'll look at you." She fixed him with her stare.

Dropping his gaze, he hugged his bony knees. "Listen to me. Leave your poor old dad alone..."

Hatred for him pulsed in her throat.

"...I've got cancer..."

She stopped. Sipped in a breath. "You were born with it. It just took a while to catch up with you." The house was screaming at her now. She covered her ears. It didn't stop. She began to pace. "You stole my life away!"

He made a noise like fear. She sprang at him, fangs bared. He flung up a hand. "What are you going to do to me?" His voice was thin as a mouse's squeal. "What, what what?" It ended in a wail.

What. What. What indeed...she closed her eyes, started to turn away.

"Candy," he said, "Candy, Candy, Candy..."

Candice Jevetta stood in the arched doorway of Grant's little suite at Birchwood.

Grant was on the couch, head in hands.

"So," she said. "You got free. Thought you would."

He jumped to his feet. "What the hell did you do to him?"

She didn't answer. She walked to the TV, picked up the remote, and sat in the armchair. She flicked the TV on, rolled through thirty channels, flicked it to a barker channel and stayed there.

She knew Grant watched her. She heard him come over to her chair and tensed for the cuffs. But he didn't put them on. He put his hands on the back of the chair instead.

"So why didn't you?"

"I don't know." It came out a little shrill. She lowered her voice. "I don't know. Buck's gotta stop somewhere."

Grant waited.

"He's dying anyway. He'll be gone in a month, two. Isn't my timing just perfect?"

He laid a hand on her shoulder. She moved out from under it.

"Aren't you afraid he'll blow the whistle on you?"

She shook her head. And even if he did, it wouldn't matter.

Grant cleared his throat. "Sometimes, I come across a little strong. I'm not sure I really mean it."

She sighed, clasping her hands.

"You really don't remember me, do you? Wil Sedgwick? Used to have kind of a crush on you. I was one of those A-V geeks and I thought you were...you know."

"What?"

"Brave. Tough. Cool."

"My father was about your age. He liked younger girls too."

"I'm not him. And you're not really younger. You just

look 16."

I'll look 16 forever, she thought.

"We could do this, Candice. Go around taking care of all the vampires and all the child abusers. We could –"

"What happened to writing?"

"That'll take care of itself."

"A one-man crusade, is that it?"

"What would be wrong with that?"

She got up from the chair, facing him. "I'm tired, that's what's wrong."

"The night is young," he said, but his eyes told her he understood.

She wandered to the window. No matter which way she squinted, no matter how full the moon, there was no way she could trick herself into believing it was sunlight on the water.

"Why not think about it some more?"

She looked at the room. The arched windows, the arched doorways. The bowl of jellybeans. His eyes, pleading with her now. "You don't have to make that decision right away, do you?"

She stared down at her hands. No silver bracelets.

She would think about it tomorrow. Maybe she could face her purgatory then. Maybe even think about getting on with eternity.

After all, she told herself, tomorrow is another day. But more importantly, tomorrow is another night.

I ventured forth into the bowels of Hell.
Granted, I had entered that place
almost an hour ago, but it was at this
time I began to realize my predicament.
Claudia and Vernon Detross were
not merely wealthy eccentrics,
they were downright dangerous.

Pet Consultation

Mia Fields

I entered the red brick mansion marveling at the ornate beauty of the woodwork and intensity of the vacuous color scheme. Stark white walls were bordered by even whiter crown and chair moldings. The coal black tile floor gave the appearance of stepping into a dream where one is in the clouds without any idea of how far reality lies below. The ceiling was textured plaster, also white. The silver chandelier above the entry offered bright light from many candle shaped bulbs. The only thing to cause hesitation was the slight smell of age or dust. I could not tell if the odor was from the house or its owner.

"We're glad you're here," Claudia Detross purred. She held out her exquisitely manicured long fingered hand. I stared at her hand but did not shake it.

Unperturbed by my lack of reciprocation, Claudia smiled and called out, "Vernon, dear. The canine counselor has arrived." Brushing back her thick dark brown hair, Claudia stepped aside allowing me to enter her home. Once in, the door was shut firmly behind me. I looked down and saw my reflection in the floor. Their housemaid did a wonderful job. Not a single smear in the marble tiles.

During the past couple weeks, I received more calls than I had all year. Business had dropped off due to Steve Fowler, another dog trainer. He had invested in some mass marketing that I simply could not afford. With the bills piling up, I really needed this job even though I went into it knowing that I would only earn a consultation fee. However, there was a good chance I might be able to convince the Detross' that they needed my training services as well. I smiled to myself knowing that Steve would have one less customer. I had often wished that he would move somewhere else, like across the country, leaving me as the only dog trainer in the area. At my last dog show I heard a rumor that he had moved to Florida. When business starting picking up I believed the rumor was true.

"Come Ms. Leaky," she stepped in front of me and led me through the foyer and into a sitting room. I followed her closely as she glided across the floor like a model who had much practice walking with a book on her head. My eyes caught on a renaissance style oil painting hanging to my right. My attention was not due to knowledge of the artist, I am not an art history buff, but more to the subject matter. A pack of drooling hounds stood around a child who played among them without fear, unaware of the canines salivating and circling. In the background the sky was dark and cloudy as though ready to rain. The artist had put so much life into the painting that I expected lightening to flash any second. When it did I knew the child would be torn to shreds.

"Ms. Leaky?" Claudia repeated, looking over her shoulder.

"Liz," I blurted, pulling my eyes away from the haunting picture and fixating on Claudia's lithe figure as she moved silently over the floor. "Please, call me Liz." I immediately envied her small bottom and slim waist.

Claudia stopped, turned and looked at me, glancing up and down. Her chin tilted up. "Of course." Her entire demeanor spoke of growing up wealthy. She carried herself well and exuded class from every pore. Wearing a floor length black gown that accentuated a perfect body, she looked prepared for the Opera, dinner at a lavish restaurant or a formal party. Anything other than a meeting with me.

The sitting room did not appear any more comforting than the foyer. The smell was also the same. The scent of age. Contemporary furniture, upholstered in lush white leather was arranged in a neat square in the middle of the room. A long couch was bordered by two arm chairs facing each other with a glass topped black iron framed coffee table in the middle. A fireplace that looked as though it had never been used was located on the far wall behind the long couch. The only spot of color in the room was a bright red Persian carpet. Woven into the priceless rug were yellow, white and pea green colored designs. I could not discern the pattern.

"Please have a seat...Liz," Claudia seemed to say with distaste. She apparently preferred to address people formally. "Vernon will be down in a minute. Meanwhile," she folded her porcelain fingers, red nails clicking against each other. "How about some refreshment?" She looked down at me from her superior height.

My eyes remained glued on her shiny fingernails, mesmerized by their perfection. Her manicure was superb. Not a single cuticle left uncut or chip in the polish. She probably just had them done.

"Liz?" Her voice although quizzical tinkled like soft music as she pulled my attention back to the moment.

"Nothing, thank you." I quickly looked away from her and stepped to one of the arm chairs. I could not imagine what type of "refreshment" she had in mind and although my mouth was dry, I did not want to find out. People of her caliber usually had Perrier or wine when they socialized. My normal drink was plain water or a diet soda, not that what I drank had much effect on my figure. But then, if I drank beer and regular sodas I could be unpleasantly surprised with a few more pounds than I already suffered with. I sat, and sank into the opulent furniture.

Claudia seated herself on the long couch, her knees close enough to touch mine. The sheer proximity of her body made me shiver. She did not lean back nor cross her legs. She kept her knees together as though glued and back straight as a board. Resting her hands in her lap, her alabaster skin appeared to float in the darkness of her black dress. I drew my legs beneath me and leaned back against the cushions. Resting my clipboard on my lap, I pulled a pen out of my handbag. I was ready to listen and take notes in order to help Claudia and Vernon make a proper decision. I had been hired to help them find the perfect pet.

I have been training dogs and various other animals for over fifteen years. While most of my job entails teaching people how to train their pets, I also offered consulting services for those who aren't sure of what they want. Most of the people who utilized this service were wealthy and educated. Claudia and Vernon Detross were of this ilk; wealthy, attractive and their lives tailored to perfection. They probably consulted with others on everything from interior design to the clothing they wore day to day. Their minds were far too busy with important thoughts to think of daily tasks. Common sense was often lost on these types. Thus, I knew they would need a pet that learned quickly and easily forgave their inconsistencies. After glimpsing the house, I knew they would also need one that was very clean.

"So...Liz," Claudia said, her full red lips briefly revealing straight white teeth. "How long have you been doing this sort of work?" She again lifted her chin, her lids drooping as she looked down at me. Brown and beige eyeshadow highlighted her large green eyes, the lashes long and lush. Not a single large pore marred her complexion. Twice a day I washed with special cleansers and toners to attain a fair complexion. I wondered what she did to achieve hers. Probably expensive salon facials.

I looked down at my large thighs straining through relaxed fit jeans. "About fifteen years," I said. I closed the fingers of my left hand around the pen while hiding my other hand under the clip board. My nails were long overdue for one of my home manicures where the cuticles were never cut and the edges of my fingers remained rough from being chewed.

I leaned forward a bit looking into her china doll face. "Do you have any idea of the type of pet you want? Dog? Cat?" Her bone structure was captivating. I could not help but want to reach out and run my hand down her cheekbones. I tightened my fingers around each other and shifted in my seat. I could not understand why I was so attracted to her. Never before had I felt any desires toward a woman.

"Well, Vernon really wants a large pet, but I was thinking more along the lines of a mid-sized one. You know, one that looks like a baby all its life. I so love them when they are rolly poly." She brought her hands together, fingers against each other, nails pointing toward me. "They flop about so." She raised her hands to each side of her face, her eyes turned toward the ceiling. "They are just so cute, don't you think?" She lowered her head and looked at me.

I nodded. "Sounds as though you've got an idea of what you want."

She returned her gaze to me. Her thick hair moved around her shoulders, framing the high cheekbones of her face. I wanted to bury my hands in her hair.

"I've had many pets. But that was some time ago." She looked down at the floor. "Time seems to go so quickly nowadays." She returned her gaze to me. "Vernon and I, well, we just moved into this place and we felt a pet would warm things up a bit."

"They do make a family," I agreed. I looked around the room, where not even a speck of dust blemished the floor or furniture. "Have you put any thought into how messy dogs can be, especially when they're puppies? There's housetraining and they go through teething for upwards of five months, which can be difficult to deal with at times. You have to watch them constantly to make sure they don't get into trouble."

Claudia nodded. "I know all about it. The pet would have my full attention. Vernon's too. We would make sure it doesn't get into trouble." She gestured demurely with her long fingered hands. "We just need help on finding out exactly what we want." She lowered her voice and leaned toward me. Shalimar perfume drifted into my nostrils. The perfume did not fully mask the musty odor, which I discovered radiated from my client. Although I should have been disgusted, I found her scent enticing. "I really don't want a big pet, like Vernon does," she continued. "Things can get...out of control. If you know what I mean. And, I'm also thinking along the lines of a female instead of a male. We had a male last time and there was all that marking." Her left hand touched her chest lightly as she rolled her eyes.

"Don't let her convince you to get a little nippy, yappy pet." The voice came from the entry. A voice that was full and deep, but not loud. "I can't abide that."

I turned and saw the most handsome man I had ever laid eyes on. He stood well over six feet tall. His long black hair was slicked back and held in a pony tail with a jeweled band. With high cheekbones, perfect triangular nose and full lower lip his face could not have been more perfect. I figured he must work indoors a lot for his skin was pale. I could not entirely discern his shape through the elegantly tailored suit, but he certainly was not overweight. Most amazing, were his bright blue eyes. Eyes that pierced my soul. I had never seen eyes so clear except with someone who wore colored contacts. The irises were tiny black dots swimming in a sea of mid-summer sky blue. I could not look away.

Shivers ran through my loins, almost as if I was orgasming. Before coming into this house I had never shivered so much in my life without being physically cold. I crossed my legs and pressed the clipboard against my lap. Sitting up straight, my back similar to Claudia's, I took a deep breath, my generous bosom briefly increasing in size.

He smiled. Not a wide open mouth smile, just a partial one. Enough for me to see his blinding white teeth and the dimples that formed on either side of his mouth. I noticed that his eyes did not smile with the rest of his face. They pierced mine as a lover who was readying to deliver an erotic kiss. Had I allowed myself, I would have swooned. That is the only way I can describe my reaction. I wanted nothing more than to rush into his arms.

Never before had a man affected me so. Most, once past my not entirely svelte figure, ended up being more an intellectual friend than a lover. Those out for sex? Well...they did not come calling on me. It had been some time since my last serious relationship and I was not counting the days until the next one. Besides once a woman is over forty it is pretty tough to attract an unattached man. I have filled my life with my pets and clients. I was happy, but had never realized how much I longed for sexual contact until I saw Vernon.

"Come, Vernon," Claudia interrupted our long distance love making. She patted the leather couch beside her right leg. "Liz," she exaggerated my name, "was just explaining how destructive pets can be."

Vernon floated over the polished black marble floor. His feet moved but, unlike most people, his body did not rock side to side or appear to be in motion with his legs. His was so quick I barely had time to register the fact that he arrived and sat close beside Claudia. Did it take ten seconds or ten nanoseconds? He was fast.

"Yes," Vernon nodded almost imperceptibly. "They can

be if you don't keep a close watch on them." He lifted the corner of his lip and then winked at me. He jerked his gaze toward Claudia. "You remember our last one don't you?"

My eyes opened wide with surprise as I wriggled in my seat. Why did he do that? This consultation was becoming more uncomfortable by the moment. I reminded myself that I really needed the money. Besides, I liked being with them. Strange, but I felt similar to being with a movie star, excited and nervous at the same time.

"Yes," Claudia answered. "He urinated all over the place. The maid had a rough time cleaning it all off the walls and furniture."

These people obviously did not have their previous dog trained. I hoped I could convince them to do so with their next pet. But despite my conflicting emotions and the dire need for income, I did not want to offer the service. Not only did I have a feeling my suggestions would not be followed, these people were having a strange effect on me. I knew that if I ever spent time alone with Vernon I might throw myself at him and that would be extremely improper.

Eager to finish, I said, "Claudia says you want a large dog like a German Shepherd but she wants a medium sized dog. What is it about the Shepherd that appeals to you? Is it the size or the bold temperament?"

Both of them stared at me attentively, winsome smiles on their lips. I took another deep breath trying not to break my focus. "Some mid-sized breeds can have very bold temperaments. Although, unless you intend to be very dominating you don't really want a highly bold dog. There can be problems when it reaches maturity such as hierarchical challenges or, if not neutered, territorial marking. Like with your last pet."

Vernon continued to stare at me, his gaze making my insides turn to jello. I had a difficult time remaining professional. Pulling my eyes from him, I glanced at Claudia, who seemed amused. Her eyebrows were arched. She clasped her hands and lay them in her lap. My stomach churned.

"Well," Vernon began. "I guess I must defer the final decision to Claudia for she will be spending the most time with it." He turned and looked at his wife. "I just don't want anything that will drive me crazy. You know I don't have patience for that. And your patience is even thinner than mine." He put his left arm around her shoulders and caressed her supple neck. "I don't mind a little hair and other mess one way or the other, but Claudia dear," he looked into her eyes where they locked, "you did just finish decorating the house. I'm sure you don't want one of those little pests that are difficult to housebreak and try to run away all the time. You know how frustrating that can be."

"Any dog can be housetrained, given the right procedure," I interjected. "It's just a matter of scheduling and letting him outside regularly. Also keeping an eye on him at all times and beginning formal obedience training right away."

Claudia broke her eye lock with Vernon and looked at me. She smoothed down her dress, caressing her long legs. I could almost feel how her silky skin slid down the satin material. I rubbed my fingers against damp palms.

"You see," she said to Vernon, waving a hand at me demurely. "It doesn't really matter what type of pet we have provided we train it. I have every evening to work with it while you go about your business and then, when you get home, we can switch so that I can get some work done."

I nodded. Now I was getting somewhere and that meant a quick decision, payment and I could go.

Vernon touched Claudia's ear. My body reacted as though he had touched mine. I took a deep breath, my heart hammering so loud I could hear it. Sweat broke out on my brow. My toes curled inside my sneakers.

"What types of pets did you have before?" I asked, gulping. I squirmed in my seat, feeling dampness in my panties.

"Oh, so many," Claudia quipped. She leaned toward Vernon and tilted her head, giving him easier access to her neck. "Dogs, snakes, iguana, one of those pot-belly pigs when they were all the rage. The only ones I really could not abide were cats. They get so jealous and deceptive. Why, the last one we had destroyed the sofa with its claws."

Vernon leaned close to Claudia and nipped at her jaw, his lips caressing ever so tenderly. I felt pressure on my face. Bumps raised on my arms while my cheeks flushed. I had never seen anything like this in real life. The movies, yes, but never directly in front of me. Caught up in their passion, I recrossed my legs in the other direction.

"Yes," Vernon said between kisses. "And the way they stare at you. Cats...are definitely...out of the question."

Claudia leaned into Vernon and rubbed her face against his. His left arm dropped from her ear to her breast where he began to lightly caress her nipple. The satin of her tight dress raised. My body involuntarily shook as I, too, became aroused. Luckily, I was wearing a loose oxford shirt and a padded support bra.

I could hardly believe their behavior. Never before had a couple started making out while I was at their house. In fact, my clients usually remained so restrained I never saw so much as hand holding. These people were highly unusual and I was very uncomfortable but could not look away. I felt as though I was part of their intimacy, feeling every caress and kiss. They wanted me to take part. It was difficult for me to control my desire to jump between them and join in versus remaining glued to my seat and finish the consultation. I cleared my throat and continued on, desperately trying to pretend none of this was happening.

"Do you lead an active lifestyle?" I managed to ask. "The type of pet you choose has a lot to do with your activity levels. If you like to remain...home a lot then a smaller less active dog might fit the bill better." I judged from the fact that both of them seemed pale and did not spend much time outdoors that they remained home much of the time. "A sporting dog such as a Springer Spaniel or any of the retrievers are very active animals and require much exercise." I broke off my eye contact with Claudia and glanced around the large room. I started tapping my left foot, anxiously wanting to leave. "Or a bird might be good. All you have to do is feed and water. Their cages get cleaned once a week. And some have beautiful sounds."

Vernon stopped petting Claudia and leaned back against the cushions. He took a deep breath and put his hands behind his head. Claudia remained sitting near the edge of the seat. The light from the overhead chandelier shone against her bare arms.

I felt myself breath easier, but was more than in a hurry to leave, I was desperate. I hurriedly concluded their needs whether I fully believed this to be the right pet or not. "From what I've seen of your beautiful home and busy lifestyle I would recommend a Portuguese Water Dog. They rarely shed, are mid to large in size and learn very quickly. Their ears fold over like that of a Spaniel and if you allow their coats to grow a bit they appear as puppies, even when fully matured." I inhaled, letting the air out slowly.

"I'm intrigued, Ms. Leaky," Claudia said. "Water Dogs." She put her right hand on Vernon's left thigh, her little fingers stretching upward toward his crotch. She glanced at my unrestrained foot.

I gulped and ripped my eyes away from her hand. "If one has allergies then this breed is wonderful," I rambled. "Better yet, their coloring would fit into your decor perfectly." I knew this was a concern among many wealthy people with professionally decorated homes. "They come in black or both black and white."

"Wonderful." She glanced at Vernon, squeezed his thigh

then returned her liquid gaze to me. "I can't thank you enough for helping us with this. I've wanted another pet for a long time, ever since my other one," she briefly closed her eyes, "passed on." I've kept a memento of him as I do all my pets. They're in the room down the hall. Would you care to see them?"

I really wanted to leave, but I had yet to be paid and reminded myself that I should remain mannerly, especially in a house where etiquette and appearance were of extreme importance. Except for their unrestrained ardor, I had yet to see either of them present themselves as less than high class, as though they came from another time and place. Besides, I hoped to be able to get closer to Vernon. Touch him. Kiss him? Worse yet, I wanted to rest my face against Claudia's chest. My feelings were in a jumble. Why would I want to kiss this man whom I barely knew, especially with his wife right there? Yet, the thought of being near Claudia while being fondled by Vernon was very appealing. I could not trust my own thoughts.

I glanced at my watch trying to intimate that I had other places to be. "I do have another appointment to get to, but I guess I could take a quick look." I stood and stepped away from the chair, my clipboard held against my chest while I slung my handbag over my shoulder.

Claudia clapped her hands with delight. "You won't be but a minute, I promise."

Vernon climbed to his feet and offered his right hand for Claudia to hold as she rose. Standing side by side, they were awesome. I had never seen two people so perfect for each other in both appearance and demeanor. Not only were they deeply in love, wore matching outfits and stood tall and beautiful, the very air around them was charged with their magnetism. Not a single person could pass these two without several serious second glances. I was drawn to them.

Claudia took a step forward, glanced back at me and took

my hand. "Come," she purred. "Come and see my collection." Her hand though smooth as silk was as cold as ice.

Clutching my belongings, I followed, mesmerized by her voice. My feet moved of their own volition, my eyes remaining fixed on the wavy brown hair falling down her back, the ends nearly to the swell of her buttocks. The short sleeves of her dress revealed her fair skin from her shoulders, giving the appearance of white stripes on either side of a black expanse of satin. I felt as though hypnotized by the movement of black on white and white on black, the non-colors interchanging, but not their shapes as they moved against each other. My eyelids drooped. I looked at the floor. I saw my reflection but not Claudia's.

I felt Vernon behind me, an electric presence drawing me closer to Claudia, sandwiched between them. I yearned to fall into his arms, feel his hands caress my cheeks and breasts. Would he utter a shriek of surprise if I did this, or would he laugh and push me away thinking I simply mistepped?

Claudia led us out of the sitting room, back into the foyer and then down a long hall where I saw swinging doors at the end. I did not notice the decor as before. Black on white, white on black, the man behind me, his hands reaching for me? Fine hairs rose along the back of my neck. I assured myself I was delusional, until I felt his hand fall on my shoulder.

I jumped.

He laughed.

Claudia quickly glanced behind at me, smiled, then turned and opened a door to our right. Reaching through the opening, she waved her hand. Soft light poured over the threshold. It was not as bright as the other rooms. I did not think much about it at the time, but looking back, if I had been in a clear frame of mind I might have thought the light came from a lamp at the far end of the room. I would have been wrong, further bruising my delusional mind.

Candelabra graced the surfaces of two tables in the center of the room. Speculation on how the woman had lit all these candles with one swipe of her hand nowhere near them threatened to draw me over the brink of sanity.

With Vernon's hand upon my shoulder, trying hard to not push myself further into him or, as my sane inner self pleaded, run out from under, I entered.

I ventured forth into the bowels of Hell. Granted, I had entered that place almost an hour ago, but it was at this time I began to realize my predicament. Claudia and Vernon Detross were not merely wealthy eccentrics, they were downright dangerous.

I pulled my hand out of Claudia's grip and turned to run. I could not take even two steps. Vernon stood between me and the door. He put his hands on my shoulders and turned me around. I felt electricity at his touch, but was well aware I was in a bad situation. My heart beat so fast I thought I would go into cardiac arrest. I gasped.

With Vernon pushing me forward and Claudia luminous before me, the candle light shining like an aura around her, I stepped further into the room. Dancing lights reflected in the many eyes all around me, giving the appearance of life where none should be. Brown eyes, black eyes, yellow and green. I saw the stuffed forms of cats, dogs, some reptiles and a pot-bellied pig. Some of the cats were of the larger variety such as lions and cougars. The canines, with the exception of one gray wolf, were mostly domestic breeds. One was a German Shepherd. I did not see any Spaniels.

The animals were arranged in rows along the walls so that anyone who entered this taxidermy museum could see all of them by walking in a circle. Their forms were made to stand upright, on all fours, mouths closed and eyes cast down. Tails peeked out from between some of the dog's legs, while the cats tails were allowed to lay down against the floor. None were formed to look vicious, as most hunters like to make their trophies. The owners of these pets wanted submission and that is what they got in the end; complete submission.

"What do you think?" Claudia turned and looked at me, her eyes glistening with pride. "You see? I've had many pets. I know how difficult they are to manage at times, but when they give me problems..." Her voice trailed off as she swept her hands around the room. "I'm not worried about our next pet though. With your help I'm sure to have a perfect one."

My mouth dropped open. I had heard of people who loved their animals so much that after the pet died a natural death they had them stuffed so that the pet could always be with them. However, those people had kept their pets with them all the time while the animal was alive. They spoiled them. Besides, when the pet was stuffed it was usually placed in a relaxed position, similar to laying on its owner's lap or before a fireplace – never standing with its eyes cast down.

Claudia's collection was gruesome. The enormity of it and the reasons it existed were beyond my comprehension. She had not loved these creatures, only used them for her own amusement and, when they caused problems, she killed them. Every fiber of my being screamed to race out of that house. I shook all over. Vernon's hands held me in check.

I looked up over my shoulder into his face. His smile was stoic, eyes cold, but I could still feel my body reacting to his touch – wanting his hands to travel downward, his lips to caress my neck.

Claudia took my right hand and firmly pulled me forward. She led me toward the far side of the room. "Come, I must show you my last pet. He remained in our care longer than any of these others, but then he, too, started to get destructive." Her eyes clouded briefly. "I just can't tolerate destructive pets."

"As I stated before, dear, your temper is quite bad," Vernon said, his voice so close he seemed to be speaking directly in my ear. "I keep telling you to take it easier if you want to keep your pets around longer." He let go of my shoulders and pushed me gently at the center of my back. I stumbled forward. My clipboard fell to the floor, papers scattering. Claudia's grip on my right hand kept me from falling.

"How would you suggest I punish for chewing problems?" Claudia asked me with sincerity as we neared the far end of the room. The sad face of a lion drew nearer, flanked on one side by a German Shorthair Pointer and on the other by a Bloodhound.

We were getting closer to the stuffed animals than I wanted to. I always had an aversion to taxidermied wildlife and seeing all these former pets in their unnatural states was very disturbing.

At first I could not speak. Claudia stared at me expecting an answer. I forced my words out. "I...you...first make sure you watch them or keep them locked somewhere...where they can't get...into trouble," I stammered. "You...can catch them...in...the act and then they know...why they are being punished." My feet staggered across the floor. My body felt very heavy. Somehow I was moving as quickly as Claudia. "If...the dog has done something...wrong behind your back, then...you take him by the...his...collar and show him while you say...no." Normally I would add a more serious means of punishment such as shake by the scruff, but Claudia did not need any more violent ideas.

"Ah, here we are, my favorite in the collection." She released my hand and lit a candle sitting in a simple silver holder on a nearby table. She did not use matches. The light revealed more than I ever again want to see in my life. My throat constricted and I fell backward. Vernon caught me in his arms. I did not feel safe. Highly aroused and as attracted to a man as I'd ever been, but not safe. He laughed. Not a verbal chuckle, only enough to make his chest heave.

"He was lots of fun," Claudia rubbed the head of her last

pet, gently touching his hair and brows. Her hand hesitated on his neck where she fingered two punctures along the carotid artery. She slid her pink tongue over her red lips, then continued to caress down his bare back and stop at his buttocks. I recognized the man she fondled. His straight red hair, brown/green skin, (the green hue due to whatever stuffing and preserving process they had used), and gray eyes were those of Steve Fowler. He had been "arranged" on all fours, like the others, face staring forever at the floor. I suddenly realized why business had picked up lately.

"He could do so much more than Vernon's shepherd." Claudia closed her eyes and touched her breast with the palm of her left hand. She turned and looked at me. "I just had to have another. And a female would be easier to train; less messy." She wriggled her nose, nostrils flaring, then rushed at me. Her face was inches from my own. Her hand touched my cheek and moved down my neck. "You're everything I wanted."

My skin responded to her touch, becoming warm as surface capillaries filled with blood. I deeply inhaled her scent of death.

"You will be good won't you?" She licked her lips and smiled. A full mouth smile. I saw large, pointed incisors. "I promise to take really good care of you."

I remain forever twenty-one, a sanguinary parasite seeking only perpetual and untainted nourishment. No smorgasbord of partners for me, pure blood free of disease and drugs is essential. I can become severely ill though I cannot die. At least not from the usual mortal maladies.

Something I Can Never Have

Lynda Licina

GWF iso GF. Race and age unimportant. Lover of the night with no earthly bonds seeking kindred spirits of similar background to establish a lineage of our own. I love dark...dark skin, dark hair, dark eyes...mysterious. Living and loving by the illumination of the full moon. A great mind, excellent health and creative spirit. Are you listening? I crave what you can give. I am Anaïs. Reply box 8267

So I neglected to mention that I'm a vampire and my girlfriend will become 'flavor of the month' or should I say year? The girl will find out soon enough.

The ad appears almost annually, those damn mortals don't live forever. The blood I give them keeps their faces lovely and young but does nothing to slow their biological clock. Quite the opposite, it speeds up the internal ticking to the extreme.

Yes, the personals method is deceiving but screening my cuisine is the best way to ensure they fit certain specifications. It's necessary that extraneous relatives are not part of the feast, I'm not into dessert or messy cleanups.

I was part of a family once, at least biologically. Mother, father and assorted siblings. (Sounds like giblets doesn't it?) Foster homes became my life at the age of two according to the few facts my adoptive parents offered before they selfishly took all further knowledge to their graves. I had nothing to do with that trip.

I've tried unsuccessfully to locate my biological mother. If I had found her I'd have only spit my hate upon her for denying me a normal childhood.

As a developing sociopath, I knew it was best to remain unattached. The streets became my family, the members changed from city to city. Life left a bad taste in my mouth. And no dinner mint can wash away the bitter aftertaste.

I met the woman who changed my life forever at twenty one. An alcohol influenced liaison climaxed in the sharing of the elixir that transformed the little girl into the femme fatale and a new reality...*Immortality.*

After that, why would I even consider searching for my family? To lose them again as I watch them die?

I remain forever twenty-one, a sanguinary parasite seeking only perpetual and untainted nourishment. No smorgasbord of partners for me, pure blood free of disease and drugs is essential. I can become severely ill though I cannot die. At least not from the usual mortal maladies.

I telephone the service for messages, three responses...not bad.

BEEP... *"Hi, Anaïs, cool name, I'm Amber. Your ad was intriguing, and I'm into you. I'm 5'7", 125 lbs., dark hair, eyes and complexion, like my name. I'm into performing art and nights, like you. No drugs, I'm healthy and unoccupied, digging someone to hang with. Been solo since 16, when my adoptive mother's life license expired. Her second husband evicted me 'cause I refused to put out. No idea where his private parts are hangin' these days. Anyway, call me back girl, I'd dig meeting you. 555-7545. Ciao."*

BEEP..."*Hi. My name is Mark. (a guy always calls.) I think we know..."*
DELETE...

BEEP... *"Hi. I don't usually answer personals but...My name is Annie. I'm older than most people who respond to these ads, 47, but you said age was unimportant. I don't look my age. I have no one in the world and loneliness is hell. My health is fair, I've had a few heart problems in the past, but I'm okay now. I'm olive-skinned with brown eyes and dark brown hair with a little grey. I love nights, mornings, afternoons, whatever. My day and evening numbers are the same, 555-4089. I work temp jobs. Hope you call, you sound nice. Bye."*

Two excellent prospects. I ring Annie.

◆

She arrives at my loft exactly at 8:00 pm, punctual. She is as she described herself. I'd have guessed her age at 35, very pretty in a non-descript way. I see sadness in her eyes when they meet my gaze.

Dinner is delivered, I push food around on my plate.

"Not hungry, nervous," I explain.

Wine and conversation flows. She's easy to talk to, she smells delicious. Annie's inspiration died young, when her babies were taken away. Authorities cited 'child endangerment' but the reality was bad luck and poverty.

We kiss, awakening years of buried passion. The hunger

is potent, lovemaking is spontaneous. As Annie orgasms, I christen her with canine penetration, her taste, divine. (They never remember the piercing, just the ecstasy.) Night evolves into morning, morning turns into months.

Annie is so unlike the soft-focus mortals I usually take from, I'm in love with my food!

Three months into happy oblivion, she is taken from me, heart embolism it's termed, clotted blood. Again happiness eludes me, why must I say goodbye so often? With no one to claim her lifeless body, she'll stay with me forever. In my 'family room'.

I drag her coffin up the stairs to the room. As long as I am earthbound, my lovers will remain exactly as they were when we said goodbyes. The vital fluid of life I have exchanged with them lingers in their veins and preserves their beauty. I lay Annie upon the satin and seal her coffin with glass etched in lillies, to frame her lovely face for eternity.

"Annie, meet your sisters. This is Candace, Elaine, Deborah, and over here, Evelyn, Crystal and Pamela. Girls: Annie. Be good to her."

> *GWF iso GF. Race and age unimportant. Lover of the night with no earthly bonds seeking kindred spirits of similar background to establish a lineage of our own. I love dark...dark skin, dark hair, dark eyes...mysterious. Living and loving by the illumination of the full moon. A great mind, excellent health and creative spirit. Are you listening? I crave what you can give. I am Anaïs. Reply box 8267.*

Two replies.

BEEP... *"I called you awhile back, guess you haven't met your dream girl yet. Well, here I am honey, it's Amber. 555-7545.* Call me damn it!"

BEEP... *"Hey, it's me, Mark. You never returned my last..."* DELETE.

I open the door when she arrives. *I'm looking in a fucking mirror!* Amber's my spitting image with attitude to match, so cool...cold...like dry ice.

Her tragic (trivial) story unfolds. She wants pity but I have none to give. My vampiric defenses are piqued but soon the hunger takes control. Instinctively I grasp chestnut hair forcing her head back, and kiss her brutally, masking the fact that I've bitten, I've tasted. Bitter, but I'll get used to it.

Amber is controlling, she moves in and takes over. Wants this, demands that. I provide her with everything, but she's never satisfied. Eventually I give up placating her and return the contempt.

It's a torturous game, who will break first? The score is even...until she discovers my room.

I can't let her go now, as much as I'd love to. Like an ill-tempered pet I must restrain Amber, she's my prisoner, nothing more. One evening as I unbind her, she pulls out a crudely-sharpened wooden stake. Scraping the point against my throat, she draws a thin trickle, precious fluid.

"Oh, is that for me? Where's the popsicle?" I ask. "Sorry sweetie, game over, *I win!*"

I rip through her jugular with unmerciful bloodthirst. Holding her inanimate body, I gaze into unseeing eyes and feed. But her blood no longer satisfies me. Like Chinese food, I'm hungry again within minutes.

Amber wasn't well-behaved in life, but she was virtuous in death. I ready her place in the room.

Something I Can Never Have

> *GWF iso GF. Race and age unimportant. Lover of the night with no earthly bonds seeking kindred spirits of similar background to establish a lineage of our own. I love dark...dark skin, dark hair, dark eyes...mysterious. Living and loving by the illumination of the full moon. A great mind, excellent health and creative spirit. Are you listening? I crave what you can give. I am Anaïs. Reply box 8267.*

When I call to retrieve my responses, Mark has called continuously using up my allotted mailbox time. *Fuck!* He's pleading.

"*Please* talk to me. Your past, I know things. Please call, 555-0741, I have to talk..."

I ring him, the relief in his voice is disconcerting. I extend an invitation for "conversation only", at my place. He arrives and I'm relieved to see that he doesn't fit the psychopath profile. Dark, rugged features with sincere brown eyes. I shake his hand, it's somehow intimate.

"Okay, talk."

He does...words spill out so rapidly I'm sure he's speaking a foreign language.

"I think we're...no, I *know* we are...related. I'm adopted. Like you. Researched endlessly. Single mom, sister, you, me. I'm the oldest. You and the other girl – were twins, well...still are. Foster homes...before we could remember. I know who they are now, mother and sister I mean. Tried contacting them with no luck, they've just kind of vanished. Still looking though. Won't give up..."

I sit on my feet, enthralled, and ask "How did you find me?"

"I saw you about eight years ago, in a bar. I just had a feeling who you were. The name proved it, Anaïs isn't common. I tried to follow you, lost you, found you, lost you, what a rollercoaster. I wanted to be one hundred percent sure before I approached. Then you completely disappeared about six years ago, but I kept searching. I saw your ad in *Nightlines* a year ago, the name thing again. I called your box number, you never called back. Couldn't find a listing for you in the phone book and when your ad wasn't running, your box number wasn't active. Recently I saw it again, I called, but as before, no response..."

I interrupt, "I deleted your calls, you're a guy, I wasn't interested."

"Finally you called. I can't wait to tell you what I know, to have my sister again." We talk into the night. I've spent a lifetime denying it but I would have given anything for the chance to meet my mother. I want to know everything. *I have a brother!*

It's late. The hunger rises. I hear his words but my body is oblivious. An appetizer can't hurt, I think. He won't remember. As a blood relative, the taste of his nectar will be infinitely sweeter. I am so hungry. Take his wrist, pierce the skin, the warm flow is pure honey.

A flood of visions, I see the past. Two girls wear identical outfits, me and my twin! Innocent children being taken. A mother in hysterics.

"Don't take my babies...I *have* to work, babysitters cost money, I have none. I work to feed them, they're my babies. please...don't take them...*pleeeease."*

I see everything with crystal clarity. She was a devoted mom. We were her life, her reason for being. I feel my hate for her being replaced by a deep love. Her face is distorted by tears but I see something familiar in the features.

Mark interrupts this visionary reunion with his shrieks.

"What are you doing to me? Get away from me, you freak!"

I underestimated the trance-hold I had on him.

"Calm down, I won't hurt you." I sense my reassurance is not being accepted. "Mark, let me explain about me...

everything. It sounds incredible but I am a vampire. Transformed about the time you said I disappeared. You didn't see me anymore because I couldn't tolerate the sunlight. I live in the shadows of the night now. We're real, and I *need* blood. I only feed, I never take more than is required, I'm not a killer. My lovers are my donors. Easier than take out!"

I laugh in attempt to alleviate his fear and revulsion.

"I want to help you find the rest of our family. But I still need to eat. In the meantime, if I could take a small amount from you now and then...?"

Mark makes me promise I won't hurt him. Why he trusts me I'll never know, but he agrees and I feed.

"What eventually happens to the people you drink from? Do they die? Do *they* turn into vampires too?"

"My lovers, as with all mortals, eventually die. But they age internally at a greatly accelerated rate as I feed upon their life essence. I'm partly responsible, for their premature death I mean, so I take care of them. Come with me, I'll show you."

As we climb the stairs I mention, "I saw this in a movie once." (I'm not sure he gets the reference.)

We arrive at the door, which I unlock to reveal a sight he is not ready for.

"My God! Eight coffins?! You've killed eight girls for your survival?"

"No! I've assured eight women infinite peace. I've used them for my survival but they're not immortal. I provide them sanctuary and sit with them every night. They're content to remain here and I'll always take care of them, that's my promise. Forever.

Mark steps into the room, over-cautiously, looking down into each coffin as we talk.

"Beautiful girls, and so young looking."

"I have taste," I respond.

I gesture at the coffin before me.

"Sadly my latest two loves met with premature ends. I

would have loved Annie forever, (at least for her forever) but she had serious medical problems and died just months after we met. Died of 'natural causes' as they say. Amber however was too much like me, beautiful but impudent. Never satisfied with the lavish life I provided for her, she was a terror. She tried to kill me. So what could I do? I had to destroy her, it's survival."

Mark begins to run from coffin to coffin, scanning the faces of my former loves.

The girls smile serenely up at him through the embellished glass.

He screams, the scream of nightmares.

"Mother! and, Amber! Oh God!" My brother turns on me with a fierceness, a killing look in his eyes. I can smell his blood, hot blood. *Food.* "You're a demon, you *are* a killer! You knew them! You've taken them from me. Forever!" His words sear my skin as the sunrise would.

I recoil. "No! I didn't know. I should have seen it in the blood vision...but they *didn't know!* I would never have... never..."

He rips a glass lid from its delicate hinges and raises it over his head.

"Is it true how they kill monsters like you? Can I slice right through your dead heart?"

He moves forward to carry out his vengeance.

What can I do?

Get him first. It's the game. It's *always* the game.

I scream, "I'm sorry...Mark, I'm sorry", and hurl myself at him.

I *always* win the game.

"Mark, don't hate me, I love you." I slash his throat to shreds with razorlike fingernails, press my mouth to his neck and drink in his memories, his dreams, his nightmares. I feed until his pulse ceases.

"I love you Mark." I lie down beside him and sleep, as the

daylight breaks over the city.

In the evening, I drag the new coffin upstairs. Mahogany for someone special. I lay the remains gently on the cream colored satin, trying to convince myself he looks at peace. I slide him into place between mother, and the sister who mirrors the image of his killer. I kiss the cold hard glass.

Downstairs I pour a goblet of wine, and locate my camera.

Returning upstairs, I sit and chat with my family. How fabulous it is to finally be reunited. I toast my guests, *"Na Zdorovye!"* and drink.

Framing three coffins in the camera viewfinder, I engage the self-timer. I cross the room and take my place among Mom, Amber and Mark. The shutter releases, the flash illuminates the endless night. I have my souvenir photo, 'Family Reunion 1998'. Together again.

> *GWF iso GF. Race and age unimportant. Lover of the night with no earthly bonds seeking kindred spirits of similar background to establish a lineage of our own. I love dark...dark skin, dark hair, dark eyes...mysterious. Living and loving by the illumination of the full moon. A great mind, excellent health and creative spirit. Are you listening? I crave what you can give. I am Anaïs. Reply box 8267.*

Looking at him now, she found herself believing him. She had no reason other than the sincerity of his gaze. She knew somehow that he, above all others, would understand. Taking a deep breath, she told him everything. She started with the bleeding, the pain and shame...

A Month of Bleeding

Tippi N. Blevins

Theresa made a quick check of the store to make sure no one remained inside and then closed the door. She flipped over the sign in the window to read "closed" and drew the blinds. This was her favorite time of the day, when she had the store to herself and the smell of the old books surrounded her. She would go to pour herself a cup of coffee and then gather the money to take to the bank. It was a much-loved ritual, something that added regularity to her life.

But first, damn it, she had to go to the bathroom again. She was bleeding heavily this month, and with the blood came a familiar sense of dread.

She was about to lock the door when a hand closed on her shoulder.

Theresa gasped and turned around. The shock of seeing someone where she had expected not to quickly dissipated and she realized that this was only a boy. No more than eighteen or nineteen. Bright blond hair a little greasy, dark blue eyes startling in the luminous white face. A coarse black sweater and loose-fitting pants seemed to swallow him. The hands that peeked out from the ends of his sleeves looked like five-winged white doves, fragile and somehow quite pretty, and clutched a small leather-bound volume of poetry.

"I didn't mean to startle you," the boy said, his voice incongruously deep. He thrust out the book. "How much for this?"

She peered at the volume. In worn gilded letters, the title read *Poems For Flesh and Blood.* She didn't recognize the author's name inscribed just below. She glanced up at the boy. "May I? I just need to open it and see if it's been priced." He hugged the book to his chest. "I promise I'll give it right back."

At last he handed the book to her, but kept his hands outstretched as if waiting to receive it again. "Please," he said, "I must have it. I've been searching for this book for a long time."

A part of her wanted to laugh – what was a long time to someone so young? But when she looked up, the intensity of his gaze startled her. She caught a minute reflection of herself in his eyes: short, light brown hair, wire-rim glasses that slid to the tip of her nose, eyes that looked too old and too tired in a face that would not be young much longer.

"This must be one of our newer acquisitions," she murmured. She fingered the well-worn leather binding. *Poems by Simon Fournier.* "I – I wouldn't know what to charge you for it until the store owner comes back in the morning."

"No!"

Theresa jerked back, surprised by the volume of this frail-looking creature's voice.

He said, quieter this time, but with the same urgency, "No. Please, I must have this book. I'll pay whatever you ask. It is imperative that I bring this book home to my master."

Theresa felt her brows arch involuntarily. His master? A

shiver coursed her spine even as she tried to shrug off her sudden feeling of unease.

"Look," she offered, "I'll set it aside for you. I'll make certain no one gets it. You can come back in the morning –"

But the boy was already grabbing the book from her and shoving her out of the way with surprising strength. She caught the edge of the desk and faught to maintain her balance. Her hand skidded into a stack of books and they went clattering to the floor.

"Hey, wait –" she called out. "Come back here!"

The boy didn't even glance over his shoulder as he disappeared through the door and down the street.

Theresa entertained a brief thought of chasing the boy down – she had seen reports on the news of store clerks apprehending criminals – but the detested, familiar dampness in her crotch held her as surely as iron bonds.

Nearly weeping, Theresa pulled herself together and locked the door.

◆

She was roused from sleep later that night by the feel of Robert's hands on her waist. She froze, stiffening, and waited for her husband to withdraw.

Robert groaned and rolled away from her. "Jesus, Theresa, it's been two weeks."

She curled into herself, tucking one fist under her chin and the other just below her belly button where the pain was the worst. "I'm sorry," she said quietly. The pain was not so bad as the wholly unclean feeling. It made her feel dirty and animal. It made her uneasy, and it made Robert short with her.

"This has been going on for months, Theresa. I can't touch my own wife two weeks out of the month. When are you going to see the doctor?"

"He's going to tell me the same thing he told me last time."

"What's that?"

"That I'll have to go on the pill." She waited a few seconds for Robert to sigh, to acquiesce, but he said nothing. She looked over her shoulder at him, saw that his jaw was firmly set and that his eyes looked like two slivers of tar. "You don't want me to go on the pill," she said incredulously.

He looked down, the muscles in his jaw still tense. "Maybe it wouldn't be such a bad idea."

Theresa sat up, ignoring the tangible rush of blood from her womb. "They make me sick, Robert!" It was the first time she could remember shouting at him; it felt good. Encouraged, she went on, "How could you ask me to do such a thing!"

He looked up, his face soft and charming again. "Baby, baby. Calm down. It was just an idea. Don't get all bent out of shape."

When he reached out to embrace her, Theresa pushed herself off the bed. Her head felt light and a pool of warm wetness formed between her legs. She felt blood cool on the inside of her thighs. *Oh God, it's really out of control, isn't it?* She looked down at the bed and saw a bright red rosette of blood where she'd lain just moments before. Her stomach turned.

Robert looked down, too, and saw the stain. His face wrinkled into a mask of disgust. "Now look at what you've done."

She was trembling. "I – I didn't *do* it, Robert. It – it – it just happened."

"It – it – it," he stuttered, mimicking her. He got out of bed and began pulling off the sheets. "Look, the mattress is stained, too. Do I have to get you a plastic liner like they get for babies who wet the bed?"

The pain in her belly twisted and snapped like a coiled snake. Between that and the horrible shame, she couldn't speak. Her eyes felt hot, as if she would cry, but no tears came.

At least she could be glad of that.

Robert glanced her way as he flipped the mattress over. "For God's sake, Theresa, go get yourself cleaned up."

She forced herself to nod and walk out of the bedroom. Her legs felt like wood. Blood, warm at first and then growing cold, dribbled down the back of her leg. She ran to keep from staining the rug, too.

Once in the bathroom, she locked the door behind her and ran a tub of warm water. She poured in a capful of bubblebath and ran more water. Avoiding her reflection in the mirror, she pulled off her nightgown and tossed it into the hamper. Her panties came off next, but they were so stained she threw them into the trash and stuffed wads of toilet paper on top to keep them hidden.

A soft knock at the door. "Theresa? Honey, I'm sorry. You know I am. I just worry about you, that's all. You know I love you, right?"

She didn't say anything.

"Honey, look, I'm going to make an appointment for you to see the doctor on Monday. Will you go? Honey? Will you go?"

The water, when she submerged herself to the neck in it, turned instantly pink.

"I'll go," she said, and the tears finally came.

◆

At work the next day she did not tell Miss James about what she had already started to think of as the *Fournier incident.* The book was probably without value anyway, she reasoned, probably something bought in a trunk at an estate sale for a few dollars. Nothing to worry over. Theresa resolved herself to finding out the book's value and slowly infusing the cash drawer with funds out of her own pocket. A dollar here and there. It would be like buying the book herself. And no one would ever have to know what a dismal failure she was.

All because of her period! Theresa hated it, hated the feeling of weakness. Surely she was anemic by now, from the constant loss of blood. She noticed how pale her skin was, saw a yellowish cast to her face in certain light. This couldn't go on forever, she thought. She would bleed to death. The idea didn't frighten her as much as it once had.

After Miss James left for the night, Theresa busied herself with tidying up the store. Books stacked everywhere in precarious paper towers. Newspapers like faded gray fortresses. She started at the front and worked her way back, in a better mood now that she was on that blissful last day of her period. The blood flow was light now, almost inconsequential. Tomorrow it would be gone entirely. Robert would be so glad...

"Pardon me," a voice said behind her.

She spun around and saw a man with hair so black it was almost blue. Soft, thick waves fell to his shoulders. Raven's wings. He was not tall by any means, but he exuded an aura of importance. Despite the shabby state of his denim jeans and the dusty sweater he wore, he looked to Theresa somehow noble.

She cleared her throat, willed herself not to stutter. "Yes, may I – may I help you?"

"I think I can help you, actually." He smiled and from his back pocket pulled out a slim leather-bound book. He handed it to her.

"The book!" she gasped.

"I'm afraid my assistant took it from your store last night. You must forgive him, he was only trying to serve me."

Theresa glanced up into startlingly green eyes. Shards of jade, they were that pure, that bottomlessly green. She remembered suddenly what the boy had said last night. *My master.* As she had last night, she shivered now.

"Thank you," she said. The leather grew warm in her hands. Like butter melting. "I'll find out how much it's worth tomorrow –"

The stranger was already reaching into his pockets again,

pulling out wads of crumpled money. He unfolded three hundred dollar bills and held them out. "Is this enough?"

"I –" She could say nothing for several moments. The store had not made three hundred dollars all week.

He unfolded another bill on top. "Is this enough now?"

"Yes!" she breathed, laughing. "I imagine it is!"

He smiled, too. Looking at him, she found it impossible to guess his age. He could have been twenty or thirty. He had an odd ageless quality, like a statue made of white marble. Lines showed around his eyes when he smiled, but a moment later disappeared and left his face absolutely flawless.

He handed her the money; the strange, cool touch of his hand brought her laughter to a halt. "Again, I apologize for the actions of my...assitant. He simply knew how vitally important it was to me to get this book. We've been looking the world over. The world is a much wider place than I'd ever imagined."

The silence that followed was somehow utterly intimate. Without words, they were forced to stare at one another. Study one another. His gaze was intense and personal. He stepped closer and breathed deeply.

"Ah," he sighed, "you smell...delicious."

She backed away, suddenly uncomfortable. "The store will be closing –"

He advanced, inhaling again. "Yes, a woman's perfume. Nothing else like it. Sweet, perfect. So pure. Intoxicating."

"Please," she said, her voice firm. She pointed over his shoulder toward the door. "Leave now."

He paused, as if considering it, licked his lips, then began slowly to back away. He gave an oddly elegant little half-bow, turned, and merged with the shadows on the street so completely that he seemed merely to disappear.

The man came back to the bookstore every night the next two weeks. She learned his name was Simon, just like the poet's. When she asked if he had been named for Fournier, he laughed and said, "Something like that, yes."

"I never heard of him," she admitted as she organized books in the history shelves. "But then I'm no expert on poetry."

He handed her books from a stack on the floor and she arranged them on the topmost shelf. "He only published one volume of poetry. He printed one hundred copies, each with gilded pages, illuminated text, the finest leather binding. But that was over two centuries ago. Rumor has it that most copies were destroyed during the French Revolution when the houses of the nobles were ransacked. Mine may very well be the last copy in existence."

They shelved books in silence for the next few minutes. Theresa had been wary of him the first couple of days – espcially after his odd remarks about her scent the first time they met. He was unusual, to say the least. He watched her with an unnerving scrutiny, as if studying her every move and nuance. What could he find so interesting about her – she who looked wholly unextraordinary, pale and drab? He once told her that she had a quiet passion, very intense, burning, but buried deep within. The remark should have disconcerted her, but instead it ignited a small ember of pride. She carried the glow like a secret gift. A quiet passion. It was something the rest of the world would never know about her.

The next night he came to help organize the romance novels. Her period had started that very morning, exactly two weeks since it last ended. The respite had been an all-too brief paradise. She had taken her newly prescribed pill, became violently ill within the hour, but went to work anyway. She had told herself she was merely devoted to her job, and that her persistence had nothing to do with Simon.

"You don't look well," Simon remarked as he handed her

a stack of well-worn books. Buxom women and muscular men made love on every cover; Theresa blushed hotly. Simon's fingers encircled her wrist. "Are you not feeling well, Theresa? Perhaps you should sit for a while? You look pale. Your skin is so cold."

"I'm just a little queasy," she laughed nervously. She didn't pull away from him. When was the last time she'd let Robert touch her for so long? "I'm all right."

He helped her up the ladder, bracing her legs when she started to weave. Her knees gave way and she felt herself falling away from the ladder. Strong hands went around her waist, steadying her. Simon hugged her close, his face in the small of her back.

"Oh, your smell," he breathed. "You're so lovely, Theresa, do you know how lovely you are?"

"Please, let me go," she said. She could hardly hear her own voice above the thudding of her heart. A sharp pain in the pit of her belly like a bear trap snapping shut on her womb. "Let me go."

He lifted her off the ladder, surprising her utterly. He didn't look strong enough.

He set her down beside the shelves. "Please, Theresa, you need to sit down. Tell me what's wrong. I will help."

Looking at him now, she found herself believing him. She had no reason other than the sincerity of his gaze. She knew somehow that he, above all others, would understand. Taking a deep breath, she told him everything. She started with the bleeding, the pain and shame, Robert's impatience, and ended with the pills that made her so ill.

Simon's jade eyes flashed. "What kind of man is your husband? How could he not understand what you're going through? He should love you all the more for what you are. You are a rare treasure, Theresa."

She shook her head. "No, no, you don't understand. Robert just wants what's best for me. He – he's really a very kind man,

Simon, you'd know that if you knew him. He's charming and romantic, buys me flowers all the time. He just gets short with me sometimes, and I can't say that I blame him –"

Simon stood. "Don't make excuses for him, Theresa. You deserve better." He held out his hand. "Come with me."

She glanced around the store. "I – I can't. The store's not closed yet..."

"Then close it."

Again she looked up into those measureless eyes and found herself turning, giving in, somehow knowing that she must go with him.

Slowly, she nodded, slipped her hand into his, and let herself be led away.

◆

From the sidewalk, the house looked dark and abandoned, a great hulking remnant of the Antebellum South. The wrought iron gates had rusted into precarious guardians. Vines of yellow jasmine grew up over the walls, scenting the evening air with thick, sweet perfume. The windows, gaping and broken, revealed the blackness of the house within.

As she and Simon approached, however, Theresa could see the amber flicker of candles through fragments of sooty glass. When he pulled open the doors, laughter drifted out. Male voices, throaty and rough. She glanced over her shoulder at Simon who nodded his encouragement. His arm went protectively around her waist. A word came to her: Shelter. She thought at first that Simon had said it, but when she looked at him she realized he had not spoken.

"Adam," he called out, startling her. The laughter ended abruptly. "Joseph, Miguel, Paul, come here."

Candles infiltrated the darkness, creating orbs of molten light in the immense ballroom, revealing the faces of those who held them. Shadows played on cracked marble floors.

She recognized the blond boy from the store two weeks earlier. He looked away when their eyes met.

"Adam," Simon said, and made a summoning gesture with his free hand. The blond boy stepped forward. "Do you still have the money I gave you? Good. Go and buy supper – steak, broth, wine, loaves of bread – and bring it back here."

Theresa shook her head. "I can't eat. I'm ill."

"Then all the more reason you should eat," Simon said. "You are too thin. Let me feed you."

His stare was so intense that she gave in immediately, nodded, looked away.

As Adam departed, the three others came forward and Simon introduced them each in turn. Joseph looked older than the others, perhaps in his early forties. His sandy hair was just a little thin at the temples. Miguel appeared to be the same age as Adam. He had very dark hair, a long, elegant nose and black eyes that seemed unusually serene for his age. Paul had long blond hair, a quick smile, and a charming manner. He reached out, took her hand, kissed it and then, bowing, retreated a step back with a flourish.

"Now you've met my family," Simon said beside her. She looked up at him, confused. "These are my brothers, and my sons."

She laughed before she could think to stop herself. "Don't be silly, Simon. How could –" But the question died on her lips. He looked at her with utter seriousness. He was either completely mad, or totally honest. She couldn't quite decide which, but a cold shiver of fear touched the flesh between her shoulder blades just the same.

Miguel spoke next. "Simon, what are you doing?" His voice was a harsh whisper. "You said there would be no death!"

Paul giggled. "He isn't going to kill her. Can't you see he's in love with her?"

"Shut up!" Simon commanded. His arm tightened

around her waist. "I didn't want her to find out like this. You two stop your bickering."

She began to tremble. "Find out what? Simon, I want to leave."

Joseph stepped forward, circled around to her left, breathed deeply as he came close. "Ah, that explains it," he said, eyes glittering. "She's in heat. He's in love with the blood between her legs."

Theresa gave a small, choked cry. Her face warmed. She struggled to free herself from Simon's embrace, and failed.

Joseph raised an eyebrow at Simon. "Were you planning on sharing her –"

In a blur of motion, Simon released Theresa and grabbed Joseph around the neck. "You shut up right now," Simon breathed. "Or I shall break my promise, and it will be your death that breaks it."

When Simon released him, Joseph stumbled backwards, lips pressed together against further words.

Theresa saw the opportunity to escape. She turned, but her legs moved too slowly, and Simon caught her wrist and drew her to him. She grunted and shoved against him, but his hold on her remained firm.

"Sh," he cooed. "Sh, my Theresa, look up at me now. Listen to my voice. See my eyes, know my intention. My Theresa, my love."

Again she found herself in a state of surrender, not quite knowing how she had come to be there, but that she wanted to remain.

◆

She woke to the scent of gardenias.

She sat up, remembering where she was, felt moisture cooling on her skin. A hand closed on her ankle and she cried out.

"It's all right," Simon said, smiling gently. "You're safe."

The room she was in glowed with the light of a dozen candles. The bed beneath her was musty, but elegant in brocade covers and satin pillows. A wash basin of water – were those gardenia petals floating in there? – sat beside the bed. She realized Simon must have been bathing her. When she looked down at herself, she saw for the first time that she was naked.

No shame.

Simon's lips had not moved, and yet she had distinctly heard his voice.

No shame, only beauty.

She found herself nodding. No shame. Only beauty. Yes, of course...

"But the blood," she began, remembering her curse. The dampness at her crotch was an insistent reminder. "I'll stain the bed."

"Please don't worry about such things," he said.

"But it – it's disgusting!" she blurted out.

"You've been poisoned by men like your husband, Theresa," he said, his brow furrowed. "You should have been a goddess."

From his pocket, he pulled out Fournier's book, opened it and read:

Do you know how sweet you are?
I shall tell you with my lips.
Do you know how like wine you are?
I am stained with every sip.

When he looked up, his eyes flickered amber. For a moment, she thought it had merely been the reflection of candlelight, but the fire had come from within.

She shuddered. "You're talking about blood, aren't you? It isn't wine at all, is it?"

He kneeled on the bed beside her, taking her hands in his. "But it is wine, Theresa. And my sons – my brothers – and I are dying of thirst."

She shook her head. "I don't under –"

"We're dying."

"You're so young..."

"We are old, Theresa, and we are dying. I promised them that they would not burn in hell for their immortal gifts. But in order to fulfill that promise, we have had to suppress our very nature. I promised that there would be no killing. No, Theresa, please, listen to me, don't be frightened. I promised them that they would live forever, until such a time as we were all called to heaven. But we are dying! Two have died already, my oldest sons who had been with me a millennia. I will die, too, Theresa, and only you can help us."

She was shaking her head. It was all too much to comprehend. Blood? Thirst? Sons who had lived a thousand years? None of it made sense. She told him so.

"Look at me," he told her. "Understand what I am."

She looked at him, into those cool green eyes, and saw in them the shadows of two thousand years. She saw spilled blood, broken promises to other sons now ten centuries in the ground. She saw a father trying desperately to right what was wrong. She saw Simon Fournier – this Simon – putting pen to paper in a Paris flat in 1773. She saw him traversing the ages, ever youthful, ever thirsting. Immortal, but dying.

When he arranged her against the pillows, she did not resist. She felt his thirst in her own body as desire. He opened her legs and drank.

◆

Robert was still awake when she got home. She looked at the clock and saw that it was nearly four in the morning. She made no excuses, offered no explanations. He was in the living room, arms crossed, face as red as...as red as blood.

"Where have you been!" he roared.

She laughed. "Oh, hush, Robert. Is that how you greet your wife? Tell me you missed me."

Confusion flickered in his face. The expression of anger gave way to relief, swelled again to fury. "Why do you smell like gardenias?"

"Why does anyone smell like gardenias? Really, Robert, this isn't what you want to be doing, is it? Make love to me."

He looked her up and down. The fury faded to uncertainty. "I – I thought your period started today."

She shrugged. "So?"

His mouth wrinkled into a wide frown. "That's – that's disgusting, Theresa!"

"That's – that's – that's," she said, mimicking him. As she walked past him into the bedroom, she said, "I should have been a goddess."

◆

They all drank from her. She came to know each of them by their kiss – that most special and sweetest of kisses. Adam had been so shy at first, probably still embarrassed by what had happened at the bookstore. Miguel was quick, a little rough, and sometimes she felt his teeth on the inside of her thigh. Paul's hair tickled her belly; he was a jovial and playful lover, teasing her blood-sweetened folds with a feathery tongue. Joseph, on the other hand, took the matter seriously, rather like a business transaction, and always thanked her afterwards. Ah, but it was Simon's kiss she loved the most. His satiation was secondary to her pleasure, and she always reached orgasm when he drank from her.

Just before sunrise, the curtains would be drawn against the murderous light and they would all pile into the same bed to sleep. She would be wakened every once in a while when one of her lovers parted her legs to take another sip. It was a happy arrangement.

Robert, however, was not happy. He no longer made sexual demands of her, but he continued to demand to know her whereabouts. He showed up one night at the bookstore, unshaven and pale, and grabbed her roughly by the arms.

"You tell me where you've been spending your days, Theresa. You tell me right now."

She narrowed her eyes. "All right, you want to know? I've been –" She stopped. What was she going to say. She tried out different possibilities in her mind, and they all sounded inadequate. She couldn't bear to say she'd been having an affair. It sounded so meaningless, so mundane.

Agitated, Robert dragged her through the door. She didn't even have a chance to get her purse. "You come home with me right now, Theresa," he said hoarsely. "You're my wife; you belong in my house."

She did go home with him that night, but she slipped out when Robert's vigilance gave way to sleep. It had been over three weeks, and she had taken the pills faithfully every morning, but the blood still came. She was afraid to stop taking them – what if the bleeding stopped? Dr. Pryce had called her problem "dysfunctional uterine bleeding", and informed her that the first couple of months might be irregular. Thankfully, she no longer felt weak or anemic; she attributed her health to the loving care given her by her new lovers. They fed her to bursting, gave her sweet red wine, and bathed her with gardenia-scented water.

She stopped going to work, because Robert could find her there, and told Miss James she needed the time off due to illness. She wanted to close herself in the old plantation, where it was safe, and where Simon and his strange sons told her over and over how much they loved her.

One morning, after the curtains had been drawn and the light was a molten sliver against the wall, she turned on her side and found Simon still awake.

"What if I didn't bleed?" she asked suddenly.

He blinked. "What do you mean?"

"What if I couldn't provide what you need – what all of you need? Simon, I'm asking you if you would still love me."

He smiled gently. "Of course I would. We all would. Now go to sleep. You need your rest."

◆

She had bled for nearly four weeks. The seasons had changed in that time. The moon had cycled again.

The day after she took the last pill for the month, the bleeding ceased. The flow did not fade to a trickle; it simply stopped. She waited for the subsequent elation that always came at the end of her period. The feeling of cleanliness. Purity. Instead, she felt hollow, a wine chalice made of flesh, and went to Simon and his ancient sons for reassurance.

"Do you have any poems for this?" she asked Simon. She was trembling; she couldn't remember feeling this way in weeks. In four weeks.

He shook his head. "Theresa, it will come again. The moon rises, and so shall you."

That night, all but Simon sought the comfort of their own beds. She missed the warmth of all those bodies. Simon held her in the crook of his arm, but made no overtures. When she caressed the flat of his belly with an open palm, he merely blinked up at the ceiling, detached and unresponsive. It was then that Theresa realized that they had never kissed mouth-to-mouth.

Rising up on her elbow, she leaned over and pressed her lips to his. He offered her a childish little kiss – a chaste peck reserved for a sibling.

Undeterred, she swung her leg over his hips and straddled him. His organ was limp against the inside of her thigh. "Make love to me," she said. "Like people do."

"I – I can't," he choked.

She moved against him. "Please."

"I can't." He rolled over, forcing her to dismount him. He muttered against his pillows, "Let's just sleep, Theresa. We can be close in a different way. This can be nice, too, just sleeping close to each other, can't it?"

"Yes," she sighed, "I suppose it will have to be."

◆

When she awoke, it was still light and the bed beside her was empty. "Simon?" she called out. The bed was still warm where he'd lain. She saw the book of poems on the pillow; she picked it up, found herself engulfed in absolute quiet. She did not know if the book symbolized a promise made, or a promise broken.

The echoing silence was shattered by the sound of cracking wood and a cacophony of shouting voices. Theresa stilled herself, pinpointed the disturbance downstairs. She heard shouting, angry male voices, heavy footfalls on the steps and outside her door.

The door swung inward and Robert stepped into the late afternoon light. Blinking, he looked like an unshaven madman. Pale and gaunt. He turned and saw her. Fell to his knees. "Theresa!"

Two policemen appeared behind him, waving guns. She heard footsteps elsewhere in the old plantation. There must have been half a dozen officers.

"What the hell is going on here?" she asked, rising from the bed. Robert rushed forward to cover her nakedness, but she pushed him aside.

One of the officers, a young blond man, averted his eyes. "Your husband, ma'am, he told us you'd been kidnapped."

"Kidnapped!" She glared at Robert.

He grabbed for her hands, but she jerked away. "Honey, they found your purse at work. You hadn't been home for days. Your boss hadn't heard from you –"

Another police officer came into the room. "Looks like someone's been living in here, all right. There's food and wine bottles everywhere."

"I wasn't kidnapped," she said, though she knew she could not tell the truth.

"Did you know this is private property, ma'am?" the first officer asked.

"I really hadn't considered it," she said, sneering.

"Then I'm afraid you're under arrest," the blond said, almost apologetically. "Anything you say..."

Theresa blocked out the rest of it. Clutching the book to her chest, she tried to will the strength of poetry into her blood.

◆

The owner of the plantation, a descendent of a man named Fournier, declined to press charges against Theresa. That night she was in jail, she caught the briefest glimpse of jade-colored eyes. Or thought she did. When she looked for him, he was gone.

As much as she hated the possibility of seeing Robert again, Theresa went back to work at Bierce Street Books. She tried not to think about the month she spent with Simon and the others in the plantation; the more she tried to remember, the less beautiful the past became.

Months went by. She stopped taking the pills and the bleeding came back, as strong as ever. It hardly bothered her now. After a month of bleeding, even two weeks seemed short. She did not see Simon again. At first she feared that being away from his influence she would begin to lose that passion inside her. But as time went by, even as thoughts of Simon diminished, the ember of pride did not. She started to doubt that she had ever seen him at the station. She began to wonder if she had ever known him at all.

When Miss James offered her an afternoon shift, Theresa took it. Sunlight was a novelty. She went to dinner in the park, bringing a sack lunch and eating on one of the wrought iron benches. Autumn had come again, and with it a sweet amber light. The sun, just setting, looked like a split-open peach, dewey and golden. She could almost taste the light.

She usually brought a book with her to read. The store was full of them. There were worlds left unexplored. She had taken Simon's poems with her on a few occasions, but where they had seemed passionate and beautiful before, they now seemed rather shallow. She was not a vessel of wine. She was not a container, a vase, or goblet. She was not empty just because the wine had run out.

Finishing her dinner, she watched as a young couple strolled through the park. She felt a momentary tug of loneliness, but it passed and she was able to stand and walk away.

◆

As she reached for the top shelf, Theresa felt a hand on the back of her knee. She glanced down.

"Simon."

"Hello, Theresa."

A long silence. Finally, she climbed down the ladder. "Can I help you find something?"

He shook his head. "Theresa, please, let me explain –"

"Sh," she said. "Nothing to explain." She was surprised at the genuine tenderness of her voice. She was not angry.

"We had to leave," he said anyway. "You understand that."

"Of course I do."

He clasped her hands. "Come back with me."

She searched his face, and found the eyes were the same stunning shade of green, the mouth was the same young, soft mouth. But something was different. "It doesn't work anymore," she said with quiet amazement. "It doesn't work."

She laughed as she went to the counter at the front of the store. Simon followed her. In the past, he had been able to look at her, utter a command, and she would acquiesce. Suddenly, she felt the tether break. She floated free.

"Please, Theresa, come back. We need you."

She turned and kissed his cheek. "Go now, Simon. Tell them all I send my love. But go."

He stared at her, pleading, for several minutes, before he, too, finally realized that their prior bond had deteriorated. That something within her had now supplanted it.

As he turned to go, she stopped him. She found what she was looking for beneath the counter.

"This belongs to you," she said, and gave him back his poetry.

A poster's a poster – only got this
one for myself because the movie was
hyped by promoters to a Mount Fuji high,
and because I like vampire stuff,
like I said. Still, for a price,
I could part with it.
Easy.

The Poster Man

Sandra Black

He'd be here any second. Any second. The guy who wanted the poster. It was almost midnight – late hour to do business, but it was the only feasible and available time for him, he said.

What kind of guy is this? I find myself pacing to and from the window, peeking out, watching for him. Rain suddenly splats the glass. The drops are big and roll crookedly down the pane transforming the night world into a surreal black backdrop. I hear the growl of thunder far off.

Then my ears hone in on the unmistakable rumble of an engine. Stark white twin beams poke holes in the wet night. He's coming! My stomach constricts. Jesus. This is nuts. The guy just wants a poster. Then why am I sweating?

The ad was a tiny boxed affair in the classified section:

Wanted: Bram Stoker Dracula poster.
Will pay top price. Call...

I'm thinkin' now. A Dracula poster? Those things were all

over the place, what with the movie a recent big-screen remake. Myself, I always liked that vampire stuff. Didn't go to this Drac movie, even though I said I wanted to see it. The more I thought about it, the more it irritated me to see that aging brat pack given star billing in a classic. Winona Ryder? Get real. Keno, Keester, Koko, whatever – naw, not in a mil! A classic needs class acts.

The guy who played Dracula, though, he was cool. I heard about that shaving scene, where he licked the razor blade. Just reached around some guy's neck who nicked himself while removing his stubble, took that razor with those cold, undulating fingers and slurped away the blood. He got some seductive high with his tongue sneakin' around that blade. I bet it sliced that sucker in half. Grows back together, though. Vampires have that schtick, you know.

My eyes shifted back to the ad. There's a Drac poster hanging upstairs in my thinkin' room. That's what I call it, the room. Do a lot of thinkin' there in that room surrounded by collections perhaps not common to ordinary John Doe down the street. The shelves are lined with dust-encrusted books with authors dating back to the 16th Century. Yellowing posters with crinkled edges of yesteryear horror flics featuring Bella Lugosi are tacked to the walls. Bella's granite eyes seem to focus on my every move. WW II knives are showcased. Blood-rusted bayonets lean against chicken feet voodoo candle holders. It's a very eclectic set-up.

I decided to give the ad placer a call. Dialing, I felt somewhat foolish. On the other hand, what the hay! A poster's a poster – only got this one for myself because the movie was hyped by promoters to a Mount Fuji high, and because I like vampire stuff, like I said. Still, for a price, I could part with it. Easy.

The ringing phone fills my head. Once, twice, it rings, now six times, then click.

"Hello?" The voice was vanilla pudding smooth and low.

It seemed as if I could hear the dull throb of a pulse.

"Yes, hello. Are you the person who placed the ad for a Dracula poster?" My voice was crackly, almost witch-like. I coughed up a frog from my throat.

"Speaking."

"Great. I've got a poster. If you want it, it's yours."

"Wonderful. Would $150.00 agree with your asking price?"

My eyes grew wide. Zoweee! The thing cost seven fifty, max, at a local head shop. And this guy...

"Of course, if that doesn't meet with your expectations..."

"No! I mean, that's fine, more than fine. But why so much? Those posters were all over the place, cheap stuff, mass produced."

A gravelly chuckle fills my head. "*Were* all over. But not anymore. I have shopped around. It's the same story – sorry, sold out."

"Well, ahhhhh, sure. Whatever. So, when would you like to pick it up?"

A wedge of silence ensued. I hear breathing like a bellows and pressed the phone harder to my ear.

"As soon as possible. Tonight. Say, around midnight, if that's not too late."

I opened my mouth to say no, that's not too late, fine, even though I was thinking different. Like he's inside my brain waves, he offered an explanation. "I'd come earlier, if I could – it's my job, a grave-yard shift."

He sounded legit, was formally apologetic, and I accepted the time and his explanation. There it was, a done deal. One hundred fifty smackers. Who woulda thunk it.

◆

The headlights quiver and steam, then momentarily blind me as the vehicle crawls into the drive crunching cobblestone and parchment-like leaves. When I can focus again, my breath comes up my throat in a weird squeak. The guy was drivin' the cliché of clichés – a black as Hell's dungeon, luxury Marquis with smoked windows eerily enhanced by curling silver exhaust and shimmering plates sporting *Dracula* as the personalized motif. Dracula? You gotta be kiddin' here. But, I'm impressed. Very impressed.

I stand still in my dark house and watch and swirl my scotch. I've already had three. There is no movement from inside the car. It just sits there, engine rumbling like a panther, windshield wipers swishing against the rain.

Do somethin', I tell myself. Turn on the porch light, act normal. I do what I instructed myself to do, go even further and open the door, looking out for my expected guest.

For several moments which almost stretch into the uncomfortable zone, there is no change in the scene. Suddenly the wipers stop, the engine becomes mute and the halogens extinguish. The night swallows up the blackness of the Marquis. Only I am left illuminated by the circle of yellow porch light. More time ticks by. The smile on my face feels phony and stupid. I let my irrational side out a notch.

Nothing about this whole scene is quite normal. Midnight business deals. Dracula plates. I swallow dry spit. Who's in that damn car? And why doesn't he get out?

There's a metallic click. I jump – just a little, but it's still a jump. So very slowly the car door opens. I can see nothing, no one, only the laser of light escaping from the interior of the Marquis. It's purple. Holy shit, iridescent purple! The triangle of light expands. I hear one foot, then another hit the pavement.

For a second, I think of stepping back, shutting the door, not going on with this. I have let all my horses out of the Barn of Paranoia. No one does business for a crummy poster at midnight, no one drives an over-sized sedan and puts *Dracula* plates on it, no one except maybe a freakin' psycho or maybe even a real live vampire.

Listen to me. How crazy can I be. Instead of regressing into the shadows, I stand my ground. A body materializes. I see the outline of a torso. No face. Not yet. I'm expecting a ghoul, a ghost, a phantom. Oh Jesus! the paranoid horses are running wild. I think I may want to be frightened. Why else the heebie jeebies? Is there a hidden thrill side to me?

He's walking toward me now, hurried steps. There's a good fifteen feet from that car to me, from him to me. Walking faster now. Why not, you idiot, it's raining. Click, click, heels against pavement. I see him clearer now. Black suit, fine material, not ordinary K-mart 2 for 1 special stuff. Head down against the rain, he has no face.

I am stepping backwards now, not at all a relaxed person. He's in the light now. It happens so quickly. His head jerks up. We are face to face, eyeball to eyeball. Pent-up breath escapes from my lungs.

He's ordinary! He's human. He's got gray hair. And he's reaching out to me, to shake my hand. He's speaking, too.

"Mr. Harris? I'm Robert...the poster man."

I extend my hand. I know there's a dumb look on my face. I try to cover up by sounding smartly casual.

"Come in," I say. "Nasty night, isn't it?"

He has entered the kitchen foyer now, brushing at the wet on him. He looks at me. He has winter-sky blue eyes. "Not so bad. Still, I do suppose it depends on individual perception." He flashes an abrupt smile. His teeth are flawless; chiseled, white, and flawless. And the voice – pure crushed velvet. The sound of him, his gleaming teeth, his haute persona are toned down by his quite portly nature. He's rather built like a plump kiwi fruit. Talk about juxtaposition!

"Here, I'll just get the poster. You can inspect it. There are no tack holes in it, you'll see."

"I'm sure it will be fine." Again, the movie star smile. Only this time his eyes light up. The blue is much, much brighter.

I walk into the kitchen proper and gather the poster from the counter top. I start to splash a tad more courage into my tumbler. A case of manners enters the picture. Do I ask him if he wants a drink since I've got one going? I mean, who knows how long this poster buying is going to go on. Sure, why not? I turn and almost screech. He's standing right there. He'd come up behind me. I didn't even hear him. The smile again. If he was aware of my startle, he gave no indication. He reached for the poster and unrolled it.

"Ahhhh, yes. This will do quite nicely. Thad will be pleased."

"Thad?"

"My son."

His son. Well, no wonder. He wanted the poster for his son. Relief is warming me along with the scotch. He reaches into his breast pocket extracting a checkbook which I cannot help but notice is ornate. It's burgundy leather with gold trimmed edges and scrolled with a Gothic design. He bends over the countertop and writes out the document handing it to me with a flourish. Subsequently his eyes travel to the drink in my hand.

I remember the forgotten manners and lift my glass in apologetic salute. "Sorry. May I get you a scotch? Sort of a buffer against the damp of night?"

"Why, yes, thank you. I believe I could use a touch."

I fetch a glass. There is the clatter of ice cubes, a splash of booze, and it's done. I hand the drink to him, and he sips, sips again, and sighs, "Just what the doctor ordered." There is a small lull of quiet between us which I eventually break.

"I'm curious," I say, "black car, unique sporty plates, man comes out at midnight for a poster..."

He laughs a low, throaty sound and lifts his drink in my direction. "I suppose the whole thing does come off as borderline hokey, but I assure you, there's a perfectly logical explanation. I am a vampire buff, have always enjoyed the macabre, the classic monsters. I have a marvelous collection of movie memorabilia plus a library hosting shelves of vampiric literature.

"The car compliments the picture. I like luxury cars. The plates might be a bit much, but they fit my fancy and the car." Mr. Poster Buyer stops to take another swallow of his scotch, after which he continues. "As I mentioned previously, I work a grave-yard slot. Since I reside alone, sometimes afterwards I go for a midnight drive to unwind before heading home. Just me cutting through the night."

Question marks wiggle in my eyes. I'm thinkin': What about your...

"...son?" he finishes for me. My jaw drops a fraction. What, he really is a mind reader? "My son is away at school."

"Oh, yeah? Where's that?"

"Transylvania University."

"What?" I can't believe this! This guy's gotta be jerkin' me around.

He bursts out laughing. The sound is resonant and full. He's really getting a kick out of this. "I know, I know," he gasps, "is this guy a nut or what? I assure you, Mr. Harris, I am not a nut. There is a Transylvania University; it's in the state of Kentucky."

I'm staring at him through a squint.

He continues. "Thad is a sophomore at T.U. Full scholarship recipient – he took the most lucrative offer."

I still don't say anything and finish off my scotch with a gulp. This whole scenario has been a rush. Totally absurd. I allow the start of a grin to come forth. It is funny. Everything. From all the suspenseful anticipation, the car, the man, even good ol' Transylvania U. What a truck load of coincidence and irony. Laughter rises within me, and I let it loose.

When my laughter dwindles and stops, I note that the poster man is looking at me but he is not laughing. There's just a twist of smile skirting his mouth. He brings his glass to his lips and with undaunted smooth and ease, he finishes the drink and sets the glass on the counter top. We are getting ready to enact the parting-scene chatter now.

"Well, this has been quite an entertaining evening," he grins, "or should I say morning. Nonetheless, it is late, and I mustn't keep you anymore. Thank you again for the poster."

"No problem. And thank you."

Robert retrieves the poster and heads for the door. He peers out. "Still raining," he says, "better dash. Good-bye, Mr. Harris."

I nod at him. "Yeah, bye."

A rogue boom of thunder crashes. The noise is unexpected and deafening. Lightning is right behind it; the bolt is incandescent and a raw crack. The lights die, plunging us into a thick darkness.

I'm unnerved and ill at ease, stumbling backwards toward the counter. Gonna get those candles I keep just for such a happening. Where the hell are they? My hands are clumsy inside the cabinets. I hear him, the poster man, breathing. He hasn't said a word. Neither have I except for "son of a bitch" when I don't latch on to those candles. The sound of his breath is louder now, like it's right next to me. I feel it, behind me, all around me.

It is an eternity of black, lengthening, seemingly a forever thing. My tongue is dry. I don't like being in this dark with the poster man.

Swoosh. The lights are reborn. I blink a couple of times. It was all in my head. He's still standing by the door, ready to depart. He opens the door.

That's when I see his checkbook on the counter, the gold edges gleaming. But he has already stepped out into the rain.

"Wait, you forgot..."

He darts back inside the door, shimmering anew from the rain. A thin, almost-sheepish-but-not-quite grin flirts with his lips. He reaches for his checkbook as I hand it to him. Our fingers touch. My breath sucks in as a shock slithers up my arm from the contact. It was too lingering, the touch, too intimate, and cold. I jerk my hand away.

His grin is a smile now, one of those knowing smiles. He touches his forehead in salute. "Adieu, again," and poof! he is gone, a streak heading for his car. The night swirls around him like a cloak.

There is a flash of purple, and he is inside his car. I hear the mellow rumble of the Dracula mobile as it comes to life, idling like a black demon. I flick off the porch light and the kitchen light. I've had it. I'm bushed and headin' for bed, one hundred fifty dollars richer.

As I walk toward the stairs, I realize he is still in my driveway, in the dark. No headlights on. What the hell's wrong now? I shuffle back to the door and stand there, peering out, looking and waiting. My eyes pop when I see pinpoints of red, head level in the driver's seat. My hand claps to my mouth squelching the yelp coming out. Then blackness; then again the red orbs. Eyes! His eyes, draped by the occasional blink. Ohmagod.

I skitter back and crash into the table edge. I curse silently at the pain and my blunder. My mind begins dancing, throwing images against my brain, like a movie reel rewinding. I remember the checkbook, the touch of our fingers as I handed it to him. It hits home now with a smashing wallop what I saw in that picture. My heartbeat barrooms inside my chest. I remember the design, that beautiful scrolling reversed, revealing a name. His name. Situs inversus. *Dracula.*

I'm giggling now, stepping backwards now. Or am I whimpering? I am against the wall with no retreat left. My lips form soundless words, but I can hear myself begging: Please, don't let him hear me. Please don't let him see me.

There is a great flash of light. He has suddenly ignited the headlights of his coach. The darkened room is now zebra-striped. Please let me be in a black stripe, dear God. The car is backing up, easing out of the drive and into the street. In slow motion it purrs away and rounds the corner. I am standing on rubber band legs. I am a knotted ball of scared.

On tiptoe, I stumble through my dark house. I do not turn on a single light. My skin is coated with sweat sheen. I chant to myself between clenched teeth: He is gone, he is gone, he is gone. The echo of my litany is different: For now, for now, for now.

Even though I am bone tired, I am very awake. I bypass my bedroom and enter my thinkin' room, my ol' sanctuary. Bella's eyes leech onto my own. I shudder and look away as I lower my body one inch at a time into the chair. Don't make it squeak. Don't. I feel very alone, no longer at ease in this room. There is no thrill side to me. I am composed of yellow fear. My eyes are frozen wide open, staring out of the window at nothing. But I know that nothing is an illusion. My ears strain for sound but are filled only with silence.

I have been duped by a monstrous raconteur. I know who's really out there. I wonder if I will ever be able to sleep again. I wonder...if I do sleep...if I will ever awaken.

I have had centuries to nurture this vanity. I don't apologize for it any more than a rose or a poem makes amends for existence. I am my own excuse for being.

La Petite Morte

D.G.K. Goldberg

"I get sick of people saying 'what-goes-around-comes-around', it doesn't you know. Evil wins, good loses, there is no divine justice or cosmic reckoning." I paused for effect. I really am a trifle ridiculous. "It – whatever the particular 'it' is – doesn't all even out in some kind of last minute, just in time epiphany. There is no justice. Nada, none, nyet. Just random chance and chaos." I walked quickly. The crisp collision of my boot heels with the sidewalk was very satisfying. I had my hands thrust into the deep pockets of my black wool jacket and my head bent down as if to shield myself from the cold. Cold doesn't bother me.

"You're just trying to cheer me up." Ted had an engagingly crooked smile. He tossed his long blonde bangs out of his eyes like a restive colt. Need I mention that he had sapphire eyes? Pretty, pretty mortal eyes, they lacked the intensity of my eyes, they were the blue that belongs almost exclusively to Scandinavian blondes. He took long strides to keep pace with my amphetamine pace. He flexed his frozen fingers as we walked. His breath came out in smoky puffs. Poor dear, he felt the cold. "Chaos then. That's all there is to it? How wonderful. I've never believed in order, I think that is why I've always wanted to die," he said. Ted was only twenty-three.

"You're young right now, I forgive you your melodrama because you are young and pretty." I looked up at Ted. The top of my head barely reached the sweet spot where his neck blended with the hollow of his collarbone.

"You're young and pretty." He spoke as if we were debating. He wound our fingers together and leaned down to kiss me. Perversely I dodged his lips.

"When I was mortal I loved the daylight, I thought there was order to the universe. We created a balance – you and I, a yin-yang sort of thing. I loved the sunlight. You have always been drawn to darkness and death."

Ted's shoulders slumped but he did not let go of my hand.

"Okay, what's bothering you now?" I asked. Men are so moody.

"Oh, I get annoyed at your 'when I was mortal' routine..." He continued to move forward through the frozen night, he clutched my hand as if I might suddenly jerk free and run from him.

"I thought you valued honesty in a relationship." Foolish boy, to fear I would leave him, I have waited years for him.

"Whatever." He sounded fed up. He really had no interest in the truth. The stars had a crystal brightness they only achieve when the air is freezing.

I decided to change the topic. "Do you want coffee then?" I slowed my march and turned to him; I was silhouetted by a streetlight. I was neither tired nor cold. I stopped beneath the streetlight because I knew exactly how exquisite I looked haloed by the misty light with bits of snow becoming diamond chips in my long onyx hair. Backlit and outlined by the night, my opal skin translucent, my eyes ash-smudged emeralds – that is the image of myself I love. I have had centuries to nurture this vanity. I don't apologize for it any more than a rose or a poem makes amends for existence. I am my own excuse for being.

"Up ahead there's a diner thing." I have adapted well to this century. I refer to everything as "thing." What a marvel am I, a post-modern vampire in Armani silk.

A wounded neon sign advertised Bre kf st ny Hou ! The gargling of late night drunken confession drifted out the glass door on waves of hamburger grease. The door swung open letting a wave of heat escape into the frigid night. A chubby girl with spaniel hair clutched the arm of her apathetic boyfriend who stared at me quite openly. The girl's chin quivered. She was wearing a slip dress meant to hang loose but getting caught here and there on pudgy bits of her. Her sigh predicted a life of high heating bills and cheap imitation leather shoes. I loved her because the hunger on her face was naked. She looked at her disinterested boyfriend as if she was starved for touch.

"Were there any justice, something very bad would happen to that young man." I spoke softly so that only Ted could hear me as we brushed past the couple into the fluorescent light.

As I rose on tiptoe to whisper to him the blue of his veins mocked me as the blood flirted just beneath the surface of his skin. My tongue kittened out of my mouth involuntarily tracing my lower lip. I felt hollow and ravenous. I pressed my hand against my diaphragm to keep the roaring beast at bay. I wanted him. I always had. In far too many ways.

I sat across from him. It was important to me that he look into my eyes.

A few spandex clad bar whores just past their sell-by dates shrieked with dead laughter as they sprawled across the counter spilling sugar and snatching French fries off each other's plates. A man in a dark suit drank bitter coffee as a woman, too obviously his wife, methodically chewed a burnt hamburger. I could tell from her relentless smile that they'd not been getting along well and she was determined not to complain about the burger. They didn't go out together often and he hadn't liked the play they'd seen. Three moderately intoxicated young men in a booth told sexual conquest lies to each other. They didn't bother listening to each other. It was three *AM*.

Ted sat across the Formica. He was blowing on his cold hands and smiling sheepishly at me. I sat as still as a tombstone. "Coffee?" he asked.

"Yes, please. But, nothing else." Keeping up appearances only goes so far.

The waitress wandered over and watched the bar whores. She seemed to suspect that they might scoop up her tips while she took our order.

"I do feel as if I've known you forever." Ted shook his head and smiled.

"That's because you have." I drilled him with my eyes. The rock and roll angst of the all-night diner was muffled by the intensity of my voice. I formed a bell jar of quiet around our table. "If you had been reincarnated in the sixties this would have been a great deal easier. People were into the karma thing then, you would have simply accepted the truth...we have been lovers before. Many times before."

"We haven't exactly been lovers yet," he said.

The coffee appeared on the table. The waitress drifted off on a wave of boredom. She had spent hundreds of Saturday nights listening to young men attempting to seduce younger women. Her feet hurt. Ted dumped sugar into his coffee.

I started to giggle. His cool was a transparent facade. He'd gotten sugar all over the table. "All in due time."

"Where do you go during the day? It's creepy. I see you almost every night but I've no idea what you do during the day, you could be living with some dude or even married. What are you? A drug runner's girl friend? A computer hacker? A CIA agent?" He had put far too much salt on his French fries.

"I told you what I am. You choose to ignore things that don't happen to suit you." He was churning his coffee furiously. I couldn't get him to look into my eyes.

"Okay. So, you want me to believe we've known each other several life times. Fine I'll play." He was finally warm enough to quit sniping at me. He quit messing about and looked at me. I am alarmingly beautiful. I have almond shaped eyes, full lips, and high cheekbones. I have the grace of a Degas dancer and the insidious sensuality of Lilith. I can be remarkably compelling.

He sucked on the inside of his cheeks. The sweet blood that pushed through his temples sang to me. He wanted me. "Okay. I don't see you during the day because you're Dracula's sister. Fine. If that's what you need we'll go with it."

"It isn't a question of need..." I reached across the table and stroked the back of his hand where the veins struggle against the flesh. I let my greedy fingers snake beneath his wrist to caress his pulse. I remembered sadness. That moment in the restaurant felt a lot like sadness. "I do love you Ted. I always have."

I looked at him until he was enraptured. I can snare him with my eyes. He believed me. He always did. Life after life he managed to believe.

"I believe you. I don't know why..." He shrugged. He was so arrogantly young, only twenty-three. Tell me what it's like. Do you miss daylight? Do you even remember it?"

"I told you I loved the light." Men never seem to listen. "Yet, I have only one real memory of daylight. The other images are abstract conceptualizations garnered from looking at photographs, movies, TV, from thinking about daylight – they are the idea of daylight constructed on the viewing screen of a mind too busy, too anxious, too alone." I really can be a pompous twit. I spend far too much time alone.

Ted leaned forward, his forearms on the table; he was drowning in my eyes. The conversation felt peculiarly intimate, as if we were having sex in the restaurant booth. I stopped talking and stared at Ted. He was able to believe me, if only for awhile.

He grabbed the check and paid it. He cupped my elbow and steered me through the door back onto the sidewalk. "You have a few more hours?"

I nodded.

"I tried to kill myself...when I was sixteen. I felt different from everyone, isolated, incomplete. I thought I would always be alone. I felt like that over and over again until I met you." He spoke urgently, as if he was compelled to pull these words from some locked place deep within his chest. I wanted to reach into his ribcage and extract his words, hold them warm and pulsing in my hand. I put my deceptively small hand on his chest. He held me by the shoulders. He was near shouting at me.

His touch became gentle. "If you're in some kind of trouble..."

I shook my head no. "I am never in trouble...not anymore, this is an unusually safe century for the undead. No one really believes in us."

"Hell, I don't care if you really are a vampire..." A few sheets of newspaper blew across the street like fallen angels rustling in the filth. Ted gulped air. He was panting like a runner. "I love you, Lizbeth, I always will."

"You always have."

"All right then. Let's go back to my place and you can tell me about it." He wrapped his arm around me as if I needed shelter from the cold and we walked the few blocks to his apartment. I stood on the steps and pretended to search the stars. "You will invite me in?" I asked.

"Of course." Yet he did not say the words.

"Well," I said, my voice a trifle sharp.

"All right," he said, laughing. "Won't you come in?"

I gave him the gift of a smile as I entered the building.

Ted was different from other students. He lived alone. His apartment building was a red brick square that swallowed grad students, single parents, pending musicians and erstwhile actresses. As we walked up the stairs we heard a baby wailing. A woman was screaming, "If your mother calls me about one more Tupperware piece I'll go postal." A tragic fool was practicing Mozart on a harpsichord.

Ted lived in a small efficiency apartment on the third floor. The room was sterile. He didn't bother cooking. We sat on the bed and I allowed him to stroke my hair. I like being stroked.

"Tell me about your memories of daylight." He rubbed my neck and shoulders, massaging them in the fashion that all young men believe will render a woman naked and willing. Who teaches them this nonsense? Women aren't aroused by relaxation. The heart of sexuality is tension. I wondered where the chubby girl's boyfriend was and what he was doing to make her unhappy. Ted kneaded my shoulders and glanced covertly at my breasts.

"I have a memory of daylight that I fondle; I take it from the recesses of my mind and experience the recall on a near visceral level." I shifted my position so that I could look at Ted. I have always been enamored of beauty, possessed by it, mesmerized. That may be why I am so drawn to Ted. He is always a beautiful man. In the presence of that elusive quality, that is Pure Beauty, I feel a torment akin to sexual arousal; every fiber in my body is magnetically pulled towards the perfect, the beautiful. The noumena as well as the phenomena can elicit this compelling longing.

"Go on..." He moved close. His breath tickled my ear. His lips grazed my neck.

"In my memory I am running through the warren of daub and wattle huts clinging to the rim of Hampton Court like dirt on the hem of a velvet dress. My callused feet slap the packed mud and offal as I plummet through the make-shift paths not yet streets dotted with the dwellings of those of us who serve the court as laundresses and swineherds. I stop suddenly."

I had not thought of my life in many years. The recall exerted its own alchemy. For a moment, I almost was a young girl, my cheeks were flushed, and my heart was hamstering. I looked over towards the whimsical chimneys of the red brick palace that sprawled like a reclining courtesan on the banks of the lazy Thames. The sky above the chimneys was such an aching cobalt, such a perfect shouting blue, the very essence of blueness that I held my hand to my jealous heart and drank the sky. I shuddered and twitched, turning off the memory.

"What's wrong?" Ted was confused. He assumed my spasm had to do with his touch. He wanted to touch me; he had always wanted to touch me. He could not save himself.

"It makes me sad. It's like remembering a long dead friend. Hampton Court was so wonderful then. If you go to Hampton Court today, you will not see it as I saw it: the brick work picked out in a riot of reds and yellows, the courtyard clattering with horses and men. You will see a well-tended museum housing five hundred years of furniture and artwork. You will not hear the screams of Katherine Howard; you will not see blood spilled on the scrubbed stone. You will not smell roast boar. You will not hear the lute or the melodic laughter of dangerous assignations."

"Dangerous assignations? Is that what you and I have?" Ted saw his opening. He nuzzled my neck, inhaling the jasmine of my French perfume. (The wonderful thing about longevity is that the way interest compounds, within a few centuries you can afford whatever you want.) He wrapped his arms possessively around my waist and pulled me back against him. I felt his erection prodding my derriere. Why didn't he feel how inhumanly cold I was?

"More dangerous that you seem willing to believe." I felt his hand inching up my ribcage towards my breast. I was a bit irritated with his hesitancy. He hadn't always been so timid. It must be a product of the era. The politically correct male is not nearly as arousing as the pirate or the highwayman or even the rationalizing Jesuit. His hand moved the tiniest bit and then he held his territorial gain. What a lousy century. A lady could grow old and die waiting to be ravished.

"You weren't always so timid Theodore." I took his willing hand and pressed it to my breast. With a sharp intake of air he jerked spasmodically and then melted against my spine. I took his other hand and placed it on my other breast.

I leaned into him and shut my eyes. He cupped my breasts reverently hardly daring to tease the famished nipples with his thumb. I had not always been so bold.

I was an innocent on that perfect autumn day when the sky wore early chill like jewelry; I did not see death or know of gifts more desolate than the grave. I saw only an infinite sky.

I started talking again. "I am puzzled by the way you slip in and out of personalities with each life. You've been a pirate, a highwayman, a priest, each of them you but each of them unique. During your last life, you were a RAF pilot. We met at a bus stop in Lincoln. I offered you a hoarded chocolate bar and you knew me at once. Yet, this time you seem hesitant to recognize me."

"Did I die in the battle of Britain?" he asked.

"No." I was frantic to switch topics. "You always come to me."

"I have been alone my entire life." He murmured.

"You are alone until we reunite. We complete each other," I pressed his hands insistently against my breasts, I wiggled back against him teasing his erection with my hips.

Ted pressed moist lips against my neck. I shuddered at the

slobber; his nervous courting of me lacked finesse. In prior lives, he would have already had my skirts over my face.

I missed Ted in his other incarnations. This timid product of the later half of the twentieth century doesn't have the passion of the pilot or the pirate. It is an era of emasculated men. I missed the eager electricity of men who took what they wanted when they wanted it. I suspect flirting with death makes a man more attractive.

The living are half-blind. They treat the transient as permanent. That which blooms, fades, and therein lies its glory.

"I haven't ever been to England." Damn would he never stop talking?

"Yes you have dear, you've lived there many times." I made circular motions on his muscular thigh. My touch is light.

"Have you?" he says.

I was fascinated by the indentation in his muscle on the inside of his leg. I was certainly not listening to him. "Have I what?"

"Have you lived in England over and over again? Known me life after life?"

"I've known you in all of your lives." I was cautious with my words.

He seemed uncertain of what to do with my breasts, could he possibly be a virgin? As pretty as he is? What a stupid, stupid century this is. Or what a stupid part of the century this is. "Lizbeth, tell me about the first time we met." He rubbed his face against my hair.

"All right then," I shut my eyes to concentrate. "Pretend you are watching a costume drama: the big screen technicolors the sky, a sash of red tulips, the silver scarf of the Thames thrown into the center of emerald grass. In the lower corner of the screen stands a slim young girl – almost a woman. Her hair is a tangled mass of sable. She is clear skinned; gypsy featured and full of the painful beauty that is youth. That was what I looked like when I was alive – there are subtle differences in how I appear today some four or five hundred years later."

"You are alive. What are you if not alive?" Ted placed another neophyte kiss on my cheekbone. I longed for a predatory male.

"Undead, I suppose." I teased the warm flesh sheathing his collarbone.

He shook his head, the glossy golden hair fell into place. "Go on then..."

"I looked down river and saw you my first love, my only love. You stood slender and tall amid the reeds at the river's edge rising godlike out of your own reflection. I felt something hot and hungry that I could not name. Your hair was primrose yellow, startling against the mist shrouding the riverbank. You shook it from your eyes as you did just then. You looked up and saw me. We were sealed in that moment."

Ted kissed me, tentatively at first, then with increasing urgency. I shifted my tongue into his mouth. I did not want him to feel my fangs just yet. He stroked my jaw with one hand while his novice fingertips explored my hardening nipple. "You make it sound so real."

"It is the only reality I know." I scarce moved for fear I would deter him. I wanted him to continue fondling me. "I have loved you through centuries, you age, you die, you are reborn. We find each other, like moths pulled to the flame."

He pressed butterfly kisses across my cheekbones while one hand ventured down to my lap. "It almost makes sense. The feeling I've always had that I was incomplete, searching. The wanting to die. I didn't want to die; I wanted to be reborn. I wanted to find you."

"That's it." I said.

"It makes a perfect kind of sense." He kissed me deeply, his tongue probing my mouth while his heated hands roamed my body.

I have survived long enough to know only one thing: we

none of us choose who we love. Reason cannot explain love. What reason would endeavor to explain reason profanes.

He lowered me to the mattress as if I was fashioned of thin china. He leaned back on his folded legs and dragged his sweater over his head giving his hair another shake. The skin stretched taunt across his bare chest. I could almost see his heart working. He unbuttoned my blouse with maddening indolence. Solemnly, like a monk kissing the ring of the pope he kissed each of my nipples in turn. I strained against him, aching for the rough heat of his tongue on my breast. "That was the first time then, in Tudor England," he asked his voice humid with longing.

"Yes, the next time, you were a highwayman." Finally he stroked the bare flesh of my hips. He pulled my hair out of the way and began kissing my body feverishly.

"A highwayman?" He rubbed his rough cheek against my belly.

"You ravished me on Hampstead heath. It was a moon lit night." I sighed recalling the force with which he'd driven into me, riding me like his Satan black horse. I had bucked beneath him clawing his back as I howled at the moon.

"I ravished you? Did I hurt you?" Damn his movements lacked authority; his touch was too gentle, insipid.

"You've never hurt me." I was very cautious with my words. "I loved you as a highwayman." I had, that had been one of our more successful liaisons, it had continued longer than many others had. I pulled his head to my breast and wrapped my legs insistently about his waist.

"I don't want to ever hurt you," he said. I wanted to be hurt. If he could not hurt me there was no harmony, no justice.

I arched against him. I grabbed at the velvet length of him and guided him inside me. As he sank into me I lunged against him wild in my thirst. He tried to slow the pace but I was desperate and wild with craving. He succumbed and drove against me as I clung to his shoulders drawing him deeper inside me. I wondered which of us was truly cursed.

He hadn't the skill born of experience to draw out lovemaking. There was no sophisticated teasing; no pulling all the way out and plunging back into me. There was the elemental volcanic thunder of need as he thrust into me as inevitable as gravity, as basic as sunrise. I shrieked my pleasure and tightened my legs to keep him close.

Breathing hard and moving ever faster his face contorted in la petite mort. It was at that precise moment that my fangs penetrated deep into his vein, from la petite mort to la mort – a poetic demise. As he spurted hot inside of me his sweet blood spurted into my frantic mouth. I drank his essence in huge gulps; his blood infusing me with the power of love lived time and time again.

I leaned back and looked at my lover as he lay lifeless, his skin like marble to the touch of my own cold hand. I swallowed the last drops of his blood and kissed him farewell. I have loved him not well but so very long and so many times. I dressed under the cloak of darkness. I crept out into winter to make my way to safety in advance of the sun's killing rays. I was melancholy and filled with bittersweet longing on my walk home to bed.

I loved him so. There was nothing left for me but the long empty years of memory and solitude until he is born again. Years of nights that feel endless, people that do not matter, countries that blur, blood that sustains but does not nourish – a wasteland stretches out before me until I am reunited with my love.

I go on only that I might find him again.

Biographies

Sandra Black - *Poster Man* - who is 'married with children' (2) and resides in Pleasant Plains, IL, has been published in various fiction periodicals including *Midnight Zoo, Aberrations, Nocturnal Ecstasy*, and Peak Output Unlimited's *Friends of the Lincoln Library's 1998 Writer of the Year Award* with an 'experimentally creative' work, *Tell Me of the Forest Where You Once Lived*, which is currently in the Milkweed Editions offices awaiting a nod. Black also writes under the pseudonym, Gates McMillan, billing him as an exmercenary now retired gardener.

Tippi N. Blevins - *A Month Of Bleeding* - lives in Texas with her extended family and four dogs. She is a sometime student and full-time writer whose works have appeared in dozens of magazines and several anthologies. To contact Tippi or read about upcoming projects, visit her home page at http://www.sff.net/people/tippi.

Dominick Cancilla - *To Die For* - lives in Santa Monica, California with his wife, Deborah, and son, Markus. He has had other tales of unusual circumstance published in *The Best Of Cemetery Dance*, the HWA anthology *Robert Bloch's Psycho's, Bending The Landscape: Fantasy* and other anthologies, as well as many magazines. Dominick would like to make clear that his writing this story in a theme park during the month of October is nothing more than a coincidence.

Margaret L. Carter - *The Pale Hill's Side* - is the wife of a Navy Captain, currently living in Annapolis. They have four sons and two grandchildren. She received English degrees from the College of William and Mary, the University of Hawaii (M.A.), and the University of California, Irvine (Ph.D.). Her first book was a vampire anthology, *Curse of the Undead* (1970). She has published several books and articles on vampirism in literature, including *Dracula: The Vampire and the Critics* (an anthology, 1988). Her stories have appeared in various small press publications, in Marion Zimmer Bradley's *Darkover* anthologies, and in *The Time of the Vampires,* edited by P.N. Elrod and Martin Greenberg. She edits a semiannual fanzine, *The Vampire's Crypt.* In her "day job" she works as a proofreader for the Maryland General Assembly. Margaret has a werewolf novel, *Shadow of the Beast,* currently published by The Design Image Group.

Sukie de la Croix - *Who Was Jane Dalotz?* - is an internationally published journalist who has been working mostly for the gay and alternative press since 1978. He lives in Chicago.

Don D'Ammassa - *Prey For The Dead* - is the author of *Blood Beast* and the forthcoming *A Guide to Horror Fiction,* as well as numerous short stories which have appeared in *Shock Rock, Hotter Blood, Borderlands 5, Analog, Asimov's, Peter Straub's Ghosts,* and many other anthologies and magazines. He has been the book reviewer for *Science Fiction Chronicle* for fifteen years, and has a library of about 60,000 books. He lives not far from Lovecraft's grave and is employed as a computer network administrator.

Mia Fields - *Pet Consultation* - has published three nonfiction books about dog training and has also written four novels: *The Tocharian, Evil, Nightmare* and *The Monster.* She resides in Virginia with her husband, Mike, son, Kyle, 3 dogs, 2 cats, 2 gerbils, 2 pigeons and a fantastic horse.

D.G.K. Goldberg - *La Petite Morte* - has spent the past year attempting to have an existential crisis and failing that having lunch. Her work has appeared in a variety of web and small press publications. She arranges her life so as to spend as much time as possible at Hampton Court. Completely unsuited to activities that are more productive, she would really like to be queen of something. Her husband manages (somehow) to tolerate the chaos, which has lately involved a coyote, a shape shifter, and a pregnant cat.

Barb Hendee's - *Night And Day* - short fiction has appeared in numerous paperback anthologies such as *DAW's Year's Best Horror Stories XX, Young Blood, Realms of Infamy,* and G*host Tide.* Her first novel, *Blood Memories,* is due out soon. She lives just outside of Boulder, Colorado, and teaches writing at the Metropolitan State College of Denver. She's a firm believer that life is just too short for cheap coffee.

C.W. Johnson - *Blood Feud* - grew up out West but now is an assistant professor of physics at Louisiana State University, doing research in nuclear astrophysics. Not surprisingly, C.W. writes mostly science fiction and has had four short stories published previously; he tells people he is working on a science fiction novel.

Lynda Licina - *Something I Can Never Have* - is Chicago's subcultural diva, writing a column called *She Poison* for a gay publication *Nightlines Weekly.* She participates in many vampire/horror related performance groups. Previously, she was editor and designer of *Screem In The Dark* magazine. She co-sponsored many vampire related events including the highly produced *Vampire Circuses* and was a member of the vampiric band *The Dark Theater.* Licina has gained a following for her witty observations about the vampiric culture at large, and one of her columns was a satire called *The Goth Makeover In One Hour Or Less* (a total impossibility). She has cultivated painful responses to the Halloween comment and wears her makeup to bed.

Kyle Marffin - *Bongo Bobbie's Bel Air* - lives in the northern midwest with his wife and family. Previous vampire short fiction appeared in *The Darkest Thirst - A Vampire Anthology,* and his debut novel *Carmilla - The Return* is also published by The Design Image Group.

Deborah Markus - *Winding The Clock* - lives in Santa Monica, California with her husband, Dominick, and son Markus. She had another tale of unusual circumstance published in *The Darkest Thirst - A Vampire Anthology* and would like to make clear that her writing this story shortly after Markus was born is nothing more than coincidence.

Christine DeLong Miller - *Friends* - resides in Defiance, OH with her husband, Rick, and has three children, (Vanessa, Jennifer and Richard). She is an avid Stephen King fan and soccer mom who can be found listening to John Mellencamp on any given day. Christine believes that if her desk isn't cluttered, she's not working hard enough.

Rick R. Reed - *Morbidly Obese* - is the author of the Dell Abyss novels, *Penance* and *Obsessed.* In addition to the U.S. and Canada, both books have been published in translation in Germany and Russia. His short fiction has appeared in the *White Wolf* anthologies, *Dark Destiny, Dante's Disciples* and *Dark Destiny III: Children of Dracula* and numerous magazines. Upcoming publications include the short story, "Moving Toward The Light" which will appear in the anthology, *The Crow, Shattered Lives and Broken Dreams,* edited by Edward Kramer and James O'Barr, published by Random House. Rick is also contributing to the upcoming Arsenal Pulp Press anthology, *ContraDictions: Queer Male Fiction.* Reed is currently at work on a new novel and lives in Chicago.

Kiel Stuart wrote *Sixteen Candles* to distract herself during a doctor's visit. She's listed in *Who's Who In The East,* was nominated for a Darrell Award, received Honorable Mention in *The Year's Best Fantasy And Horror.* A part-time filmmaker, her first documentary short should be out by the time you read this.

Night Prayers

P.D. Cacek

Stoker Award winner P.D. Cacek's debut novel is a wryly witty romp that introduces Allison Garret – thirtysomething, biological clock loudly ticking and perpetually unlucky in life and love – who wakes up in a seedy motel room...as a vampire! In a rollicking tour of the seamy underbelly of L.A., Allison hooks up with a Bible-thumping streetcorner preacher, but they'll both need more than a night full of prayers to escape the clutches of a catty coven of strip club vampire vixens out for blood.

"Further proof that Cacek is
certainly one of horror's most important up-and-comers."

Barnesandnoble.com

"The novel works...
Cacek exhibits a winning sense of humor."

Hellnotes

Trade paperback, 224 pages
ISBN 1-891946-01-3
$15.95 US ($19.50 CAN)

Available from your favorite bookstore
or on-line bookseller.

Shadow Of The Beast

Margaret L. Carter

Margaret Carter has been a fixture in dark fiction for nearly thirty years, with anthologies, critically acclaimed non-fiction books and her own long-running horror fiction periodical to her credit. And here is her long awaited horror novel debut.

It begins with a hellish night of bloodshed and horror. A nightmare legacy arises from Jenny Cameron's past – destroying her family, threatening everyone she loves – and now it's come to claim her in an orgy of violence and death.

A beast roams the dark streets of Annapolis, Maryland, a terrifying creature more animal than man. And the only way Jenny can combat the evil from her past is to surrender to the dark and violent power lurking within herself. Her humanity is at stake, and much more than death may await her under the shadow of the beast.

The Darkest Thirst
A Vampire Anthology

Sixteen disturbing tales of the undead's darkest thirsts for redemption, power, lust and of course, blood. Includes stories by:

Michael J. Arruda
Edo van Belkom
Sue Burke
Margaret L. Carter
Stirling Davenport
Robert Devereaux
D.G.K. Goldberg
Scott T. Goudsward
Barb Hendee
Paul McMahon
Kyle Marffin
Deborah Markus
Julie Anne Parks
Rick R. Reed
Thomas J. Strauch
William R. Trotter

"Succeeds quite well where so many anthologies have failed...approaches its subject with the enthusiasm and vigor lacking in collections filled with jaded veterans."

BookLovers

"If solid, straight ahead vampire fiction is what you like to read, then The Darkest Thirst is your prescription."

Locus

Trade paperback, 256 pages
ISBN 1-891946-00-5
$15.95 US ($19.50 CAN)

Available from your favorite bookstore or on-line bookseller.

Carmilla: The Return
Kyle Marffin

Kyle Marffin's provocative debut is a modern day retelling of LeFanu's classic 19th century vampire novella. Gothic literature's most notorious female vampire – the seductive Countess Carmilla Karnstein – stalks her unsuspecting victim through darkened city streets to the desolate northwoods and back to her haunted Styrian homeland.

"Marffin's clearly a talented new writer with a solid grip on the romance of blood and doomed love."

Locus

"If you think you've read enough vampire books to last a lifetime, think again. This one's got restrained and skillful writing, a complex and believable love story, gorgeous scenery, sudden jolts of violence and a thought provoking final sequence that will keep you reading until the sun comes up."

Amazon.com

Trade paperback, 304 pages
ISBN 1-891946-02-1
$15.95 US ($19.50 CAN)

Available from your favorite bookstore or on-line bookseller.

Storytellers

Julie Anne Parks

Julie Anne Parks debuts with a stunning trip through madness and horror firmly rooted in the mysterious mountain forests of her native North Carolina.

Meet Braxton DaFoe, who once ruled the bestseller lists with his novels of calculating horror. But now he and his wife, Piper, have fled to the desolate backwoods of North Carolina with nothing left between them but a loveless marriage. There they meet Ren – keeper of the legends, the Storyteller, who challenges Braxton and ignites passions that have laid dormant in Piper's heart.

But an ancient evil lurks in the dark woods. A malevolent spirit from the Storyteller's darkest tale, possessing one weaver of tales and threatening the other and everyone he loves in a sinister and bloody battle for Piper's life...and a Storyteller's soul.

Trade paperback, 256 pages
ISBN 1-891946-04-8
$15.95 US ($19.50 CAN)